Additi...
The S...
D0557830

"Channeling Willa Cather's searing descriptions of pioneer life, Jeannie Burt's *The Seasons of Doubt*--an emotionally gripping portrait of pioneer life in 1870s Nebraska--transcends the historical genre with its unvarnished look at the degradations and triumphs of life in the western territories. With exquisite detail and gorgeous prose, Burt transports you into the world of Mary Harrington, a beleaguered but scrappy and courageous woman who is trying to raise a son despite homelessness, destitution, fires, and illness. Eloquent and devastating, Burt writes with huge empathy about a lost way of life that was not kind to women."

--Lisa Alber, author *Whispers in the Mist* and *Path Into Darkness*

"Written to challenge and to reveal the courage necessary to survive... *The Seasons of Doubt* is the realism of our legacies, with our generation living the dreams of our ancestors, who came to Nebraska as homesteaders, searching for 'the better life.' Thank you for this most enjoyable book."

--Dr. Marilyn Peterson, *Associate Professor, Historian*

"*The Seasons of Doubt* is about abandonment, survival, and a young mother's determination. Her profound strength and courage in the face of rain, heat, devastation, and isolation in a world even the neighbors have fled contributes to a survival story firmly rooted in history, yet filled with one woman's obstinate determination to make a go of things against all odds. As she finds the courage to accept what she cannot change and the determination to reinvent her life,.. this ... women-centric pioneer story ...will resonate with any readers interested in Western history, women's experiences, and a fictional journey made by one special, feisty survivor."

--D. Donovan, *Senior Reviewer, Midwest Book Review*

"In her well-researched book *The Seasons of Doubt* Jeannie Burt captures early Cozad, Nebraska. I had to keep reminding myself it was a novel, based as it is on historical facts when John J Cozad, father of world-renowned artist Robert Henri, founded our town."

--Marlene Geiger, *Board President, Robert Henri Museum*

"A story of people and struggle and regret...where one woman's love of her son drives her forward against incredible odds. I was mesmerized by the beauty of the prose...a great read."
                    --Donna Croy Wright, author *The Scattering of Stones*

THE SEASONS OF DOUBT

THE SEASONS OF DOUBT is based on historical record. The story refers to real events, true locales, and actual historical as well as fictional figures. The dialog and characterizations of actual individuals reflect the author's interpretation. The work as a whole is a work of fiction.

Jeannie Burt

Publisher's Cataloging-in-Publication Data

Names: Burt, Jeannie.
Title: The seasons of doubt / Jeannie Burt.
Description: Portland, OR : Muskrat Press, 2018.

Identifiers: LCCN 2017906413 | ISBN 978-0-9895446-5-8 (pbk.) | ISBN 978-0-9895446-2-7 (Kindle ebook)

Subjects: LCSH: Frontier and pioneer life--Fiction. | Women pioneers--Fiction. | Nebraska--Fiction. | Historical fiction. | BISAC: FICTION / Historical. | FICTION / Literary. | GSAFD: Historical fiction.

Classification: LCC PS3602.U76955 S43 2018 (print) | LCC PS3602.U76955 (ebook) | DDC 813/.6--dc23.

Muskrat Press • Portland

The

Seasons

of

Doubt

A NOVEL

In Memory
of
Jan Patterson

There are moments in our lives,
there are moments in a day,
when we seem to see beyond the usual.
Such are the moments
of our greatest happiness.
Such are the moments of our greatest wisdom.

—Robert Henri
(nee Robert Cozad)

Nebraska 1873
Chapter 1

The stove almost warmed the room, though damp from the last storm still sat in it. Mary Harrington stirred a dull gravy as her five-year-old son slathered lard on a biscuit. Her husband, Edmund, had been home only two days this last time. He had said he was going to Omaha for supplies, but returned with none, neither salt, nor sugar, nor potatoes, nor wood for the winter. Their food stores were running low now.

The front door popped, Mary startled. She patted her thigh. "Ezekiel," she said, "here." The boy dropped the biscuit and ran to her. Edmund came in, swearing. He held the rifle in one hand, a near-empty bottle in the other. Ezekiel made some little noise, like an animal's squeak. His father shouted, "Runt," and staggered toward them.

Mary pulled Ezekiel's arm. "Behind me," she said.

This inflamed Edmund; he blurted something she did not understand and he stomped. It caused him to drop the bottle. Its liquid dribbled onto the dirt floor, and disappeared. "Now, look't what you made me do." The house filled with the odor of his breath.

He focused his eyes on his son like a predator on

1

quarry. He raised the rifle's stock over his head, his movement sloppy, untrue. He threw himself into bringing the gun down on them. The stock swiped the low ceiling, and sod grit rained down on him. The catch put Edmund off balance and he sank to his knees.

Mary shoved Ezekiel toward the blanket hung to demark her and Edmund's bedroom. "Out the window," she said. Ezekiel disappeared behind the blanket.

Edmund managed to pull himself up, and he spat out, "Puh! Not worth the trouble." In disgust, he took his rifle and precious bottle and wrestled himself out the door.

Chapter 2

It was so cold her son's lips had turned blue. Mary and five-year-old Ezekiel were leaving their homestead where they had lived five years. He had never known another home. The house smelled of the cold, now, of the earth of its walls, of the lacking of a fire, of a kitchen that no longer held the scent of her stews, or breads, or apples saucing. Its smell had reverted to the prairie and the cave of Nebraskan earth into which it was dug. It smelled of the must of stacked sod that made up its face. It smelled of the eternal showers of dry dust upon their heads. It smelled of the mice that nibbled through and nested in the crevasses, and the occasional snake that made its way in for the warmth; the last of which Mary had cooked and she and her son had eaten.

Three months ago, in a foul mood, her husband Edmund left and did not return. Before now, he had never been gone more than a week. She and Ezekiel had waited for him until their food and fuel ran out and they could wait no longer.

As they were loading that morning, the hinny mule had stood patient in her traces, her tail drifting in the wind. They loaded the wagon high with their things, first the trunk filled with her son's books and her letters and wedding linens, then the three hens, which they put in a cage contrived from the cooking ladle, a trowel, the

3

andiron, and the corn flail. She took what remained of her tomato preserves, pickling, withered potatoes, and the bit of grain the bugs had not got to. She considered leaving her husband a handful of potatoes, then seeing her son's razor shoulders she had brought all fifteen. She wanted to bring the rooster as well, but they had not been able to catch it.

When they had settled and braced all else, they had put in the kicking, beating doe goat, and last, to be used as a sort of gate, the treadle sewing machine. The treadle was heavy to lift, and bulky and not practical, but she could not bear to leave it to the rats and the rust. It was the only solid thing in her life.

―――――

For less than a quarter of an hour they had sat on the wagon seat as it bucked and hammered into the wind. They were already cold. At first, they had been warm from the work of the loading, but the damp sweats soon turned to chill. For a few minutes after they set out, the animals had sent up protests, the goat had bleated, the hens squawked, and the pony whinnied. Not long after, the wind took their voices and they all went quiet.

She headed she knew not where, was uncertain their direction would take them to a settlement her husband had mentioned only once. She wrenched around to look back and the house's sod face, its plank door and insufficient two windows, glared back. The hinny plodded on, until the draw curved and the house finally disappeared.

They bumped along behind the hinny. The pony

thumped along behind the wagon. The wagon's axles groaned at the rough ground and Mary worried they would not hold. She had wrapped Ezekiel in papers, then dressed them both in blankets and all the clothing they owned. And when that was done, she near buried them under the China rug.

The wagon's relentless bench banged along and they with it. She drove south toward a place her husband once mentioned might be building up ten miles away. She hoped she had heard him right; she hoped she had remembered right, lately her thinking had not been so sure. She left him a map on the table, drawing out the route she intended to take with a dot depicting where he could find them. And she penciled a note and signed it, "Love, your wife, Mary." She had drawn the words with care; he could barely read more than his own name.

If he had returned when she expected him, and if his disposition was loving as it once was, he would have brought her the mail and sugar, salt and flour, and whatever wood he could afford. He would have laid in winter supplies, cut and baled grasses to feed the animals in the shed, if they had survived the fall freeze. He would have shot rabbit and duck and mule deer for her to stew and jerk, and they would have had wood to burn in the stove through the winter.

At first, seeing no other choice, she had waited for him. When two weeks went by and he did not show, she brought out her rosary but found no succor in it. She and Ezekiel gathered grasses to feed the animals. They forked up what cow dung they could lay hands on, but they had not found enough of it to burn more than a few days. To keep warm they had fed the stove every bit of dung and wood scraps they could find, left from Edmund's work, then set upon the slats of the sow's pen after the sow froze. Mary burned pieces of the kitchen bench she did not think Edmund would notice and sawed a corner from the edge of their bed. Everything that could flame had been burnt: her apron, rags, even a desiccated rat and shells from the hens' eggs. No matter how well sod held onto warmth, the water bucket froze in a night.

When food ran short, she dug mud before the ground became too hard, and she caught frogs, which she roasted. She could hold a gun, and would have, but Edmund had taken it. She fashioned a trap for hare, but none took to it. When the pond froze over, she and Ezekiel chipped ice and brought in three pike, but no more than three ever bit. By the time they left, what was in the house to eat would have carried them less than a week.

———

Mary held her shoulder to Ezekiel's to offer what she could of her warmth. The wagon crept forward, its wheels pulling against the frozen tufts of grasses and the hills of prairie dogs. Ten miles seemed forever.

She pulled her son's cap down over the pink of his ears. The edge of the China rug buried his mouth. He had never been more than two miles off the farm, and then only when he was a toddler. She could not imagine what he was thinking.

He lifted his chin, exposed his lips. She heard him take a breath, watched as he swallowed. "Ma?"

"Yes?" she said.

"Are we going to die?"

She wished she had been ready for this, wished she had prepared a response. She paused before the answer came to her, and in that fillip of time, the pupils of his eyes shrank, yet he did not look away. "No," she said. She put her arm over his shoulders and pulled him into her.

———

They came out of the gentle hills, the only land her son had ever known. His eyes searched and teared up, she could not discern whether from the cold or from fear. They passed the Anderssons' farm and Ezekiel turned his head to look at it. He had been to the Anderssons' only once, three years ago when he had been too young to remember. When they cleared the last rise, the blast of prairie wind hit them full force. Ahead lay Nebraska's endless stretch.

Ezekiel's mouth turned white and puckered as if seeking something familiar to hold onto. She put the reins in one hand, wormed her arm tighter around his shoulders. He was small for his years and without a child's softness, his body sharp and without flesh in the way a tree branch is without it. He was midway between five and six years old, yet he no longer behaved a boy. In the last months he had begun to worry an adult's worry, to work beside her in the manner of a man, uncomplaining, dogged, adept with hammer or shovel. A child should complain. A child should whine and kick and argue. He did not. Remorse that she could not give him childhood sat with her every day.

Had she waited too long to leave? Two days ago, when the weather turned clear and without snow, she had gone for help. She had ridden the pony to the Anderssons', but the Anderssons and their six children were gone, the farm empty, the house closed, and the barn cleared out.

Leaving the farm she shared with Edmund was the first time since marrying him that she had mustered real action of her own making, and only then when choice lay between leaving, or staying and dying.

How had she come to this? She and Edmund had arrived in Nebraska with such hope. Edmund had taken two claims: a cattle claim under his name, a tree claim under hers. Their claims, strange and beautiful, lay thousands of miles from their childhood homes in Ireland. The hills rolled like a chorus of "God Be with You Kerry," and rose in swells that led down into gentle draws. Grasses, some high as the wagon, had whispered and hissed in the breeze. Wild rose mottled one hill, on another, wheatgrass and chokecherries, leadplant, bluestem, grama, and wild rye shifted and whorled at the whims of the wind. In the draw, lay a pond, fed by a stream and rounded by sedge and cattails. It had been a place of beauty and possibility then.

The day of their arrival, Edmund took the shovel and began gouging at a hill to dig them a home facing south. He determined the house should be just up from the pond. By noon their second day, he had dug a good outline.

That evening, with scents of new earth rising from his digging and a rabbit roasting over the fire, he washed in the rivulet that fed the pond. The evening had been warm, and they had slept with an insect's thin *theeeeee, theeeeee, theeeeee* calling nearby.

Each day, Edmund began work at first light. By the end of two months, just weeks before autumn, he finished the house sufficiently for them to sleep in. That evening, the eve of their moving to their own bed, Mary roasted a goose she had shot. It would be the last time to cook in the fire pit; she would have a proper stove to cook on, come the next day.

As the goose crackled and smoked, the baby had slept on a blanket laid over dry grasses a few feet away, his arms splayed out each side of his head, his tiny middle lifting and sinking. In a few moments, he would turn his head or open a hand in some thought or dream.

Edmund had washed and was groaning both in relief and in pain from his work. He took the towel and dried, then groaned again as he let himself down to lie beside the baby. He laid a blistered hand on the baby's head and said, "I love you, darlin' boy." Mary could feel what the boy felt, his pa's tenderness, the broad warmth of his touch, the steady care of his palm. The baby had made some small movement with his mouth and Edmund chuckled.

Edmund was able to afford ninety calves that first year. They fed and fattened on prairie grasses that spring and summer. He constructed a windlass near the house and did not need to dig far before it drew, sweet and clear. He sold the calves that fall, nearly doubling what he had paid. With the proceeds from the sale he bought one hundred and twenty more calves to fatten again.

Where did those times go? Where did Edmund go?

―――――

Mary's fingers ached, the mittens did little against the cold reins and the wind. Ezekiel was shivering. She handed the leathers over to him again. "You take us," she said. She wrapped an end of the blanket around his gloves, and for a moment he sat a little straighter.

The hinny plodded along, her ears held back from the wind. Ezekiel's nose ran, the mucus freezing on his lip. Mary wiped at it with the sleeve of her coat and pulled up Ezekiel's collar. He looked up at her. "We'll be warm soon," she said. He nodded, but just a little. She did not think it was only the cold that shined in his eyes.

Chapter 3

The day remained clear with a thin smear of sun bled of warmth. She had had the sense to notice the angle of her own shadow when they left midday, and had sighted direction from it. She told herself the shadow's opposite was south. For a while, as they drove, she kept the sun in their faces. But afternoon sun moved more westerly; the pace of that she could only guess. She let the light slip more and more to their right. *What was ten miles? How long did a hinny pulling a wagon need to travel it? What if she guessed wrong? What if her adjustments were sending them off course? What if she had heard Edmund wrong? What if there were no town after all?* She turned to look back, but the hills had almost disappeared, only a darkened ripple remained.

When she and Edmund and the baby first arrived three years ago, the train had let them off in Plum Creek, a small but growing town. They had bought the wagon there, and the hinny, and supplies. She knew she could find help there, maybe could find some way to support them until Edmund returned. But Plum Creek was another fifteen miles beyond the settlement she had heard of, an impossible distance now.

She searched ahead for a roof, a windmill, smoke from a fire, the dot of a farmhouse, a barn. There was nothing but prairie and low grasses covered with sharp snow. The sun, what there was left of it, was squinting-low and mean.

Wind deafened any sound but it. Ezekiel hung onto the reins as if they could hold him together. His eyes no longer teared; his mouth no longer worked but puckered in concentration or will, as his father's once had.

In minutes, dark would be on them. Then what? She could only think they would freeze.

———

The sun grew lower; darkness would settle in soon. Ahead lay the dimming line of the prairie, which the dark rendered even more endless. They had traveled for hours and seemed to have come no closer to anything. The hinny's head bobbed, the wind made a froth of her mane. The retreating horizon imparted no sense that they were moving at all. Mary allowed herself to think only of the hinny's pumping head, the flick-flick of her ears. At heart, Mary knew that if she were alone, by now she would have given up.

The hinny's stride changed the tiniest bit, and she stumbled over a mound. Mary thought the animal had come to the end of endurance. But the hinny righted herself, then looked off to the left. She lifted her head, threw back her long face, and gave out a mournful bray. Ezekiel pointed and shouted, "Ma! Ma!"

Ahead, a blemish.

Chapter 4

The sky had turned clear, the dusk swept clean of all warmth by the time Mary and Ezekiel came to the settlement. It would be dark in a quarter of an hour. There was little to the place but a handful of unpainted houses, a building the size of a barn with a small store attached, a livery, and an unoccupied structure sectioned for four businesses. Some frozen chokecherry bushes and straw grasses were all that marked something living. A train track and siding with a sagging railroad car sat to the south, and a mile beyond that spread the frozen Platte River. There was not a tree in sight, only four windmills that crackled and whined in the wind.

The door to the livery was open. By the light of a lamp, a bent, hunchbacked man worked a pitchfork. He came out, threw a load of soiled straw from the fork. He did not look up. The hinny cried; the pony blew. A horse in the livery whinnied back.

Mary took the reins. She did not know quite what she imagined the town would be: a busy old village like Macroom, in Ireland, or a city like Philadelphia where her sister lived. She swallowed a new fear: Where could she find somewhere to stay? In the dark it did not appear friendly.

On the slab-sided building was painted a sign" *Boarding, Emigrant House Hotel.* As much as they needed a place to

13

sleep and be warm, Mary certainly could not pay for a hotel, no matter how spare; she had only the money her mother had given her. The morning of Mary's wedding, Mrs. Sweeney had brought from her pocket a handkerchief tied with a string. She turned Mary's palm up and laid the handkerchief in it. The handkerchief held something solid and heavy as a watch. "My own ma gave one like this to me the day I wed your father," she said. "She told me to keep it secret, and I did." Mrs. Sweeney closed Mary's hand over the handkerchief and gave it a strong shake as if to cement what was in it.

"What is it?"

Her ma squeezed Mary's hand. "A woman should have sommat of her own."

"I have everything," Mary said.

"I hope you will always think so." But as she said it, her mother gave out a sniff weighted with doubt. "It's not much, only a one, and a one, and a one," she said. "The same your grandma gave me."

"Money?" Mary said. "But Da already gave Edmund my dower."

"But this pound, and shilling, and penny are *yours*, dear. And it is our secret."

Mary thought of her sister in Philadelphia. "Prune has one, too?" she said.

Her mother clicked her tongue but said nothing.

The bent man went back into the livery barn without giving Mary and Ezekiel even a "Hello." She was not sure he had seen them. He moved about, throwing hay into one of the pens. He did not look up, though he should have heard the wagon's jangle.

What reason could she give for their being here, just a boy and a woman appearing from nowhere on a frozen night? She felt deep inside that Edmund was alive, yet she could not admit to a stranger the shame that her husband had simply left her and their child.

Ezekiel's eyes were nervous, shifting, his head turning.

She threw back the rug, tucked Ezekiel tighter under it. He sucked in a breath that sounded frightened. "I'll be right back, son."

She went into the livery. The hairs in her nose were frozen stiff. She held her wrists inside the sleeves of her coat and tried to summon the courage to speak to this man fluffing straw. The warmth of the livery settled on her face. The barn held a warren of six pens, four empty stalls, a mow for hay, a corner filled with grain sacks. Near the door, a fire pit was flanked by an anvil and a workbench for smithing. Only two pens held animals, one with the horse, the other with a sow and eight piglets.

The man's shoulders were twisted under a lopsided hump that obscured his view of Mary. The sow snorted, but he kept working, his movements stiff and pained. Crippled as he was, she could not imagine how he could smith.

"Sir?" she said.

He huffed, then turned toward her.

"I wonder if you would be in need of a pony."

He rose up, put a hand on his back. "To board?"

"I have one to sell," she said. Her voice quivered.

"Horses we can use. Don't need ponies."

15

"It is not old."

He let himself out the gate of the pen, leaned his fork against the stall, and went outside. The wagon with its cage and goat and heap of things appeared merely a shadow, Ezekiel little more than a lump on the bench "You have a child with you?"

"Yes," she said.

"You staying in the Emigrant House?"

"No."

He rubbed the small of his back. He had not yet looked at her, but when he did, she had the feeling he was weighing her. He pointed toward the back of the wagon. "That the pony you're talking about?"

"Yes." She feared he would turn away and go back to his sow and pitchfork.

"Well, what you want for that pony?"

"Board for the hinny mule."

"How long?"

"I don't know," she said, then added, "Not long."

The goat bleated. "I don't take goats," he said. "Goats chew up a place."

"You'll exchange the pony for board for the hinny?"

He held up two fingers. "Two weeks. Hay every day, clean straw, half a bucket of grain."

"You don't want to see the pony?"

"I seen it."

She untied the pony and gave the liveryman its lead. "What is the name of this town?"

"Cozad," he said, "Nebraska," as if she were too dull to know what state. "Where you planning to sleep, then?"

16

He seemed to know she had no ready answer. He pointed across the street to one of the empty storefronts that appeared to have once been a saddler's. A weathered sign over it said *Saddles & Harnesses Made & Repaired.* "You can stay in the saddler's," he said, "for the night. But you'll need to ask Mrs. Gatewood at the Emigrant House tomorrow if it's more than that."

She was about to return to the wagon, then turned back to him and asked, "Where might I find the post office?" His mouth cracked as if about to smile. He pointed toward the train track. "The old boxcar," he said, "on that siding there. You have something coming in?"

"No," she said. "I want the postman to see if there is something waiting for me in the post office at Plum Creek." She did not add that she expected letters from her sister would be there.

"Traber Gatewood is the one to see." He swung back his head, then rubbed his shoulder. "You might find his whereabouts in the hotel."

She turned to go. "Missus?" he said, "Talk to Mrs. Gatewood. She runs most of town." He turned and took hold his fork as if this were all Mary needed to know.

"Where might I find her?"

He swung his hand toward the Emigrant House Hotel building. "She'll be there tomorrow morning. If she likes the look of you, she might come up with a bite to eat. You can stay the night in the old saddlery," he said. "After that, you'll have to speak to her."

Mary set her foot on the running board of the wagon, the raw wind billowed her skirt, and she shivered. "We have somewhere to sleep the night," she said to Ezekiel. She thought to ease him with this, but his eyes remained wide, bewildered. He had never seen anything like this town.

The saddlery door was not locked. The space was empty but for six saddle racks nailed to the walls, and a stove in one corner. She wanted to scream her relief.

She pulled the rug away from Ezekiel. "Let's get the goat and the hens inside." He untied the goat, the doe bounced down from the wagon and, as he led her, his eyes lost some of their terror.

Mary carried in the cages with the hens. As he tethered the goat to a nail on the wall, Mary set the hens on the floor. A *wood* floor. For five years, she had lived with dirt floor, dirt walls, dirt everything but the roof.

It was dark, by the time they brought in the China rug and blankets and cordoned the hens in a corner. Only a mere shimmer of light let through the windows. Mary laid out the rug by the stove, told Ezekiel to spread the blankets on it to sleep on. She put the skillet and pot, the lamp, the tomato preserves, and the rat-riddled sack of grain along another wall. They left the trunk with the books and linens and the sewing machine in the wagon.

Ezekiel's breath chuffed clouds. "Sit near the stove," she said.

"There's no wood in it."

"I know," she said, "we'll see to a fire."

He did not ask with what; they had no wood. She pulled the China rug up around his shoulders. The wind crept under the door and through the loose-seated walls. She knotted her skirts high, took one of the saddle racks in her hands, and heaved all her weight into it. The rack moved half an inch. She thrust herself back. It moved a bit more. She threw herself forward again and back and forward until the nails screamed and began to give.

"What are you doing, Ma?"

The rack swept freer of the wall. The nails groaned. Ezekiel got up and came over. He grabbed hold and together they heaved back, and pushed forward, and heaved back, and forward again until it fell onto the floor.

———

The saddle rack made for a fire that flamed hot at first, then flared out in less than an hour. She regretted the example her destruction of another's property sent Ezekiel. In another day, in another place, she might have punished him for the same kind of theft.

The warmth brought color to Ezekiel's cheeks and allowed the animals to settle. The hens mumbled among themselves and hammered their beaks at the wormy grain Mary spread. The goat let out a sigh, bent one knee, and folded herself onto the floor. She jerked, lifted her chin and gave out one putrid belch.

When Mary and Ezekiel had eaten all but two of the corncakes and some of the tomato preserves, Ezekiel curled on the rug. In a blink, he was sleeping, his mouth open, breath coming almost without sound. She lay beside him, pulled the blanket and quilt around them both, and settled her arm over him, and wondered what a good mother would do.

Chapter 5

A dull morning sun, crinkled by the iced window, threw a somber light into the saddler's room. Mary cast her blanket over Ezekiel, found a cluster of cinders in the core of the ash, poked until flame began to lick up, and then fed another piece of the broken rack to the stove. As a flame took, she gave one of the corncakes to the goat, tethered her to a window sash. As dry as the cake was, Mary would have eaten it herself, but the doe needed to be fed; they needed the doe.

The hens were mumbling, her son still sleeping in his blanket as she pulled closed the door. She had left the last cake for him.

The door to the Emigrant House Hotel was ill hung and screeched open to a hollow, echoing cavern of a room. A long table and benches sat in the middle of it. The room smelled of the sulfur of eggs scrambled some time ago and of ham. Sturdy cups and crumbs sat at places where people had just eaten. A butter plate and slices of uneaten bread on a platter lay in the middle; Mary wrenched her eyes from them.

The room was warm, plain, and smelled of new wood. Three doors led off it, one open to the kitchen, another, closed, leading to the attached store and bearing a brass plaque reading *Office and Mercantile*. The last, also closed, bore a plaque reading *Dentist*.

21

A fire snapped in a stove in the corner. As she went further in, the rich smell of onions and meat cooking wafted through the kitchen doorway. There came a woman's mumbling, her voice low-throated and rippling. Mary could not make out what she said. The smells nearly bent her in half. The woman must have heard the door. She called out, "Be there in a moment." Mary stood with her hands in front of her. Her jaws ached from the scents.

From the kitchen came the tapping of shoes, the soft rustle of a skirt. A woman a head taller than Mary floated through the doorway holding a paper written with a recipe. From the voices, Mary had expected someone young, not much older than herself. But this woman was white-haired, near sixty years old and taller even than Edmund. "Are you the one Clarence Simpson said came in last night?"

Mary's knees quivered; she tried to compose herself. "I suppose."

The woman moved along as strong and upright as a young woman. Her assurance made Mary want to back away or to curtsy. "I'm Mrs. Robert Gatewood."

Mary dipped a small curtsy. "Mary Harrington," she said, then realized she should have introduced herself as Mrs. Edmund Harrington.

"The child," Mrs. Gatewood said. "Clarence said there was a child with you." Her words were spoken slowly, strung along one to another rich and elegant, like beads on silk.

"I came in for work," Mary said.

"What do you do?" It was not said rudely or with any

22

emotion other than in service of what the woman might need done.

"I sew," Mary said.

"There's not much sewing needs doing at a hotel."

"The mercantile."

"Not much sewing there either, my dear."

Now she felt a fool, though the woman's expression seemed to imply only humor. Mary's need drove her not to back down; she had to do something to feed them and a hotel with a kitchen seemed like the place. "I plant," she said. "I grow a good garden." Another foolish utterance, for there would be no planting in winter; it was frozen crisp outside and would remain that way for months. But she did grow a good garden; she and Edmund and Ezekiel had eaten well from them over the last years.

"I see."

Mary knew she sounded like an idiot. A hiss came from the kitchen, the smell of butter on a hot skillet. "I can cook anything there is to cook."

"I have someone to cook for me, but . . ." Mrs. Gatewood tucked her chin. Her eyes bore down on Mary as if in some doubt. Mary felt like a dwarf. "I may," she said, "need a housekeeper now and then."

"Yes?" Mary pressed her hands together.

"When we have people staying," she added.

"I could start immediately."

"There isn't but one man staying right now." She waved her off. "He keeps after himself."

"When might others be coming?"

"I said, 'If they come.' We can't be certain they will."

The woman's eyes shifted to the window, opaque with steam. "We don't expect the first of them until spring." Spring? Mary's chin began to quiver. She pressed her hand against it. If Edmund did not return, she could not wait until spring. Her knees began to give in and she locked them. Her one, and a one, and a one she knew would come to five dollars and ten cents. She could buy a bit to eat with it and a room for a few days. Then what?

"Anyway, I only ever hire on unmarried girls. You have a child with you."

"Yes," Mary said.

"I can only pay you, Mrs. Harrington, if the child is a bastard."

"A bastard?"

"If you aren't married."

"But I am married."

"Your husband must agree then. The law says I will need Mr. Harrington's permission. I cannot put you on without it."

"But it may be some time before he arrives."

"How long is some time?"

"I cannot say for sure," Mary said.

Mrs. Gatewood threw her hands to her waist, elbows out as if disgusted by the circularity of the conversation. Mary took half a step back. "What do you have in your larder?" Mrs. Gatewood said.

"I have no larder. I have nothing but the wagon."

"You must have preserves from your garden."

"We ate them," Mary said, "but for two."

"You came from somewhere," Mrs. Gatewood said.

She waited, then, as if for Mary to respond. Mary rose up straighter. When she had no reply, the older woman took a breath and patted back a wisp of white hair. "I think there's some blankets might need washing. It would not be much, but it might stand you a supper."

Mary felt the thickening of her lips as they made to cry. She nearly shouted, "Do you want them washed right now?"

"Tomorrow," Mrs. Gatewood said. "And I'll pay you ahead with a bowl of stew for you and the child." She dabbed a handkerchief at her own eye. "Mr. Simpson said you spent last night in the saddlery." She did not wait for Mary to answer. "I am afraid you will need to leave it."

"When?"

"When I sell it or can get a lease on it."

Chapter 6

She washed the blankets Mrs. Gatewood gave her in a trough near the hotel where some townspeople, without windlasses of their own, watered their animals and bucketed water to their houses. The trough was built over a fire pit to guard against freeze. Now and then, Mary saw Mrs. Gatewood in the window, checking her work.

Though the hotel building sheltered her from the wind, her hands grew numb and her shoulders cramped. The blankets froze stiff as wood on the line. She was almost finished, just one blanket left to hang, when it cracked and broke as she hung it and the line shifted. The break was as long as her foot. She tried to move the blanket to cover the damage, but only broke it further. And there it was, the line gleaming right through the break.

She laid her face in her hands. Her hands were so cold she could not feel her cheeks. The wind lifted her bonnet, the string cut into her chin as if to throttle her. Until Edmund returned, her life and her son's rested on the old woman at the hotel. She had to make herself useful, to do something the old woman would come to depend on. Now, she had ruined even that.

She rolled down the sleeves of her coat, slipped her hands into them. She went through the screeching door. The heat from the kitchen hit her face. She breathed the smell of bread baking for supper. She did not call out;

27

there was no more need for decorum. She did not ask for permission to enter but went directly into the kitchen. She had lost everything. There was nothing more to risk.

Mrs. Gatewood was laying a towel across loaves that a young woman was taking from the oven. "I have," Mary said, "broken a blanket."

Mrs. Gatewood did not look up. She took another towel, covered a second loaf. She stood straight, seemed to hold in a little smile and looked straight at Mary. "I wondered what you would do about that." She took up one of the loaves, wrapped a towel under and around it, then handed it to Mary and said no more.

Chapter 7

They stayed in the saddlery two nights, then three. The goat let down her milk, but it would be three days before the hens began to lay. Mary burned the last of the saddle rack, tore another from the wall. She tried to turn away from the shapeless unknowing of when she would see Edmund again but found herself searching the street, then checking again and again.

Wind whipped through the saddlery and took with it most of the heat the stove could muster. Mary blocked the worst of the draft near the stove with the trunk, catching what she could of warmth. She set the treadle on the other side, draped a blanket over it. The make-do room kept hold of the heat a bit longer.

At the livery, she described Edmund to Mr. Simpson in case he might have seen him. She went to inquire again the next day and the next. By the fourth morning, Mr. Simpson merely shook his head when he saw her. The bread Mrs. Gatewood had given her was gone. Every morning, she pushed through the hotel door, asking about work. For supper, these four nights, Mary had thrown a potato into the fire and they had eaten it without the benefit of butter, salt or even lard. There were only eight potatoes left. The tomato preserves would last another few days. Even with the potatoes and the tomatoes, the hens' eggs, and milk from the goat's thin teats, Ezekiel's

29

stomach—and hers—bellowed.

The fifth day at the hotel, Mary pointed out the stove to Mrs. Gatewood. "I could clean it."

"It's man's work," Mrs. Gatewood said.

"I can do it," Mary said. "I've done it before." She tried to stave off the groveling in her voice, though groveling it was.

"I have a man for it."

"Does he clean the stove for a bowl of food?"

Mrs. Gatewood threw her head back and laughed. "No, a man gets paid for the work he does."

"The floor, then, do you have a man to finish the floor?"

"What is wrong with the floor? It is not a year old."

"A good varnish to make it elegant for your guests."

Mrs. Gatewood laid her hand on Mary's shoulder. "Mary, I cannot hire you."

"I could . . . exchange." The only word she could think of.

Mrs. Gatewood's head gave a small shake. "Exchange?"

"Exchange a good floor for . . ."

"I repeat, what's wrong with my floor?"

"It's bare," Mary said. This old woman had everything. She had people to do her bidding and had all the resources plus the faith that she could do whatever she wanted. The cloud of Mrs. Gatewood's hair, her grand white size, the steadiness of her certainty, allowed Mary to dare. "It is plain," she said, "unwelcoming."

Mrs. Gatewood looked down, swept one foot over it, and laughed. "Unwelcoming?" And she laughed again.

"You're not going to admit this floor is good enough until you have your way about it. Is that it?" She ducked her head, looked down at Mary. Her expression held no superiority, no belittling. "I think," she said, "I have some old resin you could use."

It was as if the old woman now saw something worthwhile in her. "Yes," Mary said, "in exchange for a bowl every evening for my boy." How had her mouth gotten such courage?

"And a bowl for you, I would think."

Mary did not dare to speak, lest she risk the conversation take a turn.

"My dear, you are as bony as your goat."

Mrs. Gatewood told her to come back at noon, after dinner was finished.

Chapter 8

There was a time in her life when Mary *knew* people in a way no one else seemed to. Her *knowing* manifested from a glimpse, or the way they stood, or took a breath, or from some scent rising from them. It came on her sudden, like a bolt, and she would know, in that moment, the most intimate and unspoken part of a person.

As a girl still in primary classes in Macroom, she had once tested the truth of her impressions. Their neighbors, the Murphys, lived not far down the road. Mr. Murphy kept milk cows that grazed along the rocky hills. While Mary's family with only four children was considered small, the Murphys had but one child, a girl three years older than Mary. Bernadette was pale; her parents kept her in the house most days, dressed in fancies and thick scarves lest she become sick and die and leave them childless.

One day, Mary said to Mrs. Murphy, "Why did your baby have to go to heaven?"

Mrs. Murphy's face whitened. "Which?"

"The one last week."

Mrs. Murphy swiped the back of her hand on Mary's cheek. "Och, what are you saying, child?" A tear came to her eye. "I never told anaone a' that. Was you sneakin' around the house, Mary?"

"No," Mary said.

Mrs. Murphy looked away and dabbed a handkerchief to her eye. "My mister dina' even know. I never told anaone." Her eyes scanned Mary's. "How then?"

Mary wished, then, that she had kept her feeling to herself or at least had indeed overheard or seen something.

"How?"

"I knew," Mary said.

"It inna' sommat a girl knows."

"The Lord," Mary said, and let the implication take care of what could not be believed; that she just knew, nothing more. She learned to keep this sense to herself.

Those understandings fled when she met Edmund. She had never been able to know him this way, to cut through whatever he kept unspoken. It was, she thought, what made her fall in love with him. But now these senses seemed to be returning, she felt a twinge of insight when she had spoken to Mrs. Gatewood, but did not know whether to trust herself in it.

———

Jars with jam and butter and a platter with one uneaten biscuit sat in the middle of the table. The cook came out, wiped away crumbs with a damp cloth, then took up the platter and jars and slipped back into the kitchen.

A pot sat near the stove. It reeked of lacquer. On the floor sat a holystone the size of her head. She shoved the first bench against the wall at one end of the room, then the other bench. The benches she could manage, but the table weighed four times more than she. There was no one to help, so one end at a time she crept the table, inch by inch like a crab. The legs howled. She waited for some recrimination for her noise, but none came. She finally settled the thing along with the benches.

Without the furniture in the middle, the room ballooned larger, the floor going on forever. She took up the holystone, knelt, and started scraping.

———

The cook left for three quarters of an hour; by then Mary had been scraping three hours, three hours when her son had been alone. She longed to see to him, make sure the room was sufficiently warm, to mumble some encouragement or comfort, but this would need to wait.

Her hands began to bleed and she asked the cook for rags to wrap them. As the cook found two clean cloths, Mary eyed the bucket half filled with slops from the breakfast; it held the crust from a biscuit, some burned ham, a scraping of mush, some beans.

The cook set a pot of tea on the table and a variety of thick, chipped cups. Mary wrapped her hands with the towels and found in the pain some relief from thoughts. The cook went into the kitchen, came back and set bowls and spoons around. Mary had barely put out table and benches for the supper when, at four o'clock, a thunder of feet stomped on the porch and six men puffed in through the door. Three of them Mary had seen at breakfast. One of them said, "What we got tonight, Hilda?"

The cook blushed and said, "Fried donkers and spuds." She went back to the kitchen and brought out a plate of meat rolls and fried potato rounds. The meat steamed as she went by and sent up the aroma of pepper and parsley.

Mary stood aside, hands folded in front of her until Hilda finally brought out two bowls and handed them to Mary. One held four donkers and another some of the evening's chicken and cheese. Mary cradled the bowls back to the saddlery.

Ezekiel had pulled himself up to the cold stove, leaning on it for whatever heat it still held. He had covered nearly all of himself, head, shoulders, back, lap, and legs with their blankets. Only his eyes and his arms and hands were exposed. He held a book. "I brought us sommat to eat," Mary said. She lit a fire and they ate without speaking. His lips sought out each bite like a pond guppy seeks bugs' eggs. He did not look up from the bowl; he ate so fast, he barely chewed. He slept, then, his face clear and pink, his lips pup-pupping at some dream. And when dark settled in and his sleep was sound, she took up her skillet and let herself out.

Five inches of snow reflected what there was of a pale moon. The wind cut through her coat and drew up a thin scrim of brittle white like a ghost whorling up. The entire town was dark; no windows glowed with lamps. There was no sound but the wind. Mary was the sole creature out. She crept around back of the hotel, lost her footing in a deep shadow, nearly fell. She toed for the steps into the kitchen, found one then slipped up to the door and cupped her hands at the window pane. The slop bucket was heaped with gristle, chewed chicken bones, leftover bread, grease, cores, and peels from apples Hilda had sauced for morning, waiting to be thrown to the pigs in the morning. She went inside, grabbed at the container, and tipped it into her skillet.

Next morning before dawn, she started a fire. And when the fire was hot, she set the skillet on the stove to heat. The smell of food warming woke Ezekiel and he sat up. He rubbed his eyes and blinked. "Come," she said, "we have something to eat beside milk and tomatoes."

Chapter 9

Mary moved the furniture again to finish the last of the stoning. Her back and shoulders spasmed and throbbed, her knees and hands felt as if they had been mauled. Her knees, in spite of being wrapped in rags, left bloody streaks on her skirt. She knew, to the heart of her, why the stone was called holy: because of the supplicant it made of one.

She swept a rag over the mess of dust stirred up by the stone, then found a bucket and mop. The relief to her knees nearly made her cry. When the floor was sufficiently dry, she pried the lid from the varnish pot. She set it on the fire. As it began to melt, the first whiff made her gasp and grab at the wall. Mrs. Gatewood closed the door to her office. Hilda closed the door to the kitchen.

Mary grew light-headed even before the lacquer was hot enough to catch onto the brush. She held her breath until she could open one of the windows. She stuck her head out and whooped air until her head cleared.

When the pot eventually burbled, she took it up and began brushing. She was able to lay down only four swipes before she thought she would vomit. She opened the door. The room grew cold, and the stuff thickened. She put the pot back on the stove. When it began to bubble again, she took the brush and resumed. She finally found a pattern that left her merely light-headed.

Around three o'clock, Mrs. Gatewood came out and told her to put the stuff away so the men would not faint when they came in for supper. "And I have a roomer upstairs." She pointed to a narrow stair of raw wood. "We don't want to asphyxiate him by morning."

By the end of that day, the floor was just half-finished. The thought of food nearly made Mary sick.

———

Some light still bled through the saddlery window. Ezekiel was spreading bread crumbs, throwing some, eating some. The hens were at his feet, their beaks tapping, wattles flapping. The goat was on her tether in the corner, grinding through some grasses Ezekiel had gathered.

Their bowls held tongue and potatoes that night. The tongue was tough. Mary would have known how to make it tender. They sat on their blankets and chewed and sopped the bread as the goat eyed them and bleated her hunger.

When they were done with their meal, Mary said, "I want you to give me your pants and your shirt." The animals had grown quiet by then.

"Why?" he said.

"I need to check them over."

He frowned, suspicious. "They're all right."

"I need to see."

He gathered his lips, took off his pants, then his shirt. He was so thin. "Put on my coat," she said. She shrugged out of it and laid it over his shoulders. As he buried himself in it, she lit a candle.

40

His clothes were in rugged shape and too big for him though it had been nearly a year since she sewed them. He had not filled out, had barely grown taller. When she sewed things for him, she had left wide seams, anticipating him to grow. Thin as he was, her wide seams needed no letting out. She cut fragments of good material from the extra seam allowance. By the time she was finished he was asleep.

She visited the hotel's slop bucket again that night.

Chapter 10

Mrs. Gatewood told her not to come until later the next morning, after breakfast. "So we can do with a few minutes without the stink," she said.

Mary went in just as Mrs. Gatewood was shutting the door to her office. The room was hot. As if trying to hurry things along, the fire was stoked high, the varnish pot already burping. She felt sick at the stink. Acres of floor still needed the varnish.

She began moving furniture. Her feet ticked in yesterday's work. The men's boots from breakfast had left a dull and dirty path from the door to the table. Sidling the table gouged arcs in her tender work. She had pictured her finished floor perfect, without blemish, bright as a new-shined shoe.

She had to be finished by the end of the day and would have to leave the blemishes to do it. She threw open the windows. An abysmal slice of wind whipped in snow, which settled in narrow drifts below the window. When the men came in for their midday meal, she covered the pot, let herself out, went to the saddlery. Ezekiel was sitting on the floor. "Ma," he said as if surprised she was there. The trunk was open, its lid collapsed back on the hinge. He was wrapped in blankets reading; books were stacked all around his legs. As if for companionship, he had tethered the goat to the hasp of the trunk, and she was lying next to him, smacking at cud. Mary had brought him half a biscuit left by one of the men after breakfast.

She sat down, leaned against the trunk with him. "What are you reading?" He held up *Ragged Dick*. "You like that one?" she said. He nodded. She stroked his arm. "Why?"

He looked down at it as if it had the answer. "Dick made himself spectable," he said.

"You mean respectable?"

"Ma, what is a boot black?"

"Someone who shines boots," she said.

"I could do that," he said, "couldn't I?"

"If someone had a boot he wanted shined." She shook the cap on his head and he blinked. "I don't think you should look up to a boy like Dick who cursed and smoked cigars and was not a gentleman." She took out the biscuit and gave it to him.

He began eating, a powder of flour settling on the blanket. His forehead gathered in the crimped concentration of an old man's. "But I could earn us money like he did," he said, "couldn't I?"

It was as if their penury, as if every step, every decision in her life had borne down on this child who understood he might only make something of himself if he were like this poor fictitious creature in a book. "You won't need to," she said. "We'll get by until your pa comes. Then things will get better." He screwed his face up and held his gaze on her as if seeking some truth.

———

She returned to the hotel. Aromas of a roasting meat wafted from the kitchen. By four o'clock, she was nearing done with the floor. There came a stamping at the door, a slapping of hats on thighs. The door screamed open, let in a cold witch's breath. The tallest man Mary had ever seen ducked through the door. He was so tall his head about hit the jamb. He held his elbows and brrred. The furrows of wool knit marked his forehead and he scratched it. He bellowed, "Ma?"

From her office, Mrs. Gatewood yelled, "Wipe your feet," like any mother to a son.

He hung his muffler and coat on a peg. "Sam Atkinson and David Claypool are with me." His voice rumbled low in his chest, a nice voice. The two other men were steadies Mary had seen coming each day for their meals. They seemed dwarfed beside him. They hung their coats then crammed gloves into the pockets and scrambled to hold their hands over the stove.

Mary kept working. She expected rebuke when Mrs. Gatewood came out from her office, but there was none. All day she had worked behind the closed door. Her cheeks were puffed and her eyes sunken.

The tall fellow pulled back Mrs. Gatewood's chair. She settled into it and blew out a breath. "I'm getting too old for this," she said. She turned toward the kitchen. "Hilda, make some tea for the boys."

Her son gave out a tired laugh. "I was thinking of something a bit stronger than tea, Ma."

She waggled a finger. "Traber," she said.

"I know," he said. "He'll have no licker in *this* town."

"Wash up before supper," she said. The men shuffled, like obedient boys, into the kitchen. There came the sounds of water being pumped, the soft rustles of hands being dried on a towel. Mary spread another gob from the brush.

The two regulars slipped onto the benches. Traber began the process of folding his legs under the table, one shin and thigh at a time. He knocked a knee and grabbed it. "Gah," he said.

Hilda came out from the kitchen. Mrs. Gatewood said, "Is the tea ready?" Hilda nodded.

"Leave the tea to me, Traber hold my chair." Traber extricated himself from the bench, legs first like unfolding a measuring stick. He stood, pulled out his mother's chair and she went into the kitchen.

Mary had heard mention of all the men's names: Sam Atkinson and David Claypool. She did not know which was which. All the men's necks were speckled with sawdust. Their hands were raw, their faces mottled from the cold. One, whose hair was red as Edmund's and parted oddly from his cap, favored a thumb with a black nail. The other had his hair thick and white as a boll. His wrist was wrapped with a bandage. He was perhaps a bit older than either of the others, but not old enough to warrant white hair.

All, including Traber, were in their twenties, not much older than Mary's twenty-two years. They had all nodded at her when they first came in but were not paying much attention as she worked. They made no comment on the stink Mary had made, nor did they complain of the cold cutting through the open windows.

From the kitchen came the squeak of the oven door,

the crackle of pork roasting, and the room filled with the aroma of crisped fat. A pan tapped onto a counter, a spoon stirred, a knife ticked. The tang of an orange wafted in. Mary's stomach roared, spit filled her mouth. She had had an orange only once while staying with Prune in Philadelphia. Prune had gotten a basket of them from a family she knew who were visiting from the south. Mary had never tasted anything so wonderful.

While Mrs. Gatewood was gone, the men mumbled about the new house they were building on West Eleventh near a street they had named L Avenue. Mrs. Gatewood came out carrying a tray with a teapot and four cups. As she passed, Mary could smell the whiff of whiskey. Traber smiled, the other two men cleared their throats. "So," Traber said, "some of your special blend, then."

"Drink up and be quiet," she said. "You'll want it when I tell you the news. Trabe, there's a telegram on my desk. Would you get it?"

He began the complicated unfolding of his legs again, the thin-legged, kneesy rising of a spider. He went into her office, brought out a yellow paper.

Mrs. Gatewood said, "Did you read what was on it?"

"No," he said, "but not because I didn't want to."

She clicked her fingers, took it, laid it face down beside her fork, then put her hand on it. The dark around her eyes seemed to deepen.

They ate, and as they did, they talked quietly. Mrs. Gatewood asked the red-haired man about Mrs. Atkinson. Mary could deduce his name. "Ach," he said, "my wife is surely ready for the baby to come." He spoke in the tones

47

of Ireland, his words carrying the green of Irish meadows, the low homes built of stone, and the scent of the sea filled her with longing.

"How many young is it now?" Mrs. Gatewood said, her voice pleasant, conversational but without spirit. The telegram lay near her fork. In some manner, by avoiding it, whatever was on it gained grave weight. The men's eyes flickered to it.

"'Tis six it will be when the new baby comes," Mr. Atkinson said.

From the kitchen came the drag of a spoon stirring, the aroma of gravy, another tapping at the edge of a pan. Hilda brought out a platter of ham sliced thick. She set the platter on the table and, for a moment, no one spoke. She went back, returned with a plate of hot baked potatoes and a bowl of sauced apples.

"Ma," Traber said, "what's on the telegram?"

"We'll eat first," she said.

They ate and as they did, Mrs. Gatewood asked the white-haired fellow about his two girls. Mary knew by deduction he was David Claypool. He had not spoken since they came in but had sat quiet, removed, working his mouth under his mustache. He was thin, his neck ropey, his suit worn at the hem and cuffs. It had been a good suit of black wool when it was new. There was elegance in his stillness, in his straight-shouldered manner. He might have been good looking but for the sharp sinking of his cheeks. He fingered his empty cup. "The girls are doing well enough," he said. He did not look up. "They are of an age to take care of the house. But they miss their mother." He blinked and his cheeks grew red. "I miss their mother."

"It will take time," Mrs. Gatewood said. "It has been only four months."

They talked about town, about the coming spring, about people they knew who were coming to look around when the weather changed. They paid no more attention to Mary and her stinking brush than they would a beetle. Their talk grew looser and more intimate with the food and the whiskey. Mary envied them.

When they were finished, Hilda cleared the dishes. The men leaned forward. Mrs. Gatewood took up the telegram, held it face out beside her cheek. "I asked you all here tonight because there is something you all need to know: I heard from Mr. Cozad this morning." She laid the telegram down, fingered back a tendril of hair. "The first immigrants are due in six weeks."

Traber blurted, "Six *weeks*?"

She nodded. "Six weeks."

"In *February*?" he said.

She ignored him.

"How many?"

"Twenty."

"Ma, that's nearly as many as we have living here now." His expression was stuck between excitement and disbelief.

She took eyeglasses from a chest pocket, pinched them to her nose, shook the paper. "Let me read."

MOTHER

Traber barked, "Mother? Mother? He's never called you mother. He wants something."

"Indeed," she said.

> MOTHER STOP TWENTY POTENTIALS
> COMING 6 WEEKS STOP MUST STEP UP
> BLDG BEFORE THEY COME STOP 6 NEW
> HOUSES & NEW BLDING FOR SHOPS
> IMMED W OF EM HOTEL STOP GET MEN
> FRM ALL DAWSON CO AND ACROSS RVR
> IF RVR STILL FROZN STOP START WK ON
> STRAW BRIDGE TO FINISH BEFORE
> THAW STOP TELL TRABER SEE PLANS I
> DREW STOP & TO FIND AS MANY MEN AS
> HE CAN STOP ORDER LUMBR FOR BLDG
> & STRAW FOR BRIDGE & GRAVEL FOR
> MERIDIAN & 8 STS STOP NOW RPEAT
> NOW STOP PAY 1$ AND HALF PER 1 DAY
> WORK

Mrs. Gatewood leaned forward, laid the telegram face down. "He left you the plans, Trabe?"

"Yes," he said. "We agreed we could have *some* houses and a new building done by the end of summer. There was nothing about a bridge."

None of the men moved, none spoke. It was as if the wind had frozen them. Mrs. Gatewood removed her spectacles, rubbed the bridge of her nose again. Traber banged down a fist. "What does he think we are? Six new houses and a new building in *six weeks*?" He waggled his chin. "Oh, and by the way, add a bridge and gravel the streets. He damn wants the world."

She placed her hands in her lap and sat back as if she had expected this. "We knew he wanted the world when we followed him here," she said, her voice softened, lowered and slowed, a balm.

"Ma, you know how long it took us to get up this hotel and it's nothing but a barn with a few rooms in the loft."

"Three weeks with a handful of men."

"He wants us to put up another building the size of the hotel *and* six new houses? That's a house a week. Not to mention a new business building, and bridge, and whatever else he happens to think up."

She grinned sideways and said, "He didn't say done. He just said up."

"And how would you define 'up'?"

"Four walls and a roof." They all laughed. It had been so long since Mary had heard laughter.

"I still don't think we can do it," Traber said.

Mrs. Gatewood held up a sharp finger that said *stop*. "And thinking like that," she said, "will prove you right. I mean it. As much as ambition drives John Cozad he has never lost faith. None of us was here two years ago. There was nothing here two years ago, no town, no hotel, no land. It's because of him we have what we have. He's my son-in-law and I love him, but he is not perfect and I know it. John Cozad may rage . . ."

Traber mumbled, "*May* rage."

". . . he may insult."

"*May* insult?"

"Traber, I mean it," she said. "But by God, John Cozad does get things done. We have a future here, it just begins a bit sooner than we thought."

She stood, put her spectacles and the telegram in her

pocket, and patted her skirt. "Enough of my preaching. Traber," she said, "take me home." She laid a hand at the small of her back. "I am tired."

————

Mr. Claypool and Mr. Atkinson stayed after. They sat quiet awhile, watching their fingers play with crumbs. The room held no sound but their breathing and the thump of Mary's knee as she dragged the brush. She could feel the pulse of their thoughts. To them, six weeks was too sudden. To her it was forever. Without work, without more food, she and Ezekiel could not last six weeks. If Edmund did not show soon, could she find something to do with the rush of new people? She did not know.

Neither of the men spoke. Then Mr. Atkinson said, "Dave, is't true where he gets money to pay all this?" He made a movement with his hands like he was dealing cards.

Mr. Claypool nodded. "Riverboats."

"Ach, then. If I knew how 'twas done, I'd do it myself and skip town."

Mary dipped the brush, maybe the last time. She swung the brush out, but not far enough. A lump the size of a marble of the hot syrup dropped, as if to a target, onto the root of her thumb. She yipped. The men stopped their talk. One of them sprang up, bent over her.

"Miss?" Mr. Atkinson asked.

She held her hand to her, stifled a cry, embarrassed.

When he saw the pot and the brush, he said, "Och, the devil's own stew."

Mr. Claypool disappeared into the kitchen. The water

pump pumped. He came out with a dripping rag, laid it on her hand. She sucked in a breath. His tender consideration tore at her. Pain held her together. "Thank you," she said. She made her voice bright. "'Tis much better."

JEANNIE BURT

Chapter 11

Mary carried Ezekiel's books against her chest. He had cried when she told him he was to go to school. The burn to her hand had stung long into the night. She rose once and rubbed it with grease from their bowls, then covered it over with cloth. The pain eased a bit, but throbbed still.

School was taught in an empty house, a temporary measure until the men could one day construct a proper schoolhouse. "I wish we never came here," he said.

"It is not far," Mary said.

He pulled back against her hand.

With all he had been through, the prospect of school seemed his heaviest burden. He cowered as they passed a woman holding her bonnet, then again as a man, leading a sorrel into the livery, dipped his head in greeting. Mary pulled Ezekiel past the hotel, past the mercantile store, past the business that sold parts for windmills.

The schoolroom was up two steps and held in what would one day be the house's parlor. A woodstove crackled in a corner. A gray chalkboard hung on a wall, scribbled with numbers—adds and subtracts—and with words drawn with care: *dog, apple, street, shirt, horse, grasshopper, million, moon.*

The teacher, a young man with hair pomaded smooth from a center part, sat at a small desk with an open book and a world globe. Five children, three boys and two girls, faced one another on benches each side of a table. In front of them lay two books they shared. The books were open as if they had just been reading. They all looked up as Mary pushed Ezekiel into the room.

The teacher stood up, came over. He was a trim man about the same age as Mary. He stood straight, his hair fresh-combed and furrowed from the comb's teeth. Ezekiel pushed back against Mary's legs. She cleared her throat. "I am Mrs. Edmund Harrington," she said. The teacher introduced himself as Mr. Young. Ezekiel slipped behind her skirts. "This is my son, Ezekiel," she said. "We are here to start him in school."

The children were all older than he and they glowed with plenty, their cheeks round and pink, their clothes clean and barely worn. The boys' straw-colored hair was combed, the girls' braided. Even sitting, two of the boys were huge, larger, even, than her husband, Edmund, though none was old enough to shave.

Mr. Young leaned down. "Ezekiel," he said. Ezekiel pushed tighter against her. Mr. Young stood back up. "I think he is too young." His voice was not unkind. Ezekiel's grip softened a bit.

Mary pulled him to the front of her. "He is a bit shy and small for his age," she said. She had never admitted it before. Sometimes, as the reality of their poor circumstance came clear, Edmund would deride his son for his small size, calling him a runt. The students continued to crane their necks. "He can read," she said. "These are some of his books." She fanned them out on the table.

56

Mr. Young lifted his brows. *Ragged Dick, The Little Corporal, The American Spelling Book, The Vagabond,* and Ezekiel's favorite, *The Arabian Nights.* Mr. Young leaned forward, took up *The Vagabond.* "Let's see." He held the book toward Ezekiel, put his finger on a page. "Read this."

Ezekiel swallowed. He was stiff as a stick, his knees squeezed together until they knocked. The other students stared and the girls covered their mouths against giggles. His face blotched. He shook his head. He had read the story many times with Mary, though he had always worried about it, and kept it hidden from his father because the boy in it was naughty. Mary wished Mr. Young had chosen another, even *Arabian Nights.* "I don't want to," Ezekiel said, his voice high and frightened. He squeezed his legs tighter and grabbed for the crotch of his pants. "Ezekiel!" Mary said. She slapped his hand away and he started to bounce.

"I don't think . . ." the teacher said.

"He can do it," Mary said.

"Show me, Ezekiel," Mr. Young said.

He stared at the teacher's finger. He wavered as if the words swam on the page. He quit bouncing and Mary knew he was about to piddle. He had piddled once at home, when Edmund came into the house after being away a few days for supplies. Mary had thought he would be away another day and she and Ezekiel were sitting at the table, Ezekiel reading aloud from a new book Prune had sent.

By then, Mary's teaching, her "pandering" to Ezekiel's

education, had become a contention between Mary and Edmund. "Waste of time learning to read," Edmund said. Mary jumped when he came through the door. He gave no greeting, instead gave out a bellow like a moose, his breath stinking of drink. He slapped the book away, took up his strop and whipped Ezekiel for disobeying.

"Oh-h-h," Ezekiel said, now. Misery lay in it.

Mr. Young stood straight. "I suspected."

"Ez-*ee*-kiel," Mary said and leaned down to him. "You've read this a hundred times." She whispered, "It is all right to read it now. Your pa is not here."

Mr. Young moved to take the book away.

A dark, wet streak ran down Ezekiel's leg. "'Accordingly,'" Ezekiel read, "'in a dark'," his voice wavery. A puddle collected at his feet. The other students pasted fingers to their mouths, but their giggles puffed out, rude and accusing. Mary hated them. But her son's predicament seemed to release him and to loosen his throat, "'and stormy night James with his three companions muffled themselves up,'" he took the book from Mr. Young's hands, "'blacked their faces and repaired to the house of the poor widow. It was agreed that James should enter the house with a club and demand the money.'"

"That's enough," Mr. Young said, his tone kind.

Chapter 12

With no work and with the end of Mrs. Gatewood's handouts, it would not be long before Ezekiel and she would be beyond mere hunger. Mary had gone to the hotel two days ago to ask for more work and had been told Mrs. Gatewood's husband had taken a chill and she was nursing him at home on their farm. Even with the few mars and tracks, the hotel floor shone.

Mary returned to the saddlery, fed the stove one more piece of rack, pumped water from the trough in the street. Two of the hens had produced eggs. She heated enough water to boil the eggs and a bit more for Ezekiel to wash in before school.

She took him to school again that day. This time, he did not resist; it was as if his experience the first day had made him fall so far, humiliated him so, he had no resistance left. When she let his hand go at the door, he did not look up, his eyes did not go to the other children, or to the teacher. He slipped into the only place left, on the girls' side of the table.

A wagon banged by, loaded with lumber. On a lot on Avenue H, a half dozen men were hammering up frames for a house.

That morning, the hotel table was set for nine. When Hilda saw it was only Mary, she said, "Mrs. Gatewood is home again today." Her face raged pink, her ears red. A bang of hair clung to her forehead. Under her arms, her dress was wet.

Mary said, "When do you suppose she will return?" If Mr. Gatewood was dying, it may be never, a thought that had knocked at Mary's door the last two days.

"I am sure I don't know," Hilda said.

The third day, she almost wept when she saw Mrs. Gatewood's office door open. She stood outside it listening to Mrs. Gatewood tell Hilda what to cook for the day. The list was long: a roast from a haunch Hilda would need to carve up, parsnips and potatoes from the cellar, and two pies. There would be fifteen to feed for the eleven a.m. dinner. The only words Hilda spoke were, "Yes, ma'am," "Yes, ma'am," her voice thick with emotion. She came out, then. Her nose was red, her chin quivering as if she was about to cry. She passed Mary without a nod.

Mrs. Gatewood saw Mary. "Yes?"

"Hilda needs help," Mary said. It was unlike her not to make some greeting.

"And you're the one to help her."

"Yes."

Mrs. Gatewood flopped back in her chair. It squawked. She seemed to give Mary's suggestion some thought. "Hilda has been able to handle things for a while. It hasn't hurt her to earn her dollar."

A dollar. A fortune. Mary's heart dropped. Mrs. Gatewood would not put Mary on to work.

Mrs. Gatewood leaned forward. The chair complained again. She sat a moment, diddling a pencil. "Hilda's cooking is beginning to bore even the men," she said. She tapped the pencil like one would after making a decision. "The weekend, perhaps," she said, "you could spell her this weekend."

"Certainly."

She looked straight at Mary then. "For your two bowls."

A demon took hold of her. She held up two fingers. "*Twice* a day," she said. How could she ask for this much more? "And whatever else comes with them."

"Whatever else?"

"The puddings and cobblers and such," Mary said.

Mrs. Gatewood sniffed. "This weekend then."

————

Ezekiel was home that afternoon when Mary let herself in. The day had cleared, sun sat on the floor of the saddlery, the same sun that warmed and gave comfort to those coming into the hotel. Here, now, the light had a fearful, sharp aspect after the news from Mrs. Gatewood.

He was sitting, legs stretched out, leaning against the wall, a book in his lap, reading. His eyes slipped from the book, not to her, but to a sheaf of green wrapped in string by the stove. She could think of nothing but what Mrs. Gatewood had just said. What would have come of them without a place to live? "I got it for you, Ma," Ezekiel said.

"It?" she said.

"The asparagus." She saw it then, the tender spears tied in string.

She went to it, bent down, took it up. "Where did you

61

get it?" She tried to settle her mind on the soft pleasure of this gift. She laid her hand on his shoulder. His shoulder was stiff.

"I found it."

"Found it?"

"It was just there."

"Whose is it?"

"Nobody's."

"Nobody's?"

"It was just there, out in the open. I picked it for you."

They ate asparagus that night with an egg and some of the goat's milk.

Chapter 13

Only a handful of men had showed for building work the first day, a dozen showed the second, then forty or fifty as the gossip spread of the pay. Noise began to fill town from dawn until dark, hammers pounding, saws snarling, lumber thwacking. Hilda would be nearly manic for the work

Mary did not have to count the potatoes they had left: two. The tomatoes were gone, and there were still three days before she'd report for work. The hotel slop bucket had dried up since Mr. Simpson had bought up ten feeder pigs and took the kitchen slops to feed them at the end of the day. She and Ezekiel ate one of the last potatoes that night and she took the rosary to bed and tried not to think when this would end.

She dreamed that night that Edmund had returned and was the man she married, not the one he became. And she woke in the morning soaked, every prurient place in her wet with her body's need.

Mary kept watch. She did not know from which direction Edmund might come, but felt it would be from the north. She imagined he would have the note she left him in his pocket and told herself it would be in the pocket nearest his heart. At times, she believed it and was certain. At times, she had to swallow fear. Train upon train began slamming in, bringing supplies and noise as

Cozad turned into a small circus of barking dogs, horses stamping, locomotives screeching. Trains and their fracas gave structure to the town's lives. Men waited at the station while brakemen jumped down. Much yelling seemed to be involved, the brakemen shouting for the conductors to stop, the conductors yelling to the engineers. And when the yelling was done, the trainmen pulled the coupler pin, dropped the chain, and left it to slap and clatter. Like ants, townsmen crawled onto the cars, threw down lumber, handed down tools, tarpaper, shingles, shovels, sheets of uncut glass. And when the unloading was done, the men jumped down and the train panted off.

Work never let up until dark. Men worked in the slip and cut of snow, and in the whipping sleet. Mr. Atkinson supervised the house building, Mr. Claypool the construction of the building next to the hotel. The bridge was to be constructed of straw, and loose straw needed baling so Mr. Claypool supervised the building of a haypress to compact and bale it. The haypress was an ugly thing and taller by twice than the Emigrant House. Its neck, an awkward mechanism of metal struts, as tall as a windlass and clad in gangling pulleys and rope, that rose up like a stork sighting a fish. A farmer brought two oxen from his farm and hooked them to a wheel attached to one of the pulleys and, as the animals plodded round and round, a weight half the size of a boxcar lifted. When the weight reached the top, a man pulled a release and the weight thundered down and pummeled the straw into bales. Over and over again all day long, the ground shook with it.

———

Ezekiel's expression was soft. He was in the room, reading beside the lamp, when she let herself in. The room was warm from the heat of the kitchen but reeked of manure and horse urine. He was filthy, his hair filled with straw and grain husk. He had taken off his clothes; his trousers and shirt lay in a filthy pile in the corner.

He took up his trousers and reached into a pocket. He brought out a nickel and held it out in his palm. His palm wept with blisters and a slick of blood from a cut. "Ezekiel, what happened to your hand? Where have you been?"

He pushed the nickel nearer her. "It's for you, Ma." He turned over his hand and dropped the coin into hers.

"But where did you get it?"

"From Mr. Simpson."

"Mr. Simpson?"

"He gave it to me for forking up some of the dung in the stalls after school. He said I was only worth a dime. He said someday when I grew, I might be worth twenty cents.

"But this is only a nickel," she said.

"He kept my other nickel so we could pay on the hinny's keep."

Chapter 14

There was no moon. Mary could not tell the time, though she felt it was not long after midnight. All night, her mind had spun. She imagined she would not remember how to cook when she took Hilda's place. She imagined she would burn everything she put on the stove. She imagined scalding Mrs. Gatewood with hot gravy. She imagined a roast pig getting up from the table and running away.

It was dark as tar when she pulled back the blankets. She held up the candle, tapped Ezekiel's shoulder. He mumbled something in his sleep. She gave his shoulder a small shake. His eyes blinked open. "Son, I will be gone at the hotel the day." He rubbed his eyes. "There's a potato in the cinders for your breakfast. Milk the goat before you leave and boil eggs to take with you to school if the hens laid." She prayed the hens had laid; she had nothing more to suggest.

"Where you going, Ma?"

She leaned over him, lifted his bang, and gave him a kiss. She kissed him again. "To work. I'll be home with dinner midday."

The town was soundless but for the slip of her steps and the worry hissing in her ears. The night was thick and close; no light shone anywhere but a dim lamp in the hotel, the stars.

She let herself in through the back. Warmth, left from the previous day, huddled around the woodstove. No aroma of cooking greeted her; it would be up to her to fill the hotel with that.

She lit the kitchen lamp. A paper lay on the counter, drawn with a line down the middle. In one column, Mrs. Gatewood had written the counts of people she expected that day: nine to twelve for breakfast, ten to fifteen for the midday dinner, and four or five in the evening for supper. In the other column, she had written what Mary was to prepare for each meal. Breakfast: bacon, mush, biscuits and gravy; dinner: roast pig (whole carcass in the cellar out back, you will need to cut sufficient from it for fifteen), cornbread (with some left for later), cream of potatoes, pumpkin pie with stiff cream tea; supper: cold meat from the pig; tea to warm the men up; jams and cornbread from dinner.

Mary took wood from the pile, stoked the coals left from the day before. She unhooked the apron from the wall and tied it around her.

The day went long. If asked, Mary would not be able to recall who sat at the table that morning, or at midday, or evening. Nor would she recall how she made it through that day. She could have only recounted that she had had something to take to Ezekiel in the middle of the day and the way his face lit when she walked in, then dimmed again when she said she could not stay. But for that, she could think of nothing but stirring, boiling, baking, serving, washing, wiping down, then oiling, baking all over again. She prepared the bland meal as she knew Hilda would have done: for morning bacon, pan fried; mush seasoned with salt; biscuits with simple gravy; pots of hot tea. For the dinner midday, she roasted the meat, made the cornbread, and salted the pumpkin for pie. Now and then she cut bits for herself she did not think anyone would notice. It held little taste. The men ate as if only because they needed to be fed. When the dinner was done midday, she ran a bowl to the saddlery, found Ezekiel huddled in blankets reading.

And when the supper of cold cuts of meat and tasteless gravy and some cold biscuits was done, when the men had all left, and the counters were still damp, Mary filled two bowls with the cuts and cornbread and let herself out.

Blue dusk sat on a cold sky. It was too cold for snow. It would be dark in a quarter hour. She expected to see the lamp in the saddlery window, but no light came from it. Since it was Saturday, he had no school; she had expected him to remain in the saddlery all day. She went in. "Ezekiel?" she called. The saddlery was empty. She set down her two bowls, laid the cornbread on top, and went out. She held open the door and called. She put her hands around her mouth and called again. The goat let out a bleat as urgent as her own. The hens gibbered. She ran out, called again.

Without answer, he showed like a shadow wrapped in his coat, his cap on his head, muffler around his mouth. Little but his nose showed. The goat wandered out the door, he drove her back in, more composed than his mother. "Where have you been?" she said, her tone harsh.

"At the livery, talking to Mr. Simpson."

She swallowed the fact that the liveryman was the sole person her son chose to go to. He had no one but her and the bad-humored man. "I brought you something hot for supper," she said, softer.

They sat, still wrapped in their coats, on the blankets. They began to eat. She took three bites of her bowl, then set it down.

"Aren't you hungry, Ma?"

She laid her hand on his shoulder. "Finish it."

"You need sommat to eat as much as me."

"As much as I," she said. "Eat your food."

She returned to the kitchen again sometime after midnight to ready for Sunday's meals. She searched for Mrs. Gatewood's instructions on the counter. She found nothing. She patted the counters, opened drawers, swung the lamp. Shadows sliced and shifted; there were no instructions anywhere. Did Mrs. Gatewood forget, or was this some sort of challenge? Her head went dizzy. She put her hand over her eyes and blocked what she could not bear to see: how to go on?

Her breath came red and ragged. Her heart sputtered. That time of night, no one else was awake. Then came the thought of her son tucked under the blankets asleep, yesterday's meals in his belly, and she took strength from it.

She could make another simple breakfast and that would be enough. Since it was Sunday, she was expected to prepare only one other meal after church let out. Mrs. Gatewood had mentioned forty. *Forty!* She gasped for air and dropped, hopeless, onto the stool. She leaned forward and put her head between her knees; she had no idea what to do.

When she could breathe again, she stood, lifted the sag that called itself an apron from its hook. Aloud, she said, "So," and her voice sounded like her own mother's.

———

In the cellar, a half-cut hog's carcass hung on a hook in the corner, a small beef calf on a hook behind it. Another door let off the room into a pantry for dairy. It held shelves of cheese, butter, milk, and cream cans. Behind that room was yet another, its ceiling hung with cabbages and carrots, onions and garlics. On the floor stood wood bins filled with turnips, parsnips, beets, and potatoes.

So much food. So much. She took up a carrot and ate it. She found a cleaver and hacked away a haunch of the hog. When it finally fell away, she lugged it up to the kitchen.

She stacked wood in the hearth, ruffled the cinders with the iron until a feeble flame took. She laid wood on the flame. How hot would this hearth cook? She had roasted lamb and boar before, but had never done anything this large. How long did such a huge ham and rump need to cook?

As the hearth fire settled, she heated grease for a bannock, whipped eggs in a bowl for a scramble, threw bacon in a skillet, and filled a pot of water for oat mush. The men came in. They sat. Mindlessly, they ate their breakfasts and drank their tea and mumbled, "Good day," too tired for more conversation, before they ambled out into the cold again to hammer up another house.

71

She wished they could stay. She wished the breakfast could last for hours. Breakfast was something she could count on, its simplicity, its reliability, the unwavering custom of eggs and mush, meat and bread. But dinner? This dinner? The ponderous weight of forty to feed made her head twirl. And she was to feed them what?

She took the mush pot, held it close in her arm, began scraping at the cracked leavings. She spooned some of the leavings into her mouth. She knew she should be hungry and tried to swallow. She had prepared the oatmeal just as Hilda would have done; the men were used to it, but it was awful. She held up the pot and looked into the gray plaster where a crack grinned. The crack opened like a mouth about to spew doubt. Faith, whatever she once had, left years ago. She had been surviving on nothing but doubt. She nicked with a spoon; bits of dried gruel flaked away.

The fire was ready. She laid her hand on the cool pig haunch on the counter; it had no voice, nothing to say. She hefted it, stood with it in her arms. The fire rack was set deep over the fire. She should have taken the rack out before she started the fire, while the rack was cold. She set the pig quarter down, rolled her sleeves high onto her shoulders. She toted the haunch to the fire, bucked it higher in her arms. The smoke choked her, the burn on her thumb flared with the heat. She threw the rump toward the rack. She had no idea what she would do if it fell into the fire. But it caught. She nudged it with the poker as the fat began to sweat.

She searched for a book of recipes she had seen Mrs.

Gatewood bring from her office when she pointed out certain pages to Hilda, but found no book anywhere.

The kitchen, like the cellar, was well stocked. She searched the shelves for some inkling as to what Mrs. Gatewood would expect for a Sunday dinner for forty people. Besides the bins filled with flour, oats, salt, and sugar, there were items Hilda never touched. Along one wall, a high shelf held jars labeled *bay leaf, dill, marjoram, rosemary, sage, thyme, caraway seed, cinnamon, clove, nutmeg, celery.* Mary had never eaten or smelled cinnamon or clove. She opened them, breathed in their strange scents. The aroma of the caraway seed took her home to Macroom and nearly made her weep. She closed the jar and put it back where it belonged on the shelf.

The pig began to drip fat. Flames exploded. Smoke filled the room; she put a cloth over her nose and her mouth. She checked the damper; it was open. She opened the door, stood waving her hands at it. She took up the towel and flapped it like a woman gone mad. The smoke shifted, the flames straightened, and the draw began to take the smoke with it.

Three times, she returned to the cellar. Three times, she filled her apron with potatoes, beets, carrots, garlics, and onions. Something outside her powered her.

She took up a mixing bowl too large to hold in one arm. She half-filled it with flour. She added oats and some meal of corn and sugar. She tapped in some of the cloves and the cinnamon and was lifted by their perfume. Her arms moved on their own as if driven by whims. Sometimes, their impulses blurted salt, sometimes currant, sometimes baking powder. She gave herself over to movement. Thoughts came packaged in doubt but her arms answered with a cup of this or a spoonful of that. When the voices whispered "eggs," she stirred in a dozen. When they breathed "mace," she pinched some in. When they said "butter," she folded in butter. And when the bowl was near full, she stirred and she tipped the batter into an acre of pans. She did not know what it was she had made.

While the pans baked, she chopped garlic. She melted butter in a pan, put the garlic in it and a sprinkling of the tops of the carrots she had minced. She stirred until the garlic turned gold. She cut the potatoes into chunks, laid the chunks onto sheets, and poured over the butter and garlic and carrot bits.

When the cakes were done in the oven, she set the pans to cool on the counter and stowed the potatoes in the oven. In just over an hour, the church bells would ring and forty people would fill the hotel, Mrs. Gatewood said she and Mr. Gatewood would be among them.

———

Five minutes before church let out, every inch of the kitchen held food: the counters, the middle table, the stove top, the shelves. Steam rose from huge cut pieces of the pig on trays, and from the platters of potatoes, the roast carrots and parsnips. Mary had hidden a good chunk of the pig and some of the potatoes and vegetables in a pot under the counter. She would have hidden some of the cakes, too, but a cut would betray her. A few minutes ago, she had set cups and bowls on the dining room table and heaped silverware on it, but had not had time to lay out the places. Children would have to sit along the floor and eat from bowls in their laps. There were only places enough for adults at the table.

She should have heard the front door. "Mary?"

She jumped and shouted, "Gah."

Mrs. Gatewood stood at the kitchen door. She wore an ermine-collared coat and bonnet pulled over her ears. "What have you *done*?"

Mary opened her mouth but did not know whether to apologize or confess.

"Lord, child, when did you get here to do such as this?" She took in all the food. She did not seem to be wanting an answer.

"There were no instructions," Mary said.

Mrs. Gatewood looked at the counter where the instructions should have been. "But . . . I thought I left them."

"There were no recipes, I looked for them."

"Lord," she said, "I forgot the recipes in my office." Her eyes wandered the buffet. She went to the cakes, untied her bonnet. "What are *these*?"

The cakes had browned in the cooking and had plumped, bits of currant speckled them. "I don't quite know," Mary said. "'Twas all I could think of."

Mrs. Gatewood took off her gloves, pinched a bit from one of the cakes and ate it. "Mary," she said. She took another pinch, bigger this time. She wiped her hands on a towel. Mary looked for something in Mrs. Gatewood's expression; nothing lay in it but the serious, business pucker she always wore.

"It's time to put on the table." Mrs. Gatewood hung her bonnet and coat on a peg. "I'll do it." She stepped toward the dining room door, then turned back. Her face went a bit softer. "It's Scripture cake," she said. "Reminds me of my mother's and that reminds me of my home in Virginia."

Chapter 15

School days, not long after Ezekiel left for school, Mary wandered down to the river to watch men stack bales from the haypress for the bridge pilings, or would bend into the wind and make her way to watch the construction of each new house. She would stand there until her teeth rattled and the cold drove her inside. She envied the men. No matter how ugly the day, no matter how much they ached, or cramped and blistered, work gave them no time to think.

It was often impossible to recognize one workman from the other, bundled as they were in coats and the mufflers pulled down over their hats that covered their faces but for slits at their eyes. She studied the way each moved, the manner in which he bent, or carried himself, or interacted with the others. Her search became organized as she went, her meanders methodical. She combed Cozad, covered every lot and clod. She learned every bush, every edifice, every horse and wagon. Men began to nod as she went by, some to tip fingers her way, and each time her heart cramped when one of them was not Edmund. When he arrived, he would be on horseback. He would not come by train.

Chapter 16

The first train of "potentials" was due in a week. It was frigid out, the dirt streets solid as rock, the wind bleeding dry one's mouth, cracking and crisping lips and exposed ears.

Mary had been cooking the weekends for more than a month. She was able to feed Ezekiel better, but had to apportion out their bowls and what else she could manage in secret to squirrel away to take home in a pot. But it was still not enough.

In three days, the men completed the first house, a small one. In another three, the second. She watched as they moved their tools from one lot to another. Building a town was an enormity she could not comprehend.

She had yet to set eyes on Mr. Cozad, but was getting an idea of the sort of man he might be. Less than two years ago, this place was no more than forty thousand acres of prairie grass, which Mr. Cozad bought from the railroad. As the men pounded and sawed, she had a great curiosity how anyone could manage this. She heard the men calculate that forty thousand meant: sixty-seven miles in any direction. In the vastness, there would be a city bearing Mr. Cozad's name, an important city to become the seat of Dawson County. He needed these men to build it. He needed families and recruited them from Ohio and Illinois. He had also convinced his in-laws to join in.

He offered the Gatewoods a section of the best farmland as incentive to sell their hotel in Virginia, and he sweetened things by funding a hotel and mercantile for his mother-in-law to own and to run. The rest of his land he would parcel out to sell to farmers and cattlemen with promises that they would become successful and rich with him. One day, when a proper home was built, Mr. Cozad and his wife, Theresa, and their sons would move here.

It was beyond anything Mary could fathom. Edmund had once been a dreamer, he once would have understood this vision of Mr. Cozad's and his version of the future. For three years, Edmund had fulfilled his own dream, had constructed the house, and the windlass, and pens, and a small lean-to barn, had bought calves he fed and sold when they grew fat. She came to realize his only sorrow was that two babies had died before taking their first breaths. They buried the last baby only days before an early, hard freeze set on them in October. The freeze lasted a week, but, in the end had taken away every hope.

All Mary could reckon with, now, was that she and Ezekiel needed to eat.

Worry and exhaustion became intimates which, left her with little but the shape of themselves. Saturdays and Sundays consumed her. But the dark of the five nights she did not work fashioned themselves into knots. She could only allow the certainty that when Edmund returned, would be a changed man, realizing what he had lost. And he would take her into his arms and return them to the farm as a family to resume the lives they had dreamed.

Chapter 17

The days were growing longer, if only by minutes, yet the weather held to the cold. Traber Gatewood received word from Ohio that in three days, on a Friday, half a dozen families would arrive on the train. Mary would not be cooking that day. Some of the potentials would stay with families already settled on farms. One large family would take the four rooms in the hotel. Two families and three men would take rooms at Mrs. Gatewood's boardinghouse across the street. Six men, including Mr. Drew and David Claypool, were assigned to take the families out on tours of the available land. The fracas, the planning, even the complaints seemed like a celebration.

Dark clouds had sat on the town for two days, but the skies cleared just as the locomotive puffed into the station. Sun highlighted the river, shone on the buildings, lightened the settling of new snow, and made a sort of magic.

The families stepping from the trains were tired, the smaller children clinging to their parents' or sleeping on their shoulders. The women shepherded the older children while the townsmen bent forward to shake the hands of the men. Mr. Claypool had drawn a family who spoke little English and was having trouble understanding. The family were black-haired, Bohemian, Mary thought, their coloring lustrous and nearly as dark as that of a bay

81

horse. They seemed to have a good hold on the word "Yass," which came with vigorous nods of their heads. Mr. Claypool began his own version of nodding and pointed and gesticulated until they finally understood to put their bags on his wagon.

A dark, elegant Pullman sat at the very end of the train. Its windows were hung with isinglass and it waited there, closed-eyed allowing no one in town a glimpse inside.

When the passengers had debarked from all cars but that one at the end, the conductor uncoupled the car, then waved at the locomotive. The train huffed ahead, leaving the elegant thing sitting like some exotic creature.

Townspeople, including all the Gatewoods, clustered around it. Mr. Owens put a stepping box under the door. The door opened; a severe man dressed in black stepped out. Everything he wore—tailcoat, necktie, and vest—was a deep and inaccessible black. A diamond flickered on his tie; a heavy gold fob rippled over his chest. His face was that of a hawk's: sharp-beaked, unsettled, aggressive. Every piece of his fine clothing fit him as if it had been sewn on. Mary did not think she liked him.

Chapter 18

Attendance at Sunday suppers had increased by a quarter because of her cooking and Mrs. Gatewood was charging almost two times more for it. When business picked up, Mrs. Gatewood began dealing Mary sundry jobs during the week. She swept. She washed linens. She sorted and shelved goods when they came into the mercantile. It was easier work, in truth, than kitchen work, but Mrs. Gatewood did not include meals with it. Mary thought Mrs. Gatewood counted the lending of the saddlery to be sufficient payment for Mary's work.

Mr. Simpson found Mary one day as she was mopping the floor. Without greeting, he blurted, "Your hinny's keep is past due at the livery. It's five dollars you owe now." For a moment, she thought to offer to sell the mule, but they would need her for farm work when Edmund returned. "I will pay as soon as I can, Mr. Simpson," she said. His forehead reddened and he made an effort to bring himself to stand straight. He drew in his mouth as if to say something more, but did not.

On Saturday, Mary roasted five chickens, made a rice pudding, baked four loaves of bread, stewed a gallon of prunes, and served sweet, clotted cream with boiled raisin cake. There had been so many that day she had coped with two seatings, two servings and two washings-up. A good deal of the new families were putting money down on land. Two of the stores facing the street bore *SOLD* signs. The mercantile was selling goods almost as soon as Mrs. Gatewood could stock it.

When all that was left of the dinner was the humidity and the dishes drying on the rack, Mary left for a few minutes. It was the quiet time of day, the brief moment when only leavings of the meals, the wet rags, the soggy towels, the sheen on the counters lay on the hotel before, in a quarter hour, everything began again. Mary had just come from fifteen minutes at the saddlery to catch her breath. Supper would be simple: simple cold cuts from yesterday's ham, apples she had sauced in the morning, and scones with lard and jam.

The store was still open when Mary let herself in the back door. Voices murmured, Mrs. Gatewood's silky trills and the voices of two other women, comforting sounds requiring nothing of Mary.

The creak of the hotel door broke the peace, then the slap of the screen and a gasp of cold, open air blew in. Often, new people to town did not realize the hotel kitchen was closed between dinner and supper but, since they were potentials, Mrs. Gatewood expected them to be served. Mary turned her back as if to hold a request at bay.

Traber's voice boomed out, "Just us, Ma. Dick Humbolt and me going to pull a tooth." Another voice, garbled between clenched teeth, said, "'Lo, Mrs. Gatewood." Mary had forgotten Traber was a dentist. It was the first Mary had seen him take anyone in for his dental service. She fixed on the humorous image of him hovering over a patient, pulling his teeth.

As she measured the flour, she heard through the walls a high voice blurt, "Gaaak," then Traber said, "Sorry, Dick." Minutes later, they came out again, went out the front door, Mr. Humbolt holding his jaw.

Mrs. Gatewood appeared not long after and stood beside Mary, clasping her hands at her waist. Mary sensed a foreboding. "Mary," she said, "I have Mr. Schultz coming at two o'clock today to look at the saddlery space. I see you have had animals in it. Please remove them and make sure there is no mess."

Mary laid down the sifter. She did not bother to brush flour from her hands, did not remove her apron. Later, she would remember the apron. Later, she would remember she had no recollection of making her way back to the saddlery, or of what she did when she went in. Only later would she realize the implication of what someone's "looking at the saddlery space" meant.

Chapter 19

A man, new to town, came to the hotel asking for work. He was not a good sort, like most of the people in town, his clothes were laden with black grease and dirt, his face unshaven but for patches, cheeks a splotch of veins. He passed Mary, and as he did, left a stream of his breath behind him that reeked of liquor. He shuffled toward Mrs. Gatewood. "I come in for work," he said. "They said over at the livery barn that you was the one to ask about it." The odor of whiskey felt like a slap.

Mrs. Gatewood remained at her desk. "What do you think you can do with the shape you are in?" she said.

"All kinds of anything you have for a man to do."

"Able bodied," she said.

"You saying I ain't?"

Mrs. Gatewood stood up from her desk. She drew herself up to her full height and said, "You dry out, get a bath, wash your clothes, and a barber and shave and you come back. He does not allow either liquor or drunkenness in town." The man gathered spit and leaned forward as if to let go. "Don't you dare," she said in a tone that broached no countering. He turned and lurched out, much as Edmund had done that last day.

———

At Hilda's request, Mrs. Gatewood had put on Hilda's sister to help weekdays. Mr. Cozad sat at the head of the table, taking a late meal the kitchen had to prepare and serve special, after the rest of the diners had eaten and left. He sat like a rooster perched on a stuffed chair shipped in special for him.

Hilda had asked Mary to bring in a basket of potatoes and carrots. Mr. Cozad turned to her, his expression tipped back and ogling, yet seeing nothing. He did nothing more and she went back to putting the vegetables into the sink.

Some commotion came from the dining room, shouting. Mrs. Gatewood came out from her office. Mary peeked up just as Mr. Cozad screamed, "This is garbage!" Hilda was standing beside him, looking down at her feet. His arm whipped out and the plate with his food flew in the air. The plate loaded with ham and potatoes hit Hilda's apron before smashing into bits on the floor. "Not fit for a pig."

Hilda gave out a cry and put her face in her hands. Her sobs turned to blubbering. Her sister stood in the doorway wringing her hands as Mrs. Gatewood guided Hilda into the kitchen. Before Mrs. Gatewood closed the kitchen door, she said over her shoulder, "Mary, would you see to the clean-up?"

Chapter 20

Mary cleared the mess Mr. Cozad made after he stomped out the door, his face flaming. Mrs. Gatewood had shut herself into her office with Hilda and Hilda's sister.

The door from Traber's dentist office clicked open. She had not been aware he was in it. Had he not heard the ruckus? It was as if he were so accustomed to Mr. Cozad's behavior as to ignore it. He ducked under the door jamb, loped into the room carrying a box filled with files, gouges, cleavers, picks, drills, chisels, pincers. His presence brought a hush in as he came. She seized onto the calm.

A dark bang fell onto his forehead. He blew a breath up and the bang leapt. "Mary," he said, "I have something for you." He set the box on the dining table and sent metals clanking. He went back to his office, came out with some letters. "I finally got to the post office in Plum Creek. They had these for you."

Her knees nearly gave way as she saw Prune's feathery script. She managed, "Thank you." The letters lay hot in her hand. She wanted to run away and read.

"Sorry it took so long," he said. "I don't get there much, with what's going on these days."

She swallowed against tears.

From his great height, he looked down on her and

remained there as if he should not leave. He cleared his throat. "I'm moving my office down by the rail tracks. To the old boxcar parked there."

"I see," she said, near unable to collect herself.

"There's a package, too, that came for you. I'll bring it up in a bit." He started to go, then popped his forehead with his hand. "Oh," he said, "Mother told me to send you to the mercantile. She wants to see you as soon as she can."

———

Mrs. Gatewood was waiting on a woman in a bonnet with tatted laces as the German women often wore. Mary had not seen her before. She pointed at a skillet high on one of the shelves. An angry red ignited her face. Apparently, Mrs. Gatewood's selection of skillets was not quite what she wanted. In reaching for it, Mrs. Gatewood's skirt pulled up and showed an ankle and her blouse let loose from the waistband of her skirt. She finally got hold of the pan. "Ah," she said. She handed it to the woman in the bonnet. "That'll do you, Mrs. Schleimer. Ah, Mary, wait there, I want to see you as soon as Mrs. Schleimer and I are done here." Her tone seemed neither welcoming nor stern.

Mrs. Schleimer shook her head. She said she wanted a different sort of skillet, which Mrs. Gatewood said she would look for when she had time to open the boxes. "Now," the woman said, "I vant to see."

Mrs. Gatewood sang out, "I will have them out just before dinner, Mrs. Schleimer," in the same tone a parent would take with a whiny child.

"Vell, I suppose I heff to come back."

Mrs. Gatewood made no apologies.

Another woman came in. Mary touched the pocket with Prune's letters in it. Mrs. Gatewood bade Mrs. Schleimer good afternoon. The new woman's name was Ruttledge. She told Mrs. Gatewood she wanted to see some of the new calicoes.

Mary tried not to fear what Mrs. Gatewood wanted. The weight of the letters at her thigh settled her some.

Mrs. Ruttledge's head was small under her bonnet. The bonnet was pink, the color of her face, and sewn with a large ruffle that further reduced her small head. Mrs. Gatewood drew out three bolts for her, laid them on the counter. They talked awhile about how maybe the lighter colors were best with spring on the way. Mrs. Ruttledge bought a dress length with a pattern of green leaves and roses. She nodded to Mary as she left.

When the store was finally empty, Mrs. Gatewood dropped herself onto the stool behind the counter. "I really am getting too old for this," she said. She smiled. Mary tried to manage a smile in return.

Mrs. Gatewood patted back a wisp of white hair. "I have sold the old saddlery," she said. "Tomorrow you and your son will need to leave it."

"I see," Mary said.

"Hilda will no longer be cooking for me in the hotel kitchen," she said. Mary tried to collect herself in order to understand why this had anything to do with the fact she and Ezekiel no longer had a place to sleep. "I was wondering if you could begin cooking for us full time."

91

Mary had dreamed of this only weeks ago. "I don't know."

"You don't know? But I was counting on you."

"We have to find somewhere to live, come tomorrow. We might need to leave town."

It came to her now, the thing she had turned away from the day Mrs. Gatewood said someone wanted to see the saddler. It had been cold that day, a storm darkening the north. Mary had gone to the saddlery and had taken the goat out to tether behind the building. She had shuffled the hens out and grained them in a small alcove buffered from the storm. They had left a mess: the goat's pellet droppings, the hens' gray and white scumble, chaff from the grains, feathers, hair all accumulated since Ezekiel had swept it. Mary picked up the leavings and with a rag from the hotel had swept out the crunch of the chaff.

Ezekiel had been there when she returned at the end of the day. The weather had turned cruel, the wind cutting, crackles of ice covered the saddlery's windows. "Ma," he said, "why are the hens and goat outside? The goat is shivering."

"Oh, get her," she said, "and the hens." She did not tell her son why the animals had been turned out, because it would bring forth something she could not admit.

Mrs. Gatewood tucked in the tail of her blouse. She frowned and chewed the inside of her lip. "Ah. I see," she said. "Yes. The saddler's. I think you are driving a bargain, Mary." Mary had merely stated the fact. There was no bargain in it. Mrs. Gatewood stood taller. "Ah, Mary," she said and sighed, a huge groan sufficient for performance.

Mary had nothing to say.

Mrs. Gatewood put her hand to her forehead. She said, "Here's my proposal: Traber is moving himself out of his little teeth-pulling room. It's awfully small, I'm afraid, no larger really than a closet." Mary had no idea why this seemed pertinent. "If you can make yourself and your son fit in Traber's room, you can have it for a while to see me through." She laughed. "That is, if you don't mind the ghosts of screams from Traber's past patients." She seemed to take pleasure in the barb at her son. "If you can stand that, it's dry and it's warm."

Mary's breath came and went.

"I want you to work full time in the kitchen. And will exchange the room and two meals a day for your work."

Mary knew the room was vacant now, giving it to her and Ezekiel to sleep in was no great imposition. The room and two meals did not add up to the amount Hilda had been paid. Mrs. Gatewood certainly had to be aware, but also aware Mary needed to feed herself and her son. It was obvious Ezekiel had been eating barely enough; even wrapped in sweaters and coat, his arms were thin as school rulers and his trousers hung from his hips. Mrs. Gatewood tipped her head and, in the manner of the gesture, Mary sensed she could do even better.

"Four meals a day," Mary said, "two for me and two for my son," Mary said. "And help."

"Help? Hire someone else?"

Mary said, "Yes." Her voice quivered; did it betray her?

"Yes," Mrs. Gatewood said. "*Some* help anyway." Her words were firm but her head gave another small tip that hinted how much she needed Mary.

Mary held up two fingers. "Two," she said. "I'll need two for help."

Mrs. Gatewood clicked her tongue. "Agreed."

———

She told Ezekiel they would have to move all their things early next morning, and after he fell asleep, she squatted by the glow of the stove.

> *Sept 15, '73, Philadelphia*
> *Dearest Sissie,*
> *I have the awfullest news, Oliver entered Episcopal Academy this morning. I am afraid I took it in the worst way. My babies! Oliver eleven, Cornelius nearly ten, they're almost grown men! They will both be lost to me too soon. I am so despondent. I told Totten when he got home that I wanted another baby. He patted my head and said, Now, now.*
> *I can admit this "tragedy" is only partly a joke. I do not know whether to be happy, proud, or downright morose. When the boys are gone, then what have I? I envy you your young Ezekiel and I hold onto the cozy thought of your sitting with him on a quiet evening teaching him his books. I will write him his own letter soon and thank him for his birthday wishes to me. Don't tell me he came up with "Earnestly happy day" by himself. You must have held his pencil as he wrote it.*
> *Aside from the tragedy with Oliver, we are doing well, tho I miss you so. Totten is greatly excited about the prospects of constructing a bank of his own in the middle of town.*

He is doing well and I am so proud of him, tho it still rankles that he took my yearning for a baby with such little regard.

Meanwhile, I eat and let out my dresses until one day someone will truly think Cornelius and Oliver will soon have a new sibling.

Write me soon, Sissie dearest. I will watch the mail every day for your letter.

Kisses, Prune

October 12, Philadelphia

Dearest Sissie, where is my letter? I have not heard from you since I sent my last. You owe me, naughty girl.

How is my dear nephew? Last you wrote, he was reading Robin Hood and you were giving him writing lessons. It means, of course, you and I will no longer be able to get things by him. And Edmund, how is he? We hope the cattle operation you wrote of continues to grow boundlessly.

Totten is making final plans on the new building. They will begin construction in spring, after Philadelphia thaws. He is so tired and distracted I find myself jealous. Imagine! I am sometimes so envious of your simple, wonderful life out there in Nebraska. I picture you now, bringing in squashes and carrots and rutabagas from your garden.

My biggest news is that Cornelius fell and sprained an ankle. He has to keep it lifted or it swells so he can't put on a shoe. I am sure it hurts but he is making a huge drama of it so that Oliver has to do his bidding.

Write soon, sweetheart, or I shall come and get you and sit

you down for a long cup of tea.
Kisses, Prune

December 23, Philadelphia
Oh, Sissie, I would wish you a happy holiday but I am too worried. I try to imagine you cozy in your home on the farm but unable to get to a post office and mail me my letter. I soothe myself thinking it, but I am so lonesome for your letter, I could spit.
Meanwhile, here at the house things are noisy, with the boys out of school and underfoot, and the dog with some kind of condition with her coat that makes her scratch and lose hair and shed on everything in the house.
Totten is gone much of the time with the bank, sometimes to New York where he collaborates with other men who are helping finance things. I have begun to want a larger home as I am feeling cramped in this one. Totten promises to work with me on it as soon as the bank opens in the new building.
I sent something for you this week to arrive later this month. Please tell me you like it, even if you do not.
Write soon, or I shall perish. And give my greetings to your lovely Edmund and my hugs to my darling nephew.
Love, Prune

Febr 24, Philadelphia 1874
Sissie! Sissie! Here it is the new year near two months old

and I am beside myself with worry. If you can take a breath, please write. I am about to have Totten send someone out to find you. I shall not be able to live if I have lost you. I am afraid the heavens are tiring of my prayers.
Forever your worried sister,
Prune

The box contained three bolts of calico: one green, one blue, and a yellow. There was also a letter addressed to Ezekiel. Mary laid it against her breast and held it there and felt tears well up, warm and soft and thankful. The envelope to Ezekiel was not addressed in Prune's usual fancy whorls, but written so to be carefully drawn-out and perfect.

Chapter 21

Before dawn, Mary tied the goat on a stake behind the hotel, near the water trough in the alcove where she had washed and broken a blanket. Mrs. Gatewood kept a low fire under the trough to protect from freeze. The alcove and the warmth should shelter the goat. Ezekiel carried the hens out, one by one, and spread the last of the grain to tease them not to wander. The animals would have to manage outside now, but Mary would have abundant scraps for the goat and she thought she could grain the hens with cracked wheat from the cellar bins. She hoped later that she might find a patch or two for the hinny to crop and save more debt to Mr. Simpson. Until then, Ezekiel would still have to lose one of his precious nickel's each day for the hinny's keep.

The moon was cold as they worked, and lopsided bright. It was not quite four o'clock in the morning when Mary put her hand on Ezekiel's shoulder and gave it a shake. He woke without fuss and they worked together in near silence collecting their blankets and teapot, their two cups, her mixing bowl, pie iron, spatula, and bowls. When they had loaded the wagon, they threw their weight against it and managed to wheel it within a few feet of the hotel. Ezekiel saw what needed done and set to it, like a man already grown.

As meager as the amount of things they had brought

with them, Traber's old office room could not hold everything. She asked what he wanted to bring from the wagon for himself and he answered, "Not much room, is there? I don't need much anyway, Ma."

It nearly crushed her. He needed so much. "Your books."

"One or two. There ain't room for the whole trunk of them."

"Isn't," she said, and for a moment felt like a mother.

Together, they brought the trunk from the saddlery. They wrestled it under the wagon, went back for the treadle. He brought out her skillet and two pots. "Ma," he said, "are we going to need the pots?"

"No," she said.

Heat from the hotel stove warmed the little room and Mary was glad. They dropped their blankets and their one change of clothes in a heap on the floor, and she spread a blanket for him to lie on. She left him reading while she went to the kitchen and made ready for work.

After school, that first day in their strange, warm room Ezekiel opened his letter from Prune and his face pinkened as he read. Some days later, when he was out, Mary read it as well.

> *September 30, 1873*
> *Philadelphia*
> *Dearest Nephew,*
> *Thank you for your lovely letter for my birthday. Your auntie Prune is proud of you. How are you doing? Do you have a pet? A dog? Or a cat? Or a pig? Hah! Pig, now*

that is our little private joke. No one has a pig for a pet. Oliver and Cornelius have a big dog with muddy feet whose name is Ruff. They like him very much, even with his muddy feet.

Your mother says you are a star reader. What is your favorite book? Please write and tell me.

Love,

Auntie Prune

Chapter 22

They had something regular, now, somewhere more permanent to sleep, a place to keep warm, food to count on. For the first time in so long, Mary could give her son true breakfasts, suppers, and something more than a corn cake in his lunch bucket for school. But for how long? Their lives balanced on the whim of one woman.

Mary never seemed to have time to *sit* and eat. She spooned up whatever she cooked, pieces of fat, bits of bread, a scoop of a sauce, which she shoved into her mouth while she stirred a pot, or set the table, or pumped water.

Ezekiel kept to himself in the room, coming out in the morning only when it was time to leave for school. He was staying out long after school let out, often slinking back well after five o'clock, when supper was done and the dining room was empty.

When Mary asked where he was all day, he merely shrugged and said, "At school."

"And after school?"

"At Mr. Simpson's."

"Doing what? Staying out from under Mr. Simpson's feet, I hope."

"I guess."

"Your dinner is ready. Wash up then come sit at the table."

"Can't I eat in our room?"

She took up a towel, dried her hands, and laid them on his shoulders. "We're alone," she said. "There's no one but us. Sit down and take your dinner at a proper table."

———

Ezekiel's breath came softly in sleep, she took up one of Ezekiel's school pencils and paper from the stationery tin and began to write:

March
Cozad, Nebraska
Dearest Prune,
Oh, I have just got your letters. They were waylaid in Plum Creek. The postmaster sent his deepest apologies.
I have so much to tell you since last I wrote.
First, we are doing well, so put your worries to ease. The biggest news is that we have moved into town for a few months to escape the frozen farm until the weather warms a bit.
We have found a small place to live and will be returning to the farm as soon as the grasses are ready to pasture. Edmund is away at the moment on a buying excursion getting ready for summer.
The best news of all is that Ezekiel is in a proper school. He spends hours studying and is doing well, the teacher says he is his best student, even tho he is the youngest in the class. He reads your books you send and studies his school readers long into the night until his head falls and he sleeps. I am so proud.
Oh thank you for the calico. I plan to start a dress for

myself with the yellow right away in hopes the gay colors bring on the summer that much sooner.

I will write more, as I have more to write. Meanwhile, our lives are a bit uninspiring, I am afraid.

My love to Totten and your precious boys.

Love, Sissie

Chapter 23

Ezekiel began spending two hours each day after school cleaning stalls at the livery; he had somewhere to be. Mary only wished she had time for him, a boy deserved more from his mother. Her hours were long; until Mrs. Gatewood hired another girl. For a week, Mary had had to work the kitchen alone.

Her legs pounded, her feet swelled and cramped when she removed her shoes before bed. Keeping her job depended not only on her willingness to work as a slave without pay, but on the savor of her cooking. She felt like a fish in a bowl, trapped in its own tiny world, stirring back and forth, getting nowhere. At night, she baked pie dough for the day's pie, kneaded and set out bread dough to rise, put a pot on the stove for whatever she would stew: stringy roosters, or chuck shoulder, or old hens. Nothing ever was done.

Attendance at her meals was rising. For that she was the fool. If she kept to the dull, tasteless meals Hilda put out, she would not have as much work to do, but she may not have gotten the job. To add to her load, Mrs. Gatewood had begun asking Mary to box something Mrs. Gatewood would take home to serve on her own table at the farm. Mr. Cozad had left the day after Mrs. Gatewood fired Hilda, and for that Mary counted her blessings. But he would be back; she would think of it then. A week after

Mary took over Mrs. Gatewood said she hired a girl.

Ula was a tall, blond, cherry-cheeked girl of fourteen whose family farmed north of town. She spoke little English but what she had hold of was sweet and eager. She took kindly to instructions, worked without complaint, but grew red-faced and embarrassed when she did not understand. Mary could have kissed Mrs. Gatewood's toes to have hired such a girl.

The trains were belching out more and more people. Mrs. Gatewood decided food baskets were required for the families to take out with them on their tours. "Empty stomachs aren't likely to be in the mood to buy up land," she said.

Mary had to leave Ezekiel more and more often on his own. Nothing could be done about it. Even working eighteen hours a day, Mary and Ula could not keep up. A boy should not be left to do his own raising. A boy should have his father. A boy should not have to rely solely on an irascible liveryman for companionship. She stirred a seasoning of guilt and worry into every pot she boiled. She and Ula worked nearly a week before Mrs. Gatewood hired on a German girl named Frieda, who spoke even less English than Ula.

Chapter 24

But for his demeanor and fancy dress, he was not the kind of man anyone would notice. He was not more than average in girth and of middling height. But an entitled, unattractive arrogance sat on him that was honed sharp as a knife. He pulled out the one comfortable seat at the table, *his* chair, and let himself into it. No word was spoken as Traber and Mr. Atkinson slipped onto the benches. People came in talking and laughing, then seeing Mr. Cozad, went quiet. They hung their coats, shuffled to places along the benches and eyed what Mary and Frieda brought out and set before Mr. Cozad. Mrs. Gatewood had ordered up a roast of hen and told Mary to serve Mr. Cozad before anyone else. "Makes him a little more patient," she added.

Mary transferred the roasted hen, still crackling from the oven, into a porcelain platter and brought it out. Mr. Atkinson sat at Mr. Cozad's right, Mr. Claypool and Mr. Drew at his left. The three men made small talk, which he did not join. He sat leaning back as they rambled on, his gold fob rising and falling with his breath, the diamond flickering. His eyes raged at them, his lips pressed against his teeth. His face was as narrow as a hawk's. She set the hen before him.

She brought his cream-whipped potatoes, and his gravy, and his bowl of honeyed carrots. She hovered behind him, waiting for him to serve himself, then wrung her hands as he bit into his food. The only thing he said was, "The gravy is tasteless. Bring me the pepper." And she brought the pepper, and waited with her shoulders forward, expecting. He shook on more pepper and took a bite. She watched his jaw, tensed at every chew, but he did nothing more than eat, smashed no plates, yelled out no screams, only asked her to, "Bring me more pepper." She gathered her hands and returned to the kitchen to breathe.

Chapter 25

Mary had never been philosophical, or deep, or any of the traits she saw as intelligent or rare. She saw this sort of depth in her son, but she had no mechanism to bring him to letting it out for others to see. She tried to pry from him an accounting of his days, but his shoulders slipped when she inquired, and he cut short his answers: "fine," "good," "yes," "no." When she asked if he had made a friend yet, he had said, "I guess so." And when she had inquired as to the name of his friend, he shrugged and she knew there was no friend. He had once been a sunny baby, a bright toddler, but had gone quiet and closed when his father changed. He had grown even more reserved since coming to Cozad.

One day, Mr. Young sent a note home with Ezekiel: *Mrs. Harrington, I would like a moment to discuss Ezekiel's attendance with you. Might you come see me at the school after the final bell tomorrow?* A rock of anxiety rose in her throat.

The schoolroom smelled of chalk and lead pencils. Warmth from the leavings of the day's fire still hung in it. Mr. Young pulled a child's chair near his desk, motioned for her to take it, and took another for himself. They sat, face to face, she straight and braced against fidgets, he with his legs crossed and hands calm in his lap. "I asked you to come today," he said, "to discuss Ezekiel."

"Yes?"

"He missed a day a while ago. He wrote me a note saying he had lost the note you wrote for his excuse and indicated he would be in trouble if I told you. I tell you now, and hope you will not punish him for it."

Missed school?

"What I wanted to talk with you about is that I am afraid he is behind the other children."

"Is he failing his studies?" she said. This was a tremendous surprise; Ezekiel brought home books and papers and spent long hours propped on his elbows, working his lessons and reading. Evenings alone with his schoolwork seemed to bring him pleasure. He had always been a quick boy.

Mr. Young held up his hands. "Oh no, he is very smart and capable. He applies himself, is never unprepared. In fact, though he is youngest, he is the best student I have. I wish the others were as adept as your son." He smoothed a pant leg that was already smooth, then looked up at her. "Can he speak, Mrs. Harrington?"

"Speak?"

"Can he . . . *talk*?"

"He read out loud for you the first day."

"Does he speak at home?"

"He is a quiet boy," she said.

"But does he *speak*?"

"Yes," she said.

"Because he refuses to speak a word to me or to any of the children."

Chapter 26

Cozad crackled. Wagons stopped. People milled. Mary saw Edmund everywhere. He hammered on every house. He baled every bale at the haypress. Every slap of the hotel door brought his shadow in.

The town crawled with people, thick as ants. People filled the rooms upstairs. Diners filled every space at the kitchen's table. The townspeople began calling the store the Bee Hive and Mrs. Gatewood hung a sign over the front door: *Bee Hive*. She sat on her stool half hidden behind brooms, and shovels, and calico fabrics, and pickle barrels. Sometimes, she hummed and counted her money. When she was not selling goods, she was bartering over the price of a house or storefront, or ordering stock for the kitchen. She kept a calendar. Past days were X'd over, the coming days when potentials were due were circled.

Attendance at Sunday supper grew again by half. The kitchen regularly cooked, now, for sixty. Mrs. Gatewood hung broadsides in both the mercantile and the hotel windows advertising "extra special Sunday" suppers and began charging twenty-five cents for the kitchen's creations. She hired yet another girl, Rose, to help with the Sunday work. Though she was well over thirty years old, Mrs. Gatewood called her "girl." Rose was a hopeful name for her, in truth she was plain-faced, of sallow gray color and thin mouse's hair that showed through to her scalp. She was near twenty years older than the other girls and she stood gray as granite as Mary explained and showed her how things would work. Rose was hired to clear and wash up so Mary, Ula, and Frieda could cook and serve. Mrs. Gatewood paid her fifty cents for it.

The gaiety of the hotel on Sundays sometimes lifted Mary, and in the quiet of a still-dark morning, she tried to believe, but she no longer knew in what. Mary was tired, yet could not manage sleep or even a yawn. Sleep required peace. A yawn required time. Her days began at three thirty and ended fifteen hours later. The compass of her days was driven by work. The compass allowed no time for anything else. She barely saw Ezekiel.

——

A mission, something Mary had to attend to, had hummed inside her for too many weeks. She had waited for a lull in work, some small break to take one day off. And when none came, one morning she finally told Ula to supervise the cooking.

The school had rung the bell only fifteen minutes before. The office door was open. Mary knocked. Mrs. Gatewood looked up. Mary gathered her hands. "Mrs. Gatewood, I need to be gone the rest of the day."

Mrs. Gatewood took off her eyeglasses. "You won't be working today, Mary?" She gave a small shake to her head. "We have potentials, you know." In the last three days, twenty families had set upon town. The hotel was full and the boardinghouse packed. Overflow families were being assigned to sleep under make-do tents. Mrs. Gatewood's tone said *How can you be gone?*

"I will be back this evening," she said. It sounded like an apology.

———

The morning light cast a low yellow the color of a buttercup. Mr. Simpson's livery was full; every pen had sows or calves in it, every stall a horse. The far corner stall held a stallion, a potent bay, who threw his head and stomped. Mary could no longer afford a pen for the hinny, so the mule lived outside in a corral with three mares. Their coats shaggy and long and clumped with mud.

The morning promised, however temporarily, a break toward spring. The light would not last. Clouds lay just above the sunrise. Mr. Simpson was forking new hay to a red gelding tied in the smithing corner. He did not notice Mary. She watched as he finished the haying, laid down the pitchfork, and tied on a leather apron. He bent over the anvil near the fire pit and began hammering a yellow-hot shoe that he held with tongs. The hammer clinked as he struck and the shoe bent a little; he struck it again. The hump of his shoulders obscured his view of her.

"Mr. Simpson?"

He jerked up, straightened as much as he could straighten, put his hand to his back. "You here to pay your past due?"

"I'm sorry," she said. "Could you carry me a little longer?"

"I don't know."

"I came to take the hinny out."

"Take her forever," he said.

"I'll be back by the end of the day."

"The bill," he said, "has to be paid."

"But Ezekiel helps out."

"And if I relied on that, I'd be dead and gone by the time your bill was clear."

———

The wagon bucked with the same zeal it did the day she and Ezekiel left the homestead. It was only four months since they had passed this way. It seemed years. She was gone less than an hour before the weather changed and a shower soaked her through. The hinny's back was slick, her sides ran wet black.

The birds were returning, their return bidding spring. Skein after skein of cranes cried their demands, their uncertain questions filled the skies day and night, their breasts clear and open to a rifle. The birds' vulnerability felt personal, now, their faith in their eternal paths, their direct and unwavering lives as certain as hers was not.

The hinny's head bobbed; the wagon rattled. The cold shook to her bones. The rain shower passed, but its passing did nothing to bring warmth.

In the distance, the hills drew her like a finger beckoning. As she drove into the first draw, her heart pounded. She tried not to dwell on what she hoped to find. With every thump of her pulse, she wanted what had once been; she wanted hope again, and security, and she wanted Edmund's soft touch.

She slapped the reins. The hinny picked up her pace. A feather of smoke rose from the Anderssons' chimney; they had returned. Where the family had gone, she did not know. To Sweden she imagined, home to visit family, and the imagining made her ache for her home in Ireland. Six pregnant cows were chewing hay at hayracks. Three men were putting in a fence for a new corral; *Mr. Andersson*, she thought, *and two of their sons, near grown.* They did not notice her going by.

She came to the gully. The low house huddled in dark misery. Had the house always been so small? As if reading her hesitancy, the hinny slowed. Mary clucked her on. The land lay bereft, dire where the wind had blown away the snow, filthy where old snow still covered it. The asparagus should be up by now. She would take some back with her. She squinted toward the patch where she had planted it. There was none but for one new white and lonely spear just broken through.

She drew up to the front door. She did not get down, but sat afraid to find what she would find.

The hinny set to cropping. Mary finally let herself down. The rough hatch door was closed like a sentry. She cupped her hands to her mouth, about to call out as though she were a stranger. She no longer felt sure why she was here, but some sense of urgency had sat on her since the day Ezekiel brought home the asparagus.

She put her hand on the door and let it lie there a moment so as to gain some sense of what lay inside it. She pushed. A dusting of sod powdered down on her head. "Edmund?" she said, though she knew he was not there.

The house was frigid and smelled of disuse and abandonment. The soundlessness surprised her, the emptiness. No matter how things eventually turned out, there had always been some sound, a lamp hissing, a rustle of Ezekiel's clothing, a sniff. Though the table and bench and chair sat where they had always sat, and the stove and counters stood where they had always stood, no pot bubbled, no rag lay drying on the counter. The roof had bent in and dripped over the bench where Ezekiel had slept and had stained it dark. Without the China rug to liven it, the dirt floor was pathetic and bare.

She lifted her skirt and went in. She pulled back the blanket to her and Edmund's bedroom. A rat had chewed a nest into the quilt she left him and had built a midden. She put her hand to her chest to feel the life of her own breath. She turned to leave. Her eye caught on the table where she had left Edmund's note.

It was gone.

Chapter 27

Mary would turn out the lamp soon, Ezekiel was turned to his side, away from her, already asleep. The homely night sounds of the rooms upstairs had become part of her, the murmurings before sleep, the snores, the tick of a door, the crackle of the floor when someone made a midnight visit to the washroom. The rhythmic thumping of a bed against a wall, the sounds of lovemaking would make Mary clamp her hands over her ears.

The hotel had been full since winter, the upstairs rooms were rented, most to families. One room, one of the hottest in the front of the building, was rented to a young, shy woman, barely out of school. Mary had seen her and her nine-month-old baby three days before at dinner. Mary did not know the woman's name, but had heard her tell another diner her husband had taken a small storefront to barber and had made a payment on one of the near-finished new houses for them to live. He had returned to Ohio to gather their things. The woman was not feeling well lately. The pasty shade of her face, the little she ate, the small rise at her stomach, and the manner in which she held her hands to cover the rise in her stomach made Mary think she was with another child.

There came that night the thin thread of a baby's crying, the hick-hick of hiccoughs. For many minutes, the baby cried. Finally, there came the prickle and creak of a door

119

coming open, a groan of feet down the steps. The baby's cries grew louder. Mary heard the mother's soft shush, which only seemed to make the crying worse. The mother's name, she remembered now, was Mrs. O'Doherty.

Mary heard the kitchen pump gushing water, then the "huck-huck-huck" of the baby's cries over a shoulder. She heard Mrs. O'Doherty hum, the baby's cries changing as he was swung one way then the other.

Mary pulled back her blanket. She blew out the lamp and let herself out their door. Mrs. O'Doherty was in her robe, her hair tied back in a braid down her back. Over her shoulder, the baby's forehead raged nearly purple. "Mrs. O'Doherty," Mary said. The woman startled. Mary reached her arms out. "May I?"

"Oh, I am so sorry to disturb," Mrs. O'Doherty said. Mary reached out, fingered, "Let me." Mrs. O'Doherty settled the baby in Mary's arms.

The baby's pitches changed a little, but gave no indication they would give up. "What is your baby's name, Mrs. O'Doherty?" The woman looked as if she wanted to join her baby in a good cry.

"Emily," she said. The baby was red-haired with thin fine fizz of it the same shade as her mother's.

Mary held the child out, and the baby looked straight at her. She hiccoughed again, head jerking, then gave out more of her loud misery. "I think she may be sick," Mrs. Doherty said.

"With lungs like that?" Mary said, and Mrs. O'Doherty's expression broke a tiny bit. "I think it might be something else, Mrs. O'Doherty. Is she your first?" Mary put a finger in the baby's mouth. The cries continued.

"Oh, yes," Mrs. O'Doherty said. "I am not sure at all I am up to another."

Mary rubbed the baby's gums. Teeth were breaking through in two places. Mary swept the soft pads of her fingers over the gums and the crying ebbed the slightest bit. She continued and the baby's fists went quiet, her cries died, and left in their place only the tiny jump of a dying hiccough. When she was limp, Mary handed her back to her mother. "Sit with me, won't you, a moment? Let me get us some tea."

They talked of Ireland. They talked of their children, they talked of where they came from. Mrs. O'Doherty was from Ballinaclash in County Wicklow, somewhat north and east of Mary's home in County Cork. Mrs. O'Doherty's diction ran thicker than Mary's and brought with it the sea and the sweet damp of home. In the few months Mary had been in Cozad, she had lost some of the lilt of her own tones to the amalgam of voices filling the air. It returned, now, and sat sweet on her tongue.

They sat until Mrs. O'Doherty's head bobbed and her lids grew thick. By the time they bid each other good night, they had exchanged given names; Mrs. O'Doherty's was Fiona and the name rolled from Mrs. O'Doherty's tongue as if it had just been delivered as a gift from home. Mary slept that night as she had not slept in a good long time.

Chapter 28

Hammers pounded almost day and night. The weather began to turn, bequeathing a hopeful day or two of warmth before another storm slammed in. The heat from the kitchen kept the hotel warm in the worst of cold weather but portended a hellish heat for summer.

Mrs. O'Doherty was coming down every night, now. She nursed the baby as they talked, and she grimaced, now and then, when a new tooth met the flesh of her breast. She spoke of her husband and their dreams: a barbershop first, then maybe a haberdashery as the town grew. They had put down on a small new house and she was eager for their furniture and things to come in. She inquired of Mary's husband and Mary said when he returned, they planned to resume working their homestead. She did not elaborate and Mrs. O'Doherty had the tact not to ask further.

Each morning, Mary rose, leaving Ezekiel in his bed. And, as the men ate their breakfast, she filled a plate with two boiled eggs, a jar of tomatoes, and a biscuit, buttered and jammed. In a bucket she would put breakfast, cheese, stew, ham into a bowl and take the plate and the school bucket in to her son. He would rise when she came in and eat by himself before he readied himself for school. It was their only time when neither was too exhausted to hold conversation. She sometimes asked him what he studied at school and he usually raised his shoulders. "Reading?" she would say and he would nod.

"Arithmetic?" Another nod.

One morning she ventured, "Do you talk with the other children?" And he slumped forward but did not nod.

"Do they talk with you?" He shook his head. "Why don't you speak to them?" she said.

"Because I don't know their language."

"Ah," she said. She laid her hand on his shoulder. "Do you talk with Mr. Young? I know he speaks your language."

"I did a couple of times," he said.

———

Her days seemed to gentle somewhat. The conversations with Fiona, her calm consistency, soothed Mary's evenings, even when the baby fussed, and she began to sleep better, dire worries seemed to weigh less.

Mary cooked the breakfasts alone, Ula and Frieda arrived later, to help with the midday dinner and supper. Ezekiel began working at the livery in earnest, Saturdays and Sundays as well as two hours a day after school forking offal. Ezekiel negotiated a better deal when the weather improved and the hinny no longer was kept in the corral. For his work, Mr. Simpson still paid him a dime every two days, but took out three cents rather than a nickel.

Even as the evenings with Fiona cushioned Mary's sleep, Ezekiel seemed to be growing anxious; he seem unable to control his legs, or his hands; they often jerked and flapped and kicked in his sleep and he would cry out.

But when Mary woke him and asked if there was something wrong, he always muttered no.

He came home late one day, limping. His hand was swollen and his cheek bore a gash. "What happened," she said.

He shrugged. "Fell."

"From what?"

"Just fell," he said. A boy his size had not far to fall. She asked him to show her his leg. Reluctantly, he pulled up his knickers to the edge of a bruise. He seemed ashamed of it.

"How did this happen?"

He shrugged again. "Just happened."

"Pull down your pants," she said, "I want to see all of your leg." A reddening swell, the size of a saucer, spread across his thigh, by tomorrow it would darken into shades of purple and black. "Did a horse kick you?"

He looked down, toed the floor, gave a half shake to his head. "Not a horse," he said. His nose was beginning to run and his chin to quiver. His injuries represented something suspicious, but she could not get him to admit anything more than that he fell.

Chapter 29

The day had begun lovely with a soft blessing of sun and breeze and April's shortened shadows. Men were going about without coats, women in soft, spring-colored bonnets. Mrs. O'Doherty was no longer feeling sick, but was certainly thickening in the middle.

The previous night over tea, Fiona had been giddy, her color high at the letter she received that day from her husband, saying that he would be on the train in less than two weeks. The baby slept as Fiona chattered on about plans for the house and about Mr. O'Doherty's—Diarmuid's—elation about their future life in Nebraska. Mary tried to share her enthusiasm, but that night as she had lain in her bed, she wept.

Three sheets of biscuits lay cooling on the counter and an eternal stew—lamb this time—burbled in a pot. It was the quiet time of day when a lull set on the hotel; the men were out working, women preparing meals at home, and the Bee Hive closed up for the afternoon for Mrs. Gatewood to run some errand in the settlement of Darr, up the road. School had just let out for the day; Ezekiel would be across the street working at the livery. The life of the kitchen, with Ula working in it, had taken on a stride, a quiet unspoken rhythm of some ease, and Mary took some succor in it.

Ula was glazing a ham which Mary would carve for Mr.

127

Cozad. His cobbler cooled on the counter. He was away more than in town anymore. Mary had heard him shout at the men, accuse them of being stupid and lazy. But he had never said more to her and, for that, she sometimes sent up a small prayer of thanks.

From the street someone screamed, "Fire! Fire!" The voice was a man's, high-pitched and gargling. "Fire in the store!" Smoke crept from under the mercantile door. Ula yipped. Mary dropped her bowl and dashed out the front door. Smoke was lifting up from behind the boardinghouse and livery.

Mary ran toward the barn. Mr. Claypool sprinted his mare down the street, his yells slicing like a razor blade. "Fire! Fire!" He whipped his mare faster. Men broke from every direction, yelling, "Where?" though smoke was beginning to obscure the view.

She screamed, "Ezekiel!" The boardinghouse next to the livery disappeared in a breath as dark as a crematorium. A window shattered, the door belched fetid black. The house disappeared, consumed by a scudding murk that drove toward the livery. Fire licked up through the boardinghouse roof, cinders flew.

Inside the livery, pigs squealed and horses shrieked. Mary ran in. "Ezeeee-kiel!" But he was not there, nor was Mr. Simpson. The animals were in a crush of panic. Horses reared and beat hooves in the stalls. Pigs screamed, eyes rolled back, white.

She dashed around to the back. The hinny's pen was open, the hinny gone. "Ezekiel? Ezekiel?"

People were running with buckets, some jumping on

mules, horses, and wagons, anything that moved. Mr. Cozad bolted from the direction of the Bee Hive, his coattails flying. "Buckets, you sons a bitches." His arm flew toward the river. "Line up!"

Men scrambled for anything that would hold water. Someone sprinted into the livery, came out on horses, bridled but without saddles. They lined up at the hotel trough with their buckets. When the line grew too long at the trough, they threw themselves on horseback and bolted toward the river. Women came from the houses, gathered their children, hustled their chickens into the pens. Men slapped at cinders with anything they could find: rags, coats, blankets.

Town was turned over to the screeches of wagons, the shrieks of animals. Nothing was still; everything moved as in a dream, all slants, angles, motion without meaning, sounds without hearing.

Sparks whorled. Fire ate the lumberyard, consumed the boardinghouse, then the livery. It licked at the stores near the saddlery. Flames sucked the air, took away breath. Mary cupped her hands to her mouth, "Ezekiel! Ezekiel!" She choked. Men ran past carrying buckets, whipping past in wagons. She screamed again, "Ezekiel!" but could hear nothing but cracks from the men's whips, and the terrible roar.

Cinders pulsed at a sill of the hotel, then blew to life on a draft. Flames took the sill. The window exploded, and the maw sucked in the fire. The fire boomed and it roared. Flames consumed one wall, then another. The blaze took the porch, flared along the horse rail.

129

Mary caught sight of Ezekiel on the wagon, fighting to hold the hinny as men loaded buckets onto it. One of the men motioned him to go, and he whipped the hinny the direction of the river. She picked up her skirt and raced after him. She made it halfway to the river until her legs could run no farther.

He was swallowed by a billow of smoke. When the smoke cleared, he and the wagon, loaded with buckets, were scrambling back up over the railroad tracks on the way to the fire. He was in the greatest peril in the middle of town. A searing heat hit her as she stood, useless, watching as flames danced and as time and time again her son left with a wagon loaded with empty buckets and returned with them sloshing. She prayed until panic bent into a pattern.

In less than two hours, it grew certain that saving the middle of town was impossible. The men turned to the homes in the path of the wind and cinders. They coughed and they threw water. And Ezekiel sat among them vulnerable, a tiny figure no more than a grain of salt. One of the men—Mary could not see who it was—leaned in to him once and ruffled his hair. He must have said something. Ezekiel ducked his head and he grinned.

———

Dark fell, black, sooty, a velvet filth. Mary sat on the bare ground upwind of the smoke. Before it turned dark, she found a patch of new grasses for the goat, then she waited, fidgeted, and listened for the rattle of the wagon returning Ezekiel to her. Where the fire had been, cinders flickered alive with the breeze and, for a moment, revealed the silhouettes of Traber Gatewood, Mr. Simpson, Mr. Atkinson, Mr. Claypool, and Mr. Holbrook. Mary listened as they spoke among themselves. Mr. Holbrook took off his cap and held it in front of him as if in prayer. "I think we have done with it," he said.

They were quiet then. They had not been able to save Cozad. The fire had consumed all of the middle of town. A defeated silence lay on them.

Someone said. "There ain't nothing more we can do tonight, it looks like."

Traber said, "Sam you still here?"

Another voice came from the dark. "Yeh."

"The houses are still standing. Could you get a couple men to make sure if the wind starts up, you dowse the cinders if they blow that way?"

"Yup," Mr. Atkinson said.

One man—Mary could not make out who—said, "Anybody know where Mr. Cozad went? I ain't seen him for a while."

Another coughed and cleared his throat. "He left for Plum Creek." It was Traber, his voice rough as a rasp. "To talk to the sheriff. Somebody died in the hotel."

"Who was't?"

"I haven't heard."

Mr. Atkinson said, "A drifter, I hear. T'was a fellow come in last night, drunk."

Mary held her hand at her stomach. She stepped forward. "Who?"

"Mrs. Harrington?" Traber said. "You're here?"

She grabbed his arm. "Who?" Sound barely came from

her mouth. "Who?"

"I don't know, Mrs. Harrington. I only heard it was somebody."

"I need to know." She dug her fingers into Traber's arm. "Tell me, was it my husband?" She began a silent cry.

From the back someone coughed. "Was somebody named John O'Neil, I hear."

Mr. Atkinson came up. "I heard that, too." He coughed, cleared his throat. "It was not Mr. Harrington, Missus."

———

The embers glittered and hissed. In the dusk, she found where Ezekiel had scattered their things before he took the wagon. She unrolled one of the lengths of calicoes and spread it for some sort of bed to lie on. She sat down and listened and waited. They had no room, now, nowhere to stay; all but what they wore and stored under the wagon had gone up in flames with the hotel.

"Mrs. Harrington?"

The man's voice startled her. She must have gasped.

"Sorry," he said. She would have heard him coming were it not for the crackles and hisses.

She squinted into the near dark and pulled herself up from the ground. Mr. Claypool stood a few feet away, holding a platter covered with a cloth. "Mr. Claypool," she said. He had washed up, his face clean, his white hair shown like a ghost in the sky light. In another time, another circumstance, Mary would have bothered to smooth her hair.

He held the platter toward her. "My girls made an extra bit, just some scones and creamed meat. I thought you might could use it."

"Oh my," she said, then had to swallow before she could manage to say more. "Thank you," and she wanted to add, but could not fathom what. "You are kind," she said, but more words stuck in her throat.

He held the platter toward her. "That boy of yours," he said, "he did a man's work today. I thought he might be hungry."

"Yes," she said and took it. "Thank you, Mr. Claypool."

As he was about to leave, she added, "Could you tell me if anyone has seen Mrs. O'Doherty and the baby?"

"The Schultzes have taken them to stay out at their farm until her husband returns."

———

Just after dark, Ezekiel finally showed. The sky was overcast, the clouds lying low and lit orange whenever a flame still took hold and burned. She took the hinny's reins as he clambered off the wagon, then led him to the calicoes. "Here's our bed for the night," she said. "Mr. Claypool brought something to eat." She patted the ground where she had put the food. "I'll stake the mule."

In the dark, she unhitched the hinny, led her to where the new grasses were.

The clouds cleared and allowed the light from the moon. Ezekiel was sitting on the calico, scooping up the food with his hand. He blended, nearly disappeared for the dark filth on him. He finished the food and lay back. He coughed and spat. "Ma," he said.

She lay back on the calico. She said, "Let's sleep, now." The ground was rough and she shifted her hips.

A thunderhead cracked off toward the east, a familiar sound she tried to make sense of. She heard him take a breath. "Ma?" he said again. She wished she could see him but could make out only the barest outline.

"Tomorrow we'll pack up and return home to the farm," she said. It was all she could think of.

"No." He said this short, almost a bark.

"Your pa surely will come home soon."

"We have to stay here," he said, his voice fixed. She heard the rustle of his clothes and felt the bump of his hand moving against her hip. "I got something," he said. He laid his hand on her stomach. She felt him open it, then felt him take it away. She patted where his hand had been, picked up three coins. They were heavy. "Where did you get these?"

He did not speak for a moment. "Pa," he said then rolled away.

"Your father?"

"Yuh."

"When?"

He coughed again. "A long time ago," he said. His voice was tight. "It's thirty dollars."

"Oh my goodness, but *when?*" She waited. He did not answer. "*When* did he give them?" She wished she could see what was on his face.

"A long time ago," he said again and his voice went away as if he had turned his back to her.

"When?"

"When," he faltered, "when he was making the whistle." His voice was hollow as if he were making this

134

up. "For my birthday." Ezekiel had brought the whistle with him when they left home, Mary had found it in the pocket of his coat.

The year Edmund made the whistle had been the last of the good years. He had bought his first calves over two years before then; they were to be the start of his becoming a cattleman. By Ezekiel's birthday early in the summer, the grasses had grown thick and the calves were beginning to thrive; her garden was rich, the four hundred saplings she had planted, on the tree claim Edmund had put in her name, were taking root, some tall enough to show over the crest of the hill.

Before winter, Edmund sold the fattened calves at a good price and had spent all the money from the sale on the new calves he intended to feed through the winter and to sell the following spring. When the second herd sold for even more, he bought more calves and began drawing out plans for a proper house. There would be four rooms and a water closet upstairs, and three rooms downstairs with a hearth at one end, just like the Anderssons'. He would put a water pump in the kitchen, just like at the Humes' in Philadelphia.

Edmund had chosen a particular stick to fashion the whistle. He sharpened his knife, hollowed out the pith, drilled five holes for the fingers and one more for a slot at the mouth. It took him a good part of two days to finish it. When it was done, he gave the whistle to Ezekiel. "Try it," he said. And Ezekiel blew out a sound that made Mary giggle. Edmund ruffled Ezekiel's hair. "Do the fingers." Their son leaned against him and Mary could feel what passed between them as Ezekiel tooted and diddled the fingers and came out with sounds sweet as a bird's.

"What do you say?" she had said.

"Thanks, Pa," he answered.

That winter would prove to be the last. Within months, the freeze would wipe out the calves, and take their future with it. The hope, the blisters, the strained back, would be for nothing. Edmund would find succor in the relief of drink.

The breeze shifted, now, and carried a strangle of smoke. Mary coughed. Ezekiel took a breath. "He gave it me when he still loved me."

"He always loved you," she said. She closed her fingers around the coins, held them close to her chest and wondered why, all this time, Ezekiel had kept this from her. He snuffed back a breath that was thick and wet, and he said no more.

―――――

Town still smoldered. Now and then, a flame caught and licked up but then died out in the ash. The heart of town was gone: the hotel, the post office, the mercantile, Gatewood's boardinghouse, McIntyre's hardware store, the new drugstore, the windmill business, the livery, and Schultz's implement store. Left behind were the smells of singed hair, char, cooked dirt and ash, the puck and scrape of shovels, the hisses of scorch when the men wetted it.

At its whim, the fire had picked what it wanted and ignored the rest. It took the livery but ignored the haystack out back. It took the porch and front of the barbershop but left the chair and the back shelves with lotions and oils. It ate or bit into every stick of the hotel but left a shed untouched. All that remained of the hotel were the hearth and the stove, which pricked up from the ruins like blackened fingers. Someone had opened the pens in the livery and let loose the sows, and they rooted about, now, at the edge of town.

All Mary's animals had survived, but the hinny had suffered some burns to her back and her withers twitched now and then. Her head drooped with exhaustion. Ezekiel had gone out again, just after the sun came up, to see about helping. Mary found the bucket they had stored under the wagon. In the brigade of buckets, theirs had gone unused and forgotten. The trough in front of the hotel was singed but still held water. Mary held the bucket under the nozzle. She let out a breath when the pump drew and began to spit.

The hinny guzzled so fast she choked, her thirst made Mary want to weep. Three times, she had to return to the pump, and three times, the hinny drank all that was in the bucket. When the hinny was through, Mary took water to the small pen where she had closed up the hens and the goat. She let herself in; they gathered at her feet. The hens clucked, but the goat was too stricken to speak.

Mary filled the old skillet with water for the hens. They dipped and tipped back their heads. She set the bucket down for the goat. The goat bent her head into it and drew in. They all depended on her, everything depended on her. It seemed a burden she was not up to. She barked a sob. The goat looked up, her eyes filled with misery. Mary patted the doe's head and let out a soft cry and the goat dipped her muzzle and drank again.

Chapter 30

Once again Mary had to prevail on Mrs. Gatewood, perhaps ask for a favor from Mrs. O'Doherty, or Ezekiel would not eat. Others in town would have something in their larders and cellars to count on and may spare a bit of preserves or jerked meats. Mr. Claypool's kindness had carried her and Ezekiel through the night, but she could not depend on charity.

Nothing in town resembled what it had been. People wandered around the burn, arms crossed, faces blanched. Where there had been buildings and industry and the sense of structure, there were black timbers and ash. Where there had been streets with horses and buggies, and a place to find a warm meal, or a scythe for sale, or a spindle of thread, there was nothing more than a memory. People gathered their hands and pinched their lips. They shook their heads and said it was strangers who did it, strangers who had been seen around the hotel the day of the fire. And they put their heads together as to whether it started at the boardinghouse or the hotel. It had spread so fast it could have started anywhere.

Mr. Cozad returned from Plum Creek. He asked Traber to gather the men in the middle of Eighth Street where the burn was concentrated. The men's faces were drawn, and they stood like shadows, some wearing the same clothes they had worn while they fought the fire. Mr.

Cozad wore a top hat and a full-tail coat. "Get to work, men. We're going to make it grand the next time."

Mr. Atkinson said, "Maybe it's time to admit . . ."

Mr. Cozad swung around. "What, Samuel? *What?*"

Mr. Atkinson could not return Mr. Cozad's eye. "It dunna look good," he said, "Mr. Cozad." Like everyone else, Mr. Atkinson depended on a town where he could make a living.

"You give up now, you son of a bitch, and I'll know you as a coward." Mr. Cozad pushed back the coattails. "Don't quit on me now, men," he said and, for the first time, Mary heard his voice soften. "We're going to build." He swung his arm in a circle. "Houses," he said. "Businesses. Schools, churches. Stay with me, men. I give my word I'll pay as I always have for a good day's work."

Mr. Claypool stepped forward. "Half the houses in town are already emptying out."

Mr. Cozad raised up his hand, signaling stop. "Dave, I won't listen to that damned talk. It won't work with me. Act like men. We're going to fill every one of them and we're going to build more and we're going to fill them, too. "We start tomorrow. Joe, you take some men, clean up this place. We have potentials coming in and it looks bad. Dave, you gather men, put them to work. Start building another house.

"We got nothing to build with," Mr. Claypool said. "Everything burned."

Mr. Cozad pumped his fist. "Traber, get the goddamned brickyard running. We'll rebuild with brick this time. No son of a bitch can burn a brick. Sam, get to work on stores. Build a bank. Build a place for a good barber, maybe two. Build a post office, a general store, somewhere to sell tools. And by God, put up another hotel. We can't have people seeing us down. You all know how we do it. Now, get the hell busy."

The next day, Mr. Cozad boarded the train. "Headed for the Mississippi to get funds," Traber told the men.

Chapter 31

Mary hoped to see Mrs. Gatewood, Ula, or Freida and approach one of them for help, for a barn to sleep in, or a place to bathe. But they had all left town, scattering to their farms.

She shoved the trunk and the treadle under the wagon and laid the calicoes beside them. She sent up a little prayer of thanks Ezekiel had not taken the things exposed from under the wagon when he moved it to fight the fire. She moved the hinny and goat to a new patch of grasses. A light rain settled the smoke some, but the stink and black had worked its way into everything, clothes, the prints of her fingers, and hair until there was no other scent.

All day, Ezekiel trailed behind the men. They started cleaning where the livery had stood, worked their ways up the blocks. Ruin lay everywhere, in lengths of charred wood, in crimped and ruined metals of flues, in heaps of ash, and in tumbled brick. She watched the men break into teams, some made piles of ruin that others threw into wagons and took away. Ezekiel was the only child among them; she saw him pick up a shovel and pitch and scrape along beside the men. None of them chided him or motioned for him to get out of their way. They worked all morning, then midday they broke and sighed and puffed exhausted cheeks as they leaned against the wheels of the wagons. Some lay under, out of the drizzle. Ezekiel lay with them. One man, unrecognizable from the filth, took something from his lunch pail and shared it with her son.

Ezekiel returned in the late afternoon. He lay on the calico and slept. After dark, Mary got up, slipped out.

———

Even with the rain, heat still rose from the burned ground. She sat at the edge of the place where their room had been, turning her face from the heat. She swept a stick in a wide arc, hoping it would catch on something that might have survived but it was too hot to continue. She rose. Not but a few feet away lay the mouth of the cellar. The door was gone, the steps filled with the rubble of black char and ash. She stumbled toward the hole, toeing along, arcing her arms like a blind woman. She felt no heat come out and did not think she could see tracks in the ash. The night was damp, the air too dense to allow the moon or stars. She nearly fell where the first step should have been. She squatted and eased one foot, one leg, a second foot, the next leg down into the familiar.

She felt around, patted the walls, fingered for the shelves. She found the beets and carrots and filled the pockets of her coat. She followed the stink of rotting potatoes, patted along the wall to the bin. She filled her skirt with them, too rushed to remove the vines. Around the potatoes, she put some of the cornmeal, and when she could manage no more, she felt her way up again and out into the night.

Chapter 32

Mary squatted again at the edge of the hotel burn. By midday the following day it had cooled some. She snaked the stick a wide swath, furrowing through the ash. The men were working nearby, cleaning up where the livery had stood and working their way toward the ruin of the boardinghouse. They would begin clearing the hotel lot soon.

The stick left tracks where she swung it. Then it hit something almost out of reach. She pulled the stick toward her, but it lost the prise on whatever it was. She lurched the stick out until it caught again. It brought in a warped tin cup from the kitchen. She set the cup aside. Like a water witcher, she swung the stick again, and it struck something hollow. She pulled but it resisted, so she grappled with the stick. By the sound, she knew what it was: the tin that held what was left of the stationery and her letters from Prune.

The box was too hot to touch. She grasped it in her skirts, threw it to her side. All its loveliness had been burned off, its sweet roses, its swirls of painted ribbons. The box was the gray of the world, now. She blew to cool it. A storm of ash rose, then drifted away. She opened it. The letters, were dust. What was left were three gold coins Ezekiel had

145

given her and a jumble of pennies and nickels.

Chapter 33

School was suspended until things settled. Mrs. Gatewood showed in town the day after the fire. Mary had tried to approach her, but Mrs. Gatewood waved her off, too busy with business and orders to the men. The trains began delivering carloads of lumber and Ezekiel hung around as the men began throwing together a small structure for a store and staking out the outline of a new hotel.

At night, under the wagon, listening to the sounds of her son's soft breath, hopelessness grabbed on. Mary prayed so hard for Edmund to come that her belly cramped. The memories of their once life, their songs, their tendernesses carried her. Some powerful force was keeping Edmund away, she thought likely it would be some work he found, and thinking it relieved her some.

———

It still drizzled. She moved the wagon a few feet back from the stink. She dug a pit and lined it with rock and scavenged wood she laid in it for a fire she started with cinders. She put the skillet on the fire and covered two of the potatoes with the pot to let them bake.

But for what she and Ezekiel wore, every piece of their clothing had gone with the fire. She scrimped small pieces from the calico they slept on, a brown mottled with blue chrysanthemums, the most colorless and plain of all. She pushed away the thought of her one and a one and a one in the trunk. She could find them under her linens in the same leather pouch her mother had given her. All else, every penny, was her son's.

She set a day, two days from then to make a decision. For two days he would be safe. After that, would she be able to find work? She had to do something; without work how long could they last?

She set the treadle on the ground. She nearly cried when she found the scissors in its drawer and saw that the machine still had thread. She brushed the floor of the wagon as well as she could and laid out some of the dullest fabric. She cut a shirt and knee pants for Ezekiel. The cutting and the sewing became a salve and, for the first time in forever, her gut let go its cramp.

When Ezekiel returned that midday and they had eaten the potatoes and beets, she told him to take off his old clothes and wash up in the water in the bucket.

"Here?" he said.

They were in the open. There was no privacy. "I'll hold out my skirt, then. You go behind it."

Ezekiel stood damp from his wash, unclothed but for his drawers. The wind kicked up and set him shivering. She saw, then, a burn on his shoulder. He had not complained, and she would not have

148

noticed. "What is this?" She reached to touch the scab and he pulled away. "Does it hurt?"

"Not so much as the one on my head." He dipped his head. She pushed away his hair. The scab was ugly.

"Your hair could have caught fire," she said.

"I slapped it."

"Let me see your hands." He held them out. The pad on one palm had a small red spot where there had been a blister. "Why didn't you say something?"

He shrugged. "All us got burned, I guess."

He dressed and she fussed to take in a seam of his shirt and wished she had honey to put on his burns.

The following day, she cut a shift for herself and sewed it. When it was done, she climbed up on the wagon, slid under the seat, and hid from view behind the sideboards. Her elbows knocked; her knees hit the bottom of the seat. Slivers caught in her underskirt, punctured the backs of her arms.

She knocked around until she was finally shed of her dress. She threw it aside and slipped into the shift. She wore the shift as she bent over the bucket to put her old dress in water to soak. She took up Ezekiel's old trousers; he had worn them so hard that the knees, the rims of the pocket, and the button fly had gone to thread. She turned them inside out, found some bit of clean allowance along the seams she might be able to use for patches. She shook them. Dust flew and she choked. She shook them again and a bit of paper flew out. She caught it before the wind took it away. The paper was folded into a bit not much larger than her thumbnail. It was dirty, as if it had been in the pocket a long time.

With the tips of her fingers, she unfolded it so as not to rip it. It fluttered in her fingers: the note she had left for Edmund.

Chapter 34

Mary had never heard of tornadoes—Ireland did not have them—until Prune brought them up as a warning to keep Mary and Edmund in Philadelphia. "Ah, Edmund," she had said, "you know there's tornadoes in Nebraska and they can sweep you right up and throw you down and kill you." Edmund had swatted his hand as if he were swatting a fly. But Nebraska did have them. The first had come just weeks after they arrived. It had fingered the distance, brought a fuss of winds, then had swept by. A second, months later, had come as fall cooled the nights. Edmund was gone to Plum Creek for supplies, hay for the calves through the winter, and sugar and flour for her. The thing had crept in on a day already taken by a misery of humidity and thunders.

She had been working in the late garden. The pumpkins lay bright as flares among the gray leaves. The baby was wrapped at her chest, sleeping. The barrow sat nearby half full, waiting to be wheeled to the cellar. The skies were iron gray and the wind strong but no more forceful than on many other days. Since coming to Nebraska, she had grown to hate the wind's relentless screams, its unpredictable pitch.

She brought up the hacking knife, whacked at a stem the size of her wrist. It was then that her skirt lifted, covered the baby, and enveloped her face. The skirt pasted itself against her nose, her eyes, her mouth. She could not breathe, she could not see. She turned her back and the skirt whipped from her face and stood away from her like a flag. Suction pulled the breath out of the day, lifted her, gave her feet no purchase. It sucked her face, her lips, the lids of her eyes. The baby screamed. Bits of prairie pricked at her arms, her bared legs. Her eardrums felt stabbed. She managed to turn toward the house but could not make a step. She dropped down, began to scrabble like a crab. Ezekiel wailed, then the thing sucked his voice away.

As she crawled, a piece of the roof lifted and was lost to the black. The sow squealed in the pen. A hen was lifted then consumed. The thing took another who rose squawking as if outraged. Mary threw herself to the ground, flattened herself over the baby. She turned to her side and pulled, side-stroke, toward the cellar door. She grabbed the handle, but the hatch pressed down with a weight she could not lift. Then, as if it had somehow changed its mind, the hatch flew up and swept from her hand. The door wavered there a moment as if making up its mind. Then, it creaked and the jamb splintered and the door whipped and was lost with the hens. On her behind, she scrambled down into the safety of the dark.

It was as if she were in the eye of that tornado once again, captured in its still tunnel, dark as death, winds blasting around. It was as if she were no more than a prickling bit to be funneled up, helpless to whatever the thing threw at her. If it was true what she had heard said, peace lay in the eye of a tornado, but there was no peace. She had no peace, no relief, no answers. There was only the whine of her doubt: Did Edmund even know where she was? Had he passed through town? How had Ezekiel got hold of the note? Had Edmund given it to him? Had Edmund even seen the note at all?

It pressed against her under the bodice of her chemise. She knelt by the bucket, the same bucket she had used to boil their eggs that morning, and sank Ezekiel's trousers into the water. Five times she had emptied the water and still it ran black. For a moment, the homely chores brought relief, and she was convinced the only thing to do was to return to the farm. But if they did, how could they live? Or, she could move them to Plum Creek, leave Edmund another note, draw him another map pointing to Plum Creek, hoping he might understand and know they had left Cozad. But how would she be able to take care of them any better in Plum Creek than she could here?

"Mary?" She turned, held up the trousers in her hand like a trophy. She remained kneeling, a run of mud coursing up her sleeve. Mrs. Gatewood rode up on her mare. "Mary," she said again. She looked tired. She had lost her town, more even than Mary had lost. She wore a lace blouse but no bonnet against the sun. The wind shifted her pile of white hair, billowed her skirt. She held back a tendril of hair, then pulled up her cheeks in a half-smile meant to speak encouragement. The brackets around her mouth, however, spoke exhaustion. She sat to the side of the saddle, the side with her bad hip braced over the pommel. She rubbed the hip.

Mary said, "Uh," and stood. The pants dripped down the side of her shift. She could think of nothing else to say.

Mrs. Gatewood said, "Uh," a sort of pain that might have mimicked Mary, but did not. She slid down, took a breath. When her feet found ground, she said, "Mary, how are you faring?" Her face was pale, her eyes lined red, the lids thick and soft. Mary was aware of what Mrs. Gatewood saw: a thin, pitiful woman, face gruesome with filth and sleeplessness, hair pinned, dust dull, and roughly back. Mrs. Gatewood touched her shoulder. "Mary," she said. She wished Mrs. Gatewood would stop repeating her name; it drove misery deeper. "I came to say that the Bower house has gone vacant. Why don't you stay there?"

"We have naught to pay for a house to stay in," she said, not quite a lie. Even with Ezekiel's money, she could pay rent only a while.

"I will need you to cook," Mrs. Gatewood said.

"Cook?" Mary said. The kitchen was gone,

nothing left of it but soot and ash and the stove

"The men will begin on a temporary kitchen in the morning." Mrs. Gatewood's voice took on its edge, her tone of certainty and expectation that surely Mary would comply.

"I will need to be paid," Mary said.

Mrs. Gatewood sighed. She waggled a finger. "In exchange, you can stay in the house."

"And still have bowls from the kitchen each day." It was not a question, though her voice was soft.

"Yes."

"Is that different from pay?"

"It is since you have something to eat. The house is empty so I am getting no money for it. I am sorry, dear, it is the best I will offer." Mrs. Gatewood put her hand on her forehead and said the oddest thing: "Oh, Mary, I just don't know."

Chapter 35

On her own, Mary loaded their things onto the wagon. She unpacked the trunk, set the books and linens aside and carried it, empty, into the house, then carried the things as she could up the steps into the house. She could not manage the treadle alone, would have to wait for Ezekiel's help with it.

The conversation with Mrs. Gatewood rang with a sense of the old woman's exhaustion and cracked confidence. The one thing Mary had come to count on and that allowed her to sleep was that Mrs. Gatewood would always know what was right and sufficient and sound. The lack of it shook Mary now.

———

The Bower house sat up three steps. It contained a hall, parlor, sitting room, dining room, and kitchen downstairs. Upstairs had three bedrooms and a small room for a wash closet. The house seemed enormous. But a sense of a sadness filled its thuddingly bare wood floors that pounded under her feet, and the walls that echoed with her breathing. The windows stared out onto the street, uncovered and naked. Mary had heard nothing about the Bowers, but was aware that when they left, Mrs. Bower was not well. Out back was a shed and a small coop. Mary put the hens in the coop. She gathered dry grasses and fluffed them in the shed for the goat.

Mary and Ezekiel were among the few who were staying. After the fire, parades of people waited to get onto the trains back to where they had come from. All but three of the fifteen houses were empty, now, their windows blank and sightless. Mr. Atkinson and Mr. Claypool and his girls were all who remained, living in two of the houses. The third was occupied by a family who would leave it, after they completed a house of their own on their new farmland. Only those three houses had curtains in the windows, and calves in the pens, and pots of geraniums and pansies by the front steps.

The house held the sense of being someone else's. And as she spread blankets for their beds, she thought of the questions she should ask Ezekiel about the note, but knew she might not want to know the answer.

———

Their first night, by the light of a candle borrowed from Mrs. Gatewood, Mary found a pencil and lined paper among Ezekiel's books in the trunk. And she wrote:

> *Cozad*
> *April 30, 1874*
> *Dearest Prune,*
> *I will write just this page, as we have spent the last*

few days in a dust of drama here in town. Before I
go into it, let me say we are all right.

Two days ago, a fire took out the center of town. Its
few businesses burned down including an emigrant
hotel, a general store, post office, livery, and some
small shops. A man died, though I knew him only
by name. All else were unharmed but for cinder
burns. The houses in town, all but two went
untouched except for smoke and a cinder burn or
two. Our house made it through.

We have decided to stay in town, in order to help it
rebuild. There is much work to be done. Men are
kept busy from sunup to well after dark.

Your nephew seems to have taken all in stride.
School has been closed for some days but will resume
again tomorrow, and he has already begun
complaining. He says he knows everything the
teacher has to teach and that he is learning nothing
at school. Alas, your nephew's independent spirit
takes after his aunt. He is a smart boy, but he still
has to go to his classes.

You can see I have run out of paper. I close with a
kiss. Please write soon.

Love, Sissie

Chapter 36

The men cleared the hotel rubble until all that was left to remember the old building was bare ground and what did not burn: the stove, the old hearth, the chimney, and the hand pump. They stood like sentinels in the black soil. The men laid in a floor around the pump, hoping it had not cracked and would still draw. They hammered out four walls in the street, by afternoon, had put them up. Twenty-four hours later, the structure had rafters and, by dusk, a roof. The men determined that the pump was not cracked, but that the seal would need repacking, something they could not get to until later. Mary would be expected to pump and carry water from the pump at the trough and to have a meal ready to serve by dark.

The structure would be temporary, would serve only until another permanent hotel could be built. It would have but one room that would hold the kitchen and a table of splintery boards and two rough benches for eating. It would have a door in front, another in back. In the corner of the kitchen section, a plank on two sawhorses would make do for a counter, until a full kitchen with counters and sink could be built.

Mary had free access to the cellar again. The steps

161

down to it had been cleared, a new door built. Before the fire, Mary and the kitchen girls had depleted most of the stores in it, and the barrels were empty or near empty and the shelves almost bare.

She swung a lamp, now. The barrels with the potatoes were a crawl of pale vines, the bottoms soaked wet with rot. The smell made her hold her stomach. There were still a few days' worth of squashes, and a small, three-pound brick of cheese, a half barrel of dried peas and another of red beans. Insects had got to the flour. It had been Ula who had baked the breads, and Mary had not been aware of the ruin. The flour needed severe sifting before she could use it. The sole plenty was pickles, the barrel still swam with pickles.

The herbs, the salt, the pepper, the spices had all gone up in the fire. Mrs. Gatewood brought in a cup of salt and pepper and some bacon and oats from her own kitchen at their farm. "This is what I could spare," she said. "It's not much, I'm afraid." It was the first time ever that Mary heard regret and perhaps apology in Mrs. Gatewood's voice. "For so long, I depended on your cooking, I did little to stock my own kitchen. Mrs. Drew is bringing three dozen eggs from their farm, and I have ordered supplies, though I am at a loss as to where you will put them. Will you find enough to feed them now, Mary?"

"Yes," she said, "but not for long. When will Ula

be coming?"

"She is not coming." Mary's heart clamped. "She's taken to work for her family on the farm. I'll find a girl, Mary, but you will be on your own until I do."

Three men came to eat that evening. Mary served them pease soup, eggs scrambled, oatcakes with clotted cream, and pickles.

Chapter 37

April was giving way, spring weather creeping in, but undecided and hesitant. The winds were gentle some days, mighty others, as if playing a game. The skies sometimes opened up and fuzzed puddles in the streets. Children stamped in them, women lifted their skirts. The Platte River coursed wide, and people muttered why had it not rained like this the day of the fire. The birds began to settle and, after the silence of winter, their voices came on a welcome.

Then one day, in a lull between meals, a bay gelding and rider appeared. The school bell had not yet rung out class; Ezekiel would be home soon. Mr. Simpson had built three pens where the livery had stood and was taking in animals again and Ezekiel was back with a pitchfork. Since the fire, Mr. Simpson had quit reminding Mary what was owed on the hinny.

The day was as ordinary as any day got anymore, clear, the sun burnishing the roofs silver, shimmering on the puddles. The gelding had a broad blaze, and one high white sock that rose up a rear leg to its hock. Though the gelding was not lame, the white leg gave it the appearance it minced. Edmund's horse.

165

Mary dashed toward it, but as she did, the rider turned away. His back was thick, his shoulders sloped and coarse; he had none of Edmund's grace, or narrow elegance. The rider made a gruff sound in his throat and kicked the gelding. It threw its head and then bolted. They rode on the road toward Denver.

Mary inquired of Mr. Simpson, asked about the man, if he had boarded a bay with a blaze and white leg. She had tried to calm her voice when she asked it, but he must have sensed her alarm because he reached out as if he might touch her arm.

"No," he said. He withdrew his arm.

"Did you see such an animal?" she said. He shook his head no. She asked Traber; she asked Mrs. Gatewood; she even inquired with the men when they came in for dinner. Though a couple said they had seen the gelding, none knew who rode it.

Mrs. Gatewood set up an office in one of the new houses. The house was just up the street from the hotel rebuilding. She set a desk in the front window to catch the sun and often sat gazing at something above the horizon. She ordered carload after carload of goods to replace what the Bee Hive had lost: garden seed, calico, milk churns, hammers, saws, mops, nails, plowshares, threads, scissors, flowerpots, hoes, coffeepots, teapots, brooms, hammers, watering cans, washboards. Mary could not fathom how Mr. Cozad could support this; he had spent a fortune and had lost a good part of it. But he had not given up; and without a sense of how it could be, his determination fortified her.

Mrs. Gatewood told Traber to order a carload of paulin and rope. When it came, there was nowhere to put the paulin but in piles along the railroad siding. He ordered three carloads of lumber and had men dig up soil at the new brickyard. Like everyone, he was growing drawn. Under the breadth of his forehead, his face was giving way to cheek and jaw bone. He was everywhere, supervising men at the lumberyard, ordering supplies, putting in a cable for a telegraph, digging ground with the men at the brickyard, sewing up gashes, setting bones, pulling teeth, seeing to the mail. One day, he stood in the middle of Meridian Street, unmoving, as a wagon went by. He seemed as if in a dream.

Mrs. Gatewood had Traber cut poles. She told him to have his men put up a small temporary structure hung with the paulins on poles; it would do, for a while, for a new general store.

Chapter 38

Traber brought Mary a letter, addressed to Mr. Edmund Harrington. "I think this belongs to you," he said. The envelope was of heavy paper, the return from the "Law offices of Franz Hoffman."

Mr. Edmund Harrington;
I am in receipt of an inquiry from a client interested in discussing the possibility of purchasing the homestead claim taken under the name of Mary Harrington, your wife. Please see me at your earliest convenience about this matter. Sincerely,
Franz E. Hoffman,
Attorney at Law

Mary laid the letter aside.

————

Once, as a girl in Ireland, Mary had seen four boys from her school playing down by the Sullane River. Somewhere they had found a sheep's bladder and had filled it with water and were throwing stones at it. As she watched, they threw half a dozen misses, then finally one boy's stone hit perfectly on. The thing shot water. Bits of it flew up, out, right, left, everywhere. The boys yelled and clapped and yipped, and knocked the winner's shoulder. But it was the explosion Mary thought of now, the dizzy flying of bits and activity in every direction, almost a violence of movement.

Like the bladder, town lay in pieces as if it had exploded, movement never stopped. Wooden stakes poked like quills where men were to build. Huge patches of earth lay bald by the brickyard where men had skimmed the soil. They wetted the bare earth, made mud of it which they slapped into molds they called greens. They stacked the greens to dry. And when they were dry, men laid them into triangular tunnels as long as a street. And they threw wood in and set it afire and the kilns glowed and hissed and pinged all through the nights.

Days after the fire, Mary heard that Mr. O'Doherty had come for his wife and baby and had taken them back to Ohio. The news left Mary bereft until a few weeks later, the O'Dohertys showed again. She had not yet seen them, but the small house they had bought had curtains, now, and a sow in a pen out back.

Behind the Bower house, their animals went back to a hens-and-goat kind of normalcy; the hens laid and the goat gave and Mary and Ezekiel had eggs, again, and milk. Some days she had the urge to kiss them. With the warmth and the rains, weeds began to break through. The hens grew fat on the hatch of bugs and the worms and the goat's milk grew rich on the weeds and the grasses.

Mrs. Gatewood hired a new girl, Aibreann O'Donnell. Aibreann was fifteen, her family from Donegal. The O'Donnells had just bought up land for a farm east of town. Though Mrs. Gatewood said her name as it was written, Aibreann pronounced it the Irish way: Abrawn.

Mrs. Gatewood paid Aibreann half a dollar for a day's work and Mary knew, when she had time to think of it, with her own lack of pay she earned every splinter of rent one would pay for the house Mrs. Gatewood lent her. As she and Aibreann worked, they spoke of home until Mary could only just bear the pain of it.

Chapter 39

The days grew longer, the weather soft and pleasant, though it would not stay that way for long, the sweats of humidity would soon set in.

School let out for the year, and, with it, memory of her summers growing up, her mother seeing to tea parties for the neighbor women, cricket on the lawn for the children who screamed chants as they played Plainy Clappy and Mr. Fox. The best Mary could muster at the end of a day, now, was to splash water on her face and try to make some kind of conversation with her son.

At times, she inquired as to what he did to occupy himself during the day. He normally shrugged and said, "Worked at Mr. Simpson's," or, "Watched the men." But one day he said, "I worked down at the bridge."

"You worked at the bridge?" she said. "What can a boy do building a bridge?"

"I got the wagon to help with the building of it."

She corrected, "You *have* the wagon."

"Me and the hinny can haul." She had no more energy to correct him again. "They pay me," he said. He pulled some coins from his pocket, held them to her in the flat of his palm. His face reddened, proud. "You can put them in the box," he said.

"Get it then," she said. She did not add "sweetheart" but thought it.

He went to her room, brought out the scorched tin box. He set it in front of her carefully, now, as if the box were a Magi's gift. She opened it. All the money he had earned, nearly five dollars of dimes and nickels, were sorted neat and even in stacks. The three coins from Edmund sat in a corner by themselves. She laid her hand on his shoulder. "Your da would be proud." She felt him stiffen.

———

They had a table again, a three-legged one Ezekiel found somewhere and dragged home. They set it in what the Bowers would have called the dining room, and Mary tried to imagine the room was hers. For the fourth leg, Ezekiel found a stool, likely from one of the abandoned homes, to put under it. She did not ask where he got it, and he did not explain.

Another package arrived from Prune. In it were two magazines, *Godey's* and *Collier's*, and a book for Ezekiel that Prune wrote was new and just published. The book was called *The Adventures of Tom Sawyer*. It must have been funny; Ezekiel smiled as he read and laughed outright once. At the end of the day, Mary barely had mind enough to read through Prune's letters much less page through a *Collier's* or a *Godey's*. There was a time she would have consumed those journals much as her son consumed the books now. Ezekiel had read his new book by the end of the week.

Out back of the house, the Bowers little garden patch was being consumed in weeds. Among the dandelions and thistle, a row of their kale had survived the winter. In the lull of an afternoon, Mary and Ezekiel began working the patch. Mary spent twenty cents on seed at Mrs. Gatewood's. Ezekiel brought home buckets of manure and straw from his job.

They worked side by side quietly, with only a grunt now and then at a difficult weed, or the *chiss* of the shovels. The cut of the hoe made for conversation. When he was a baby, she had set him, swaddled, in the shade of the wagon as she worked, and while she dug and planted her saplings he played with his hands and made the sounds a baby makes. He was barely walking when he learned to put seed into a small hole and to pat it in. When he was old enough to hold a trowel, she showed him how to use it. He learned which was weed and which was not. The garden, the damp, the intimacy of hard work and blisters surrounded her, and she knew it did him.

Nearly every day they were out, now, pulling weeds or running the bucket to water. The garden began to fuzz sprouting greens, tender and young. It rained most mornings, and the patch was dark and moist.

Finally, the radishes were up and full. Mary pulled one. She stood, laid her hand on her back. She wiped the radish on her apron, put it into her mouth and held it there for a moment. Ezekiel pulled another, bit into it. "Ma," he said, "good."

"Heaven," she said. They ate all the ripe radishes before they even made it into the house.

The next day, they woke to a killing frost.

Chapter 40

She and Prune had once had a cat. It was buff colored and had a long, fluffed tail it waved back and forth like a flag. Their mother said it was a mousing cat, but she let the girls play with it. Soon, it was no longer relegated to the cellar where the mice were but was sneaked into the house by the girls.

They named it Ossian, which meant fawn. It was a wonderful cat and loved to chase a string tied with a hen's feather. The cat's nails scritched and slipped but her eyes never left the feather until, suddenly, she would quit and would stand on a wobble of legs, her eyes shifting, her head jerking as if her world were still spinning.

Mary's world whirled, now, like the cats', numb and endless. The more she did, the more things came to pieces. The earlier she came to the kitchen, the more Mrs. Gatewood expected. She learned that The Family were to arrive in days: Mr. Cozad, Mrs. Cozad, and two boys ten and twelve years old. The day Mrs. Gatewood came with the announcement, Mary and Aibreann were getting supper on the table. Aibreann nodded and ducked and paid shy attention to the bowls she was toting to the table. "Mary," Mrs. Gatewood said, "my daughter will be coming in on the fifteenth." Her face was gloriously lit, her eyes keen. "Mr. Cozad will bring her and their sons to stay for the summer."

It was told as an announcement of something Mary should prepare for. "I see," she said.

"Mrs. Cozad has a bit of a sensitive constitution and will require some special dishes from you. I will write out a list."

The Cozads would stay at the Gatewoods' farm through the summer, the boys would spend a good part of their days in town. Mrs. Gatewood planned activities, but the boys would play and swim and ride ponies she bought specially for them.

A handful of people met the family at the train: the Atkinsons, the Claypools, and the Drews. The men were dressed in Sunday suits, the women in bonnets with ribbons. For three days, the family rested at the Gatewoods' house outside town, and Mary did not see them. Then, on one particularly hot day, Mrs. Gatewood came to Mary and told her to prepare tarts and iced sugar cream and to bring them down to the river. Mrs. Gatewood would have a tent set up with chairs and a table, and she would see to it that Mr. Simpson would drive her and the food. This last, Mrs. Gatewood said, as if it should be no trouble for Mary at all.

Mrs. Gatewood wrote out a recipe for the cakes, and when Mary said she had never made iced creams, she showed her and Aibreann an iced cream maker she sold in the store and wrote out how to use it. While Mary prepared the cakes, Mrs. Gatewood told Aibreann to go to the new ice house and bring back a chunk of ice in a wheelbarrow.

Mary covered the ice and barrow in a blanket and took

178

a sledge to it. And when the ice was crushed, Aibreann spun the contraption and poured in salt and ice and cream and sugar. Mary saw the blisters on Aibreann's hands as they carried the container to the wagon and wrapped it in three blankets against melt.

Mr. Simpson drove. Mary held a basket with the cakes and plates and bowls in her lap. In back of the wagon, sat the lump of blankets coddling the iced creams. Mr. Simpson made no comment, nor did he look at her. Mary thought the crook in his back might not have allowed him to turn his head. He did keep clicking his tongue. His manner spoke for him. "This is idiocy," it said. Mary agreed.

The tent had been set up on a spit surrounded by clusters of cattail and sedge, which jutted out into the cool breeze off the water. Just upstream the men were building the bridge. Seven people stood in the shade under the tent: Mr. Cozad, Mrs. Gatewood and her husband, Traber, and David Claypool and his youngest daughter, and Mrs. Cozad, dressed in fine yellow lawn.

A pile of jackets and ties were thrown on the river bank. Three boys in shirts and rolled-up pants were wading into the water, all three near their teens. One of the boys, particularly thin legged and tall with a ruffle of thick black hair, tripped on something and went down on a knee, sopped up to his thigh. From the tent, Traber cupped his hands around his mouth. He shouted, "That'll cool you some." Mary had never heard Traber laugh full out. It was a deep, rolling, wonderful laugh.

She got down from the wagon. A breeze stirred and the

paulin lifted, then sank again as if taking a breath. While Mr. Cozad stood in the shade beside his wife, Mr. Claypool and Mr. Simpson brought down a table, set it under the tent. Water rose and flew, arcs like lace as the boys splashed and shouted.

Mr. Claypool and Mr. Simpson brought the chairs, settled them around the table. Mary carried down the basket with the cakes. She shook the cloth, laid it out. The boys were becoming loud. Mr. Cozad hissed, his eyes pinkened. He threw up a fist. Mrs. Cozad touched his arm and softly said, "John." He looked at her. Her head gave a minuscule shake. "They are just boys," she said.

Chapter 41

They came up from the south. They blackened the sky. At first, no one in town took much note; after all, dark walls of dust were part of life. The first clicked in and settled on a pot of geraniums, then another and another until their greenish wings and their backward knees covered the plant and they consumed every leaf and stem of it. The things settled, then, in the millions.

Mary joined everyone, crazily swatting their hands, flapping blankets. Some people set fires in the middle of the streets, burning papers, rags, straw, anything. Mary had nothing to burn.

The locusts were ravenous. In the snap of a finger, they consumed every bean in a garden, every flower, every weed, every blade of grass. Mary felt like her childhood cat, standing dizzy, wobble legged, her head spinning. The bugs were everywhere. She batted them from her hair, blew them from her nostrils, spat them from her mouth. Her broccoli, which had survived the frost, lasted no more than two minutes. Nothing survived the bugs, not her peas, her brussels sprouts, cabbage, mustard, sorrel, and radishes, none of it. They ate gnats, they ate flies, and mosquitoes. They ate clothes on a line. They ate the handles off hoes and bales of straw and the hair off horses' backs. Chickens glutted themselves on them and grew fat, horses kicked and twitched, dogs barked long into the nights.

The Pentecostals prayed to the Lord and took credit when the hoppers left four days later, but the Pentecostals' prayers proved successful only when there was no more left in Dawson County to eat.

Every able-bodied adult, child, ox, and plow horse launched into a frenzy of replanting.

Chapter 42

By the end of summer, Mary had trained and lost four girls in the kitchen. Only one, Elsa Bjorkman, had stayed. She was thirteen, a tall girl who spoke English with a crooked lilt that Mary could sometimes not understand. Her family had come in the year before. Elsa knew Ezekiel from the school, but did not pick up the conversation when Mary inquired as to how they might have interacted.

It was two years, now, since Mary and Ezekiel had lived in Cozad, two years of thoughtless hours peeling, and baking, kneading, lighting the stove, setting out plates, filling bowls, serving, taking away, only to clean and mop and start over again day after day.

It took the labor of three people to cook and serve and clean up now, with attendance such as it was, an endless rotation of girls needing training and watching over. The days when the Cozads ate at the table, the kitchen was expected to serve two, sometimes three, different meals, maybe a haunch ham and roast and special sweets of fruits and creams for Mr. Cozad and the boys, and, on the days Mrs. Cozad's stomach was tender, the kitchen was ordered to provide lettuces and lamb with a light gravy. Everyone else ate stews, and beans, and biscuits.

In these two years, Mary felt as if her feet had never met the ground; she forever felt as if she were dangling with nothing to grip or to give her substance but work. She had always taken a moment each day to step out and gaze every inch of the street, in case Edmund showed. Then came a day she forgot.

———

It was hot, the sun bearing down. Both doors were flung open to a morning without breath. Another new girl, Anna Cranshaw, had begun work the day before. She barely knew how to cook more than eggs and biscuits. Anna was out back, peeling potatoes and beets farmers had brought in from what they had been able to grow after the bugs ravaged the country again this year. All were stunted. Elsa was loading baskets into the cellar. Mrs. Gatewood had ordered a lamb for The Family. A leg sirloin had been roasting since three thirty that morning; a shank for the others was braising on the stove.

Ezekiel was growing. Though he would never be a large man, it would not be long before he was nearly Mary's own height. She saw him one day working in the livery, his boy's narrow back bent at a shovel as he cleared offal from a pig's pen. He was strong, able to do a man's work now. When he was not cleaning pens for Mr. Simpson, or carting bricks at the brickyard, he seemed to disappear. Where he spent his time she did not know. By the time he came home of an evening, his clothes reeked of dung. The work was hard, his hands blistered, his legs sometimes cramped and, as she rubbed them, she would see bruises on his arms, his calves, his shoulders. One evening he was limping. She asked what happened. "I bumped it," he said. She told him to let her see his leg and his face reddened with anger and he said, "I told you I bumped it."

In the evenings, he ate what she brought him from the kitchen, then would go to his room and close his door. He read if he could keep his head up. The comparison to the lives of the Cozad boys clamped at her. He deserved what they had: time for play, respite from work. He deserved fine-tailored suits, and ponies, the freedom to laugh, someone to listen to him and to ask what he did each day.

If Edmund were here, Ezekiel might not be living like this, nor would she. She turned away the thought; their lives were what she was making of them and therein lay a ponderous weight.

Chapter 43

School was set to start again in two weeks. Mrs. Cozad was leaving soon with her sons to their home in Ohio. By the end of the summer, the kilns at the brickyard had produced enough brick to begin work on a new hotel when the weather warmed in the spring. A stack of brick lay where the men would also construct a bank.

Ezekiel's teacher, Mr. Young, called to ask if she could come see him before school started up. "For just a moment," he said. She feared the worst.

The school had been moved; the house where classes were held last year had been sold. Classes were moving to one of the newer, smaller, unfinished houses until it, too, could be sold.

Mr. Young was in shirtsleeves, hanging the chalkboard when she went in. The room was a tumble of new desks, not yet put in rows. His jacket was draped over one. His own desk was shoved out of the way against one wall, a briefcase, some books, tablets, pencils, and erasers arranged as if ready to be distributed. "Welcome, Mrs. Harrington," he said. His greeting seemed genuine but did not ease the cramp in her stomach. He swung his hand around the room. "When classes begin, the children will have desks this year," he said with a hint of pride.

He picked up his jacket, put it on. He pulled two desks from the tumble, set them face to face, and motioned for

187

her to take one. They sat. "Thank you for coming," he said. "It seems strange, doesn't it, a school without children?" He grinned. It was a kindly grin.

"Is something wrong?" she said. He was losing his hair. It settled her some.

He gave his head a tiny shake. "Mrs. Harrington," he said, "Ezekiel is a very astute young man. You should be proud of him."

"I am," she said. Her throat tightened.

"I would like to ask your permission to assign him to help new students."

Help new students? "How?"

"To learn to read."

"They don't already read?"

He laughed and it was a nice laugh. "No. And a lot don't even speak English," he said. "Though your son has said a thing or two lately, he's still awfully quiet. I think it would be good for him, if he was willing, to tutor some of the children. He is a wonderful and quick boy and a challenge for me to keep ahead of him. If he would do it, it would be a big relief to me so I could work with the children who are slower than he, or who don't speak the language."

When she told Ezekiel Mr. Young's proposal, she did not know what to expect. His response was curious, flat, unimpressed. He gave a little shrug. "I guess," he said, "I will."

Chapter 44

The morning was still, the sun throwing long, late-summer shadows. For the second time, she told Mrs. Gatewood she would be unavailable for work; she needed the day off.

She waited until Ezekiel left for school to get the hinny from Mr. Simpson.

The hinny's head bobbed, her ears flicked at sounds Mary could not hear. For a few miles, a fair groove of road marked the way north out of town. The road soon petered out. Scattered along were signs of new settlers: a sod house here, a plowed patch there, yards filled with pens holding hogs and calves. Aside some houses, hutches with rabbits and hens, an acre of alfalfa that had been cut, another farm with a mangy patch of cut wheat, or maybe oat straw. Most farms had not been there last time she rode through.

The wagon staggered and pitched. Had the ground been so rough before? It made her sick to her stomach. Her teeth clamped and rattled and made her bite her tongue.

The Anderssons' house was surrounded, now, by fields, fresh sowed. The fields were patchy. To the side of the Andersson house, a garden with yellowing squash and pumpkin vines spread along a fence had been mostly harvested. Like everyone, the Anderssons had been riddled by locusts; the bean vines barely reached halfway

189

up the stringers, a section of corn showed some cobs barely bigger than a thumb. She swallowed a packet of guilt over her satisfaction that the Anderssons, with their beautiful farmhouse, their pens full of hogs, their field of alfalfa, had not been spared.

Their house lay dark in its depression, helpless, dry, and abandoned. The trees she had planted around the house, the willows, the maples, and a row of cottonwoods were nothing more than bare sticks. She searched for a bit of green and found nothing but one branch of a cottonwood with life.

The door had lost a hinge and sat slanted as if drunk. She got down from the wagon, set the hinny to crop. She tucked a strand of loose hair into a pin. Her fingers searched for another to neaten, a habit reborn now that she thought of Edmund again.

She entered the house as she had once done hundreds of times. It held the musky scent, not of a home, but of a hole. Little had changed since she came out before. The mouse and rat track was thicker, and a thick rodent smell sat upon it. She had brought a note, written on Prune's fine paper. She had once more drawn a map that showed the way to Cozad and she had written on it in hopes he could make out what it said:

> *Edmund, dearest*
> *It has been nearly a year since you left. I doubt you know where to find us. Your son and I are living in the town of Cozad. Before we left the farm, I wrote a letter to you but I since have learned you may never have seen it. I am leaving*

*another in hopes you are well and will return to see it and
know where we have gone.*
Your loving wife, Mary

She laid it on the table.

The hinny cropped and shook her head against flies.
Mary put her foot on the wagon to go but turned back for
a last look. She had noticed no sign that anyone had
passed into the house but the slant of a blade or two of
grass where she had tamped them. But there was a sign: a
path worn bare leading to the sod lean-to. A bald spot in
the ground had been worn smooth around a stake where a
horse had been tethered. Tied onto the stake was the knot
from a rein that had been cut, as if someone had had no
time to untie it. She took a breath, held it until she could
hold it no more.

She lifted her skirt and let the path draw her. She laid
her hand on the lean-to as if the touch of it could give her
an answer. She peered into the dark until her eyes lost the
glare of the sun.

Someone had been here. The quilt she left for Edmund
lay on the ground, rumpled as if recently slept in. There
were indications of a struggle, clots and black-brown drips
of old blood, a mess of bottles and tins, dry but smelling
of whiskey. Dried vomit was spewed on the wall, the signs
of drunk sickness that caused Edmund to become who he
became.

Violence, ruin. In the middle of it, lay, broken, the
whistle Edmund so long ago made for his son.

Chapter 45

A few weeks into fall, the trains quit spitting out potentials. The piles of beets and corn and baled hay that had been heaped at the siding since harvest disappeared. Three men, whom Traber particularly favored, planned to stay on through the winter. They rented another one of the vacant houses to bunk in and took their meals at Mary's kitchen. But most others left town when the first real snows came in, some going east to find factory work, a few to the Gulf to fish, but many, those who had their own saddles and mounts, set out for Mexico to ride with the cattle drives. No one wandered the streets, now. Mrs. Gatewood closed her store and hung a sign: *Open Wednesdays if weather permits.*

Mary had only a handful to cook for. She worked alone, the rest of the kitchen girls had been let go. She served the regulars three meals a day. Mrs. Gatewood filled the barrels in the cellar with an economy of potatoes, and beets, and red beans, told Mary to serve chicken and pig no more than three times a week.

Ezekiel had little work. Every day after school, he continued to report to Mr. Simpson, but he took in few animals in winter, and farmers waited until spring to bring in their horses to trim and shoe. The sole place in town where there seemed to be life was out at the brickyard. The kilns still fired the brick the men had pressed earlier in the year. To protect themselves from the wind and snow, they built a wind shield of misfired brick and braced up a rudimentary roof. The furnaces popped all day and all night, even in the thickest storm, and the ground around the kilns ran wet with black mud.

Mary had not asked Ezekiel about the note, though she suspected he knew she had it. If she asked of it, she was certain he would not give her an answer; there was so much he kept away from her. After school and on the weekends, he began hanging around the brickyard. She said, "Don't pester," but knew he would not obey. Though the house had a stove, she had no wood to feed it. And at the end of each day he brought home two hot bricks wrapped in a blanket. They wrapped the bricks in wool and slept with their feet pressed against them. In the morning, they dressed in their beds as their breaths froze and sparked in the lamplight like diamonds. When they had dressed, he followed her the four blocks to the kitchen and sat inches from the stove as it warmed. And as she began making the breakfasts, and kneading the breads, setting a pot of beans to boil, and putting something into his bucket for school, he sat at the table alone with his books and he read. Once, she asked how his tutoring was going at school. "Fine," he said.

In the evenings, after she cleared the table from dinner, the men bunking in the rooming house often sat and made small talk and played pinochle. And if one had a cigar he lit it and passed it around and filled the room with the thick smoke. She could feel their aloneness, the loose-endedness of their lives, the way time stretched, and how they made do for family, and she lingered listening to the shuffle and taps of their cards, sharing the slap and guffaw when one won.

———

A stomping came at the door. It was midmorning; the breakfast men were gone; the rack was filled with drying dishes. The door opened, a whip of wind rustled in. Traber stood in the door in all his startling height. His shoulders were heaped in snow, his cap was pulled down over his brows. He looked like a bear.

He took off the cap, shook it. He rumbled, "Cold out." He laid a letter on the table. "I have something from the post office for you, Mrs. Harrington." It was addressed not to her, but again to Mr. Edmund Harrington. Traber would have seen that. "Thought I'd bring it now rather than later." He shivered. "B-r-r-r," he said and left out the door, taking his kindness with him.

The embossed return address was from Mr. Totten Hume, Pres., Philadelphia National Bank & Trust.

2 November 1875
Philadelphia

Dear Edmund,
I hope my letter finds you and Mary well and that you are enjoying your time in Cozad and are continuing to enjoy the prosperity Mary writes us about. Prudence says it is surely music to her soul to know you are so happy as Mary's letters convey.
Well, besides a hello to you and Mary, here is my news.

Prudence and I have just received a wonderful surprise. A notice from the Customs has come to me saying that they are holding a trunk from Ireland come for Prudence and Mary from their brother Ciaran back in Macroom.

I am including the document that you must sign for it to be released to us. Could you scribble your name on the line indicated and send it back to me? I'll see that the authorities clear it.

Needless to say, Prudence is puffing with impatience. Ciaran did not elaborate as to what might be in it, but Prudence is sure it is their mother's linens and perhaps some of her fine crochet. She is driving us all mad with the suspense of it. Please rush your signature and save our boys, and me, my wife's torment.

Yours,

Totten

She had no heart to answer Totten's letter that night; she did not know what to say. Her lies were closing in. She dashed out a letter to Prune that she dated a week before.

Dearest Prune,

Oh for the winter, dreary snows with their endless wind and cold. Housebound is not for me. I wish you were here at my table with a cup of good (hot) tea. We continue to excel, your nephew continues to grow and do well in his school. He sets off like a man with his lunch pail each morning and he makes me proud. He is such a good student that his teacher has put him to work tutoring other *children to read. Imagine! Some of his <u>students</u> are nearly twice his age. I cannot imagine that their mothers did not sit them down and read to them until they were hoarse, as our mother did with all of us.*

The town has grown until we can barely recognize it, tho it is quiet now that it is cold. The only industry that continues with the winter is a brickyard just outside town that fires brick even in the worst freezes.

In the last year the settlement has gone from six houses to nearly twenty and has rebuilt nearly half what was lost to the fire. I will be glad when the weather clears and the men are back whacking away with their hammers. Their work does make its own sort of music.

Write soon, dearest.

Your loving and lonesome Sissie.

She was a coward. Her secrets and lies were nothing more than bookends for her shame.

Chapter 46

The ground was still frozen when the first potentials were due to arrive in a week. Traber put every man available into constructing the new hotel. Several tons of brick lay in stacks near pegs laid out according to Mr. Cozad's drawings. He demanded the hotel be done by summer; his family was coming again in June and he wanted them to stay in it.

With the prospect of potentials, Mrs. Gatewood had ordered a beef from one of the farms out of town and had bought a huge, fat hog from Mr. Simpson to have butchered, as well. When Mrs. Gatewood told her Rose would be back to help, Mary inquired as to Ula and Frieda, but their families had put them to work on their families' farms. She tried to dissuade Mrs. Gatewood about Rose; no matter how Mary had tried to make Rose's effort pay off, she was always more trouble than she was worth. But Mrs. Gatewood insisted: Rose would be hired.

The kitchen was yet to be stocked—spices and dried fruits had been ordered. Until they came, there was little to choose from, and it took a great deal of thought to dream up what to serve. Some of the cellar was replenished: one shelf was piled with cheeses, a barrel was filled with flour and another with oats. But there was little of anything fresh. Soon, gardens would begin to bear. Mrs. Gatewood had ordered the men to hammer up a kitchen shelf for the spices and dried fruits when they arrived, and they came to do it just as Mary was finishing the supper. Rose had not changed, she stood about, hands at her waist, head turning side to side watching, still the same old impediment to the doing of cooking. After three days of it, when Mary told her to stir the gravy, Rose said, "With what?"

"A spoon!" Mary screamed.

"Where?"

At the end of Rose's first day, Mary was exhausted. Being around the woman absorbed what bit of vitality she had regained during the winter quiet.

———

It was dark when she let herself into the house that night. She hung her coat on the peg, then dropped into a chair. Her hands seemed too heavy to lift, and she sat there, her fingers in her lap as red and thick as bangers. Ezekiel would be upstairs, either reading or asleep. She sat there awhile, listening to nothing, not even her own thoughts. She lifted her chin, swept a hand through her hair, and noticed a corner of paper torn from a page of a school tablet. On it were three seeds and a note written in pencil in Ezekiel's heavy precision.

> *Mrs. Gatewood gave me these. She said you ought to plant them. She gave them free. They are two apples and a lilac.*

Chapter 47

At Mr. Atkinson's request, Mrs. Gatewood hired his oldest daughter, Theadosia. After helping her mother care for her younger children, a sister and five brothers, Theadosia was capable and, bless her, willing. Rose stood in the middle, her hands gathered under her breasts as Mary and Theadosia moved around her as they would a piece of furniture. Rose seemed to be able to carry out one instruction at a time, and that she did slowly. She did not seem to remember from one day to the next how to repeat an activity even as simple as kneading the doughs for the breads. Mary did not know if Rose was merely lazy or was unable to hold a thought on her own.

After a few days, Mary mentioned to Mrs. Gatewood they could make the kitchen more efficient with someone other than Rose. But Mrs. Gatewood did nothing; Rose hung onto her job and her dark face, her sighs and resentful posture sucked air from the kitchen. Mary tried not to dislike the woman.

Some days, Mary did not even think of Edmund, others she thought of little else.

The new hotel began to take shape. By the end of April, the first floor of it stretched along Eighth Street, and the men were putting in sills for the windows and jambs for the two doors. In the back, they were constructing a frame kitchen off what would be the dining room. In all, the intent seemed to be to fashion a lordly structure.

Early summer, another scourge of locusts wiped out everything down to the ground and again farmers rushed to replant. Mary and Ezekiel coddled what survived in the garden and set out new seed. She planted the two apple seeds out back and the lilac in front. They would benefit someone else. Mary envisioned a family with children and chickens and birthday celebrations. Would they share the apples with their neighbors? Maybe take a nosegay of lilacs? Mary would never know, that would happen long after she and Ezekiel lived in the house.

Two days before the arrival of The Family, Mary was told she had to move everything to the new kitchen.

Chapter 48

Cozad had a new, proper hotel. The day of the move into it, without Mary's telling her to, Theadosia put a pot of stew on the new stove and baked three sheets of scones. The stew bubbled as Theadosia and Rose went back and forth from the old kitchen to the new, shuttling skillets, pans, plates, cups, spice jars, pots, cutlery, sugar, salt, pepper. Mary had to find places to put it. She had little time to think, other than tomorrow The Family were arriving and somehow, between normal meals, the kitchen would have to start putting out specialties, as well.

The new kitchen was like a cavern, larger by three times than the old one. There was no hearth; in its place was a new stove beside the salvaged old fire-dimmed one. There was space enough for five girls to work, if Rose stayed out of the way. Mrs. Gatewood said she was talking to two more girls who might want work.

When the men began coming in for their supper at four o'clock, Mary was still figuring out where things should go. Plates were stacked three feet tall on one counter, pots clatter-stacked one on another on the floor, sacks of corn, and oat, and flour still leaned against the cupboards, waiting to be binned.

Mary pulled up a stool, shoved aside some pie tins. The tins were old and bent and did not settle one to another. Theadosia was knocking a spatula at a metal sheet, trying to get up a stuck scone, while Rose threw herself into the water pump handle, its spout coughing up nothing but air. Rose's skirt caught on the tins and they hurtled over and crashed to the floor. Mary sat, stared at the rack of butchering knives. The image came to her of picking up one of the knives and slashing to bits everything in sight. She covered her ears with her hands. Theadosia picked up the tins as Rose continued to pump. Mary told Rose to put the scones on platters and take them out to the table. She took them out, then returned to hover again. "The jam," Mary said, "and the butter."

"Where?" Rose said.

"Where do you normally put them!" Mary screamed. Theadosia's shoulders shot up.

"Oh," Rose said, her voice flat and calm as if she were screamed at every day.

———

The hotel had two doors in front, one that let into a hotel parlor, the other to a small stairway up to the nine sleeping rooms. The smell of its newness hung in it, in the scent of plaster and new mortar and of wood not quite cured.

The dining room, meant to seat and feed crowds, consumed a good part of the lower floor. The space of that room was eaten up by a special-built table from Pennsylvania. At the far end clustered four excelsior wing chairs reserved for The Family, and along both sides of the table ran benches for anyone else.

The Family were due on the train at 11:32. All morning long, men had been scrambling around the hotel like ants on a hill, Traber calling out instructions for fellows to bring in furniture: desks, chairs, files for the hotel office, wood chairs for the hotel parlor, mattresses, iron bed frames for the cool downstairs rooms The Family would take. When the men had put the Cozads' beds together, they began carting more up to the hot rooms on the second floor for renters.

After a thunderstorm in the morning, the day had turned hot as scorch. The kitchen walls ran with humidity, the ceiling dripped. The bodice of Mary's shift leaked with her sweat.

Mrs. Gatewood had requested a refreshment for The Family when they arrived. Three pies were cooling on the counter, one of peaches, one of lemon, and another of strawberry. Mary got Rose out of the kitchen by having her churn iced creams, one seasoned with cinnamon, the other with mint. There would be tea, Rose's iced cream, and a goat cheese brought in from one of the farms made special for Mrs. Cozad's tender stomach. More seemed to hinge on The Family this year, but Mary could not think what.

The hotel doors and windows were all braced open. Flies fizzed in, dabbed at the pies. The girls swatted at them, which sent up a swirl until they settled back to dab at the pies.

———

The Cozad boys had grown since Mary last saw them, the youngest now a gangling stretch of a boy. Though he was three years younger than his brother, he would likely be taller by the time they returned to Ohio in the fall.

Mrs. Cozad was paler, her hair more streaked with gray. She came in on the arm of her husband, wearing a dress of lawn the color of peaches. He toured her through the building, pointed out this and that. The Cozad boys followed Mr. Cozad. He kept referring to it as *our* hotel. The thrown-back carriage of his shoulders didn't seem like arrogance as he stroked his wife's hand and called her dear. His eyes did not dart and shift; his forehead did not blaze red; his voice held no edge; he seemed calm with her and docile as a house pet.

When the tour was done, the parade wound around the table. He pulled out the chair to his right, held it for his wife to gather her skirts and sit. He eased her in. "Too close," she said, and he positioned her back an inch. She nodded but did not say thank you.

Chapter 49

Another letter came from the attorney saying the offer to buy her claim had been renewed and asking for Edmund to contact him immediately. Again, she folded it and set it aside; nothing had changed, it still required Edmund's approval to answer.

When not at the livery, Ezekiel had begun taking small jobs for Mrs. Gatewood as she had them: painting, cleaning, sweeping, sorting, shelving. Mary often caught him at the corner of her eye, slipping from the new store addition through the front door near the Cozads' parlor.

Mrs. Cozad collected her boys in the parlor every morning. The parlor was a small room, buffered from the noise of the dining room and the all-day rustle, thumps, clicks, and greetings from the hotel office. The parlor was stuffed with more furniture than any other room in the building: There was a snug collection of two desks, a table in the center, a rocker chair bracketed by a small round table on one side and a basket filled with tatting threads and shuttles on the other. The room had no shelves yet, and books were stacked in a pyramid against a wall, more spilled onto the floor. The lovely clutter nearly made Mary weep; she could only dream of such a place. It had been no more than a chimera that Mary and Edmund and Ezekiel could have lives like this one Mrs. Cozad shaped, one filled with a grace of quiet and calm and study.

Each morning, Mary prepared minted soda water with shards of ice for the boys and set out a pot of ginger tea for Mrs. Cozad. The boys would be at their studies by then, reading, drawing, looking through a Pasteur scope at greenish glass plates half the size of a playing card, on which they put drops of liquid.

As Mary brought in the tray, the boys would continue discussing the subject their mother dictated for the day. They ran through their maths, they debated politics, examined what they read in the papers. A recent discussion focused on the country's history, since in a few days it would celebrate its one hundredth birthday.

They often laughed at the same jokes; they sometimes shared the same opinions, but sometimes they did not. And when they disagreed, their mother insisted they back up their arguments with fact. When one of the boys spoke, their mother listened. She questioned and waited as they conjured their answers. Intelligence and care filled the place, and Mary had to turn away and force herself not to compare these boys' schoolroom to the plainness of the rudimentary lessons Ezekiel found in his. Each day after Mary set down the tray, Mrs. Cozad lifted her lower lids as if she had just returned from somewhere desperate and lonely, and she said, "Thank you, Mrs. Harrington," and Mary found it difficult to hate her.

Chapter 50

The kitchen sweltered. The back door lay open to the flies and whatever breeze it could catch. The windows were never closed, even in thundering storms. Mrs. Gatewood hired two more girls. Things were so hectic Mary could not remember either of their names. Rose often disappeared to the cellar where she sat in the cool until someone came to get her. Mary wondered if the woman was perhaps smarter than all the rest of them put together.

A few days before the Fourth, Traber shuffled in midmorning. A pot of ginger tea steeped in a pot on a tray with a small creamer and a pot with honey. As she waited for the tea, Mary was crisscrossing dough strips on peach tarts for the Cozads' supper; she would fizz soda water into glasses for the boys just before she took the tray to the parlor.

Traber shouted, "Sis?" Mary startled: Sis was her own nickname growing up. He gawped around as if his sister might be sitting right there and he was not seeing her. His hair stuck to his forehead, a streak of black filth ran from between his eyes down his nose. His shirt sleeves were rolled, revealing long, stringy arms which he moved with some grace. He was attractive to her and Mary knew that, were she not married, she would allow herself to notice even more about him.

209

From the parlor, Mrs. Cozad said, "You needn't shout, Traber."

He drifted off toward the sound of his sister's voice. Mary poured the soda water, picked up the tray, and followed him.

"Uh, Sis," Traber said, "I have something I want Bobby for." He stood in the door, each hand on a jamb.

"We are in class," Mrs. Cozad said. "Behind you. Someone wants in, Traber."

He twitched back. "Uh, excuse me, Mrs. Harrington."

Mary slipped into the room. Ices tinkled in the glasses.

"You're *filthy*, Trabe," Mrs. Cozad said. "I don't want you in here."

He leaned in the doorway again but did not enter. "It is a hurry sort of a deal," he said.

"What, then?"

"We need a broadside printed."

"Who's we?"

"Me," he said.

"Can't it wait?"

"Has to be done this afternoon for David to deliver. Just got the printing press running." An ugly machine of gears and pulleys had been moved into a small back room of the hotel and Traber had been working on it, ticking around with tools and grunting all morning.

Bobby popped up from his desk, went to stand between his uncle and his mother. "Ma?" he said.

"You can't dawdle," she said.

"I won't."

The broadside was delivered two days before the Fourth.

COZAD
COME ONE–COME ALL
GRAND CELEBRATION
ONE HUNDREDTH BIRTHDAY
OF THE UNITED STATES
FOOD, DANCING, RACES

———

The entire county was coming for the hundredth-birthday celebration, plus nearly thirty potential families who were scheduled in that same week. Mr. Claypool complained, "They might as well bring in a circus." Even without the celebration, the number of hotel guests, alone, would be too large a crowd to feed inside the hotel.

Mrs. Gatewood expected to house everyone who came and to sell them a meal. To put up the numbers of potentials expected, she requisitioned boxcars to be fitted with cots and parked on the siding. People could rent a cot in one of the boxcars for a dollar a night. A family of five would pay five dollars unless they could double up. But even the boxcars would not hold the crowds expected, so she recruited a good share of the wives in town to board and sleep the overflow in their houses.

For the hundredth-birthday celebration, the new butcher in town hired men to kill, skin, butcher, and dig pits for three steer carcasses to roast. The flouring mill ground a half ton extra, and men set up a dozen tables outside. There would be contests: sack races for the children, horse and mule races for the men, and pie and quilt competitions for the women. A band would play: three fiddles and a fife and three empty barrels to bang on for drums.

Men would oversee the roasting of the three steer carcasses. Pies, pickles, cakes, preserves would be up to the community women to bring and to compete for prizes; at least the kitchen didn't have to deal with all that. But serving the extras, the salads, the drinks, the dainties of frosted scones, and of course the cleaning up would be up to Mary and her girls.

Men set up the paulins, which had been stored away since after the fire. They hauled the big table from the hotel out to the picnic grounds for the buffet and arranged smaller tables under the paulins, out of the sun, for seating and for the cooking contests and for the ladies' competitions of quilts and laces. The Pentecostals did their part by sending up a loud ration of prayers for a dry day.

Mrs. Gatewood ordered thirty pans of biscuits, three dozen cakes, as many hens as could be found to kill, pluck, and fry, potato and vinegar salad mixed with Mrs. Schleimer's special bratwurst, iced creams with strawberries, ices in troughs to chill watermelons. There had to be enough of everything to feed three hundred; more would be expected of Mary's kitchen than ever.

―――――

The dizziness came on her quietly as the girls were cleaning up. Something about the ring in her ears, the din and light of the day, the glare of heat, the movement, made the ground come at her. It grew difficult to walk, so she dragged her feet. One of the kitchen girls—she would not remember who—asked the simplest of questions, and she could not make her way through to answer it. The girl stood there, head tipped, holding something in her hands, meat, Mary thought, or was it something else? "I don't know," Mary said, and the girl wandered off somewhere with the thing still in her hand. Mary remembered an arm around her shoulders, a high elbow given her to grip, Traber's rumbling and kindly voice saying, "Mary, let me get you home." The soft rumble of his voice, the sharp offering of his arm gave her something to do, somewhere to go; it had been so long since she had had that.

———

She slept three days and nights. Mrs. Gatewood paid for Dr. Chase to attend to her. Dr. Chase told Ezekiel to keep wet rags on her face and to pat them on her neck, her arms, legs, and her chest. The boy brought hot broths from the hotel kitchen and, when her bed became wet with her sweats, he removed the sheets and washed them. These things she learned later from Dr. Chase. Traber had carried her home after the celebrations, and it had been he who found Dr. Chase, but it was her son who had tended her. The intimacy made her blush. He was eight years old; no boy should be burdened in such a way.

Chapter 51

After several weeks of heat and humidity so dense it sucked one's breath, there came a morning dry and cool. Mary had been at work again for some days. For a brief few hours after the respite she went about work renewed and with some clarity. It was not long until, again, her legs dragged and stupefaction weighted her. The kitchen had suffered the days she was gone; the girls had not kept stock on the shelves or flour in the bins. The floor was streaked where they must have let things go, then had slopped around a hurried mop before she returned.

The day began as usual; the Cozad boys and their mother had gone into the parlor half an hour ago. In the three days Mary had been sick, the parlor had been transformed. Two high-back excelsior chairs clustered in one corner, now, a rocker near the window with basket of Mrs. Cozad's tatting threads and shuttles beside it. A vase of fresh zinnias and ivy sat on a side table. A rug with figures of roses was spread in front of the rocker. There were proper shelves, now, for the boys' books. When Mary took in the refreshments that morning, the boys were sitting at their desks in a stream of light from the window. The scene could have been one in a painting.

Ezekiel had been hanging around the hotel ever since The Family returned. Sometimes, Mary caught him hiding behind the door, pushed against the wall, his head tipped

215

as he listened to the lessons. He had once avoided the hotel, had once begged her not to have to eat his meals where there was even a hint someone might expect conversation from him. She had never seen him as much as she did that summer.

Seldom did Mr. Simpson take a meal at the hotel. In fact, Mary remembered seeing him in it only a time or two when some conflict of Mr. Cozad's required the men of town to come in for a meeting. But the last two days, he had shown, and had sat on the long bench and smelled faintly of pig droppings. He had brushed his coat free of straw and mostly free of dust, and he sat at the place with a view toward the kitchen.

Mary felt tender toward him, even with his rough manner and his grouse's face; he had been a solid soul in her son's life. He sat awkwardly, the hump of his shoulders setting him off center. He spoke little to the others and gave out little expression at all, his intent centered on ladling a good portion from the platter the girls set out. He looked up only when Rose poured milk into his glass, and Mary noticed a bit of color came to his face.

He showed again a third day, early, as if to make sure to secure his place with the view. Mary had assigned Rose to rounding up and plucking three hens for a stew. It required Rose to work outside for the clouds of chicken feathers the plucking always stirred up.

Mr. Simpson did not come in again the following day, but did the next. That morning, Mary had started to tell Rose to spend the day sorting bins in the cellar. "The

216

potatoes," she said, "are much going to rot, and we need the room for fresh coming in."

Rose had let out a small, wheezing yip when Mary said it and had diddled a corner of her apron in her hands. "I was thinking," she bent her head for a good look at her feet and kept her gaze there, "I might serve the platters and bowls today." She did not look up. Her cheeks reddened the length of her long face. She was near forty years old and blushing like a girl.

Good Lord, Mary thought, *if I am so attuned to people, how did I miss this?* "You serve the platters, then. I'll have someone else do the bins."

Rose squeezed a sound from her throat that could be taken for, "Thank you."

Chapter 52

The season still hung with heat, but shadows were beginning to lengthen and thin. There was nothing unusual, nothing of note about the day until Ezekiel bumped in the side door with a stack of wood in his arms so high he had to sidle to see. He struggled around the dining table, through the room, and toward the Cozads' parlor. Mrs. Gatewood had apparently asked him to tote in wood to lay in for a first freeze.

The view to the parlor and into it was open through the dining room. Mary often took a moment to still herself and take in the peace of it. Ezekiel stood at the parlor doorway. Mary knew he would have knocked but for the heap of wood in his arms. She watched, her hands covered with flour. Mrs. Cozad said, "Come in, won't you, please?" She had not used Ezekiel's name; Mary did not believe she knew it.

The boys had been discussing some book they had just read, and Mary had paid little attention. Bobby was sitting on his desk in front of the open window, a strip of sun burnishing his hair a crow's silver-black. He turned. "Ezekiel," he said. *This boy knew her son?*

Ezekiel lumbered in, his shoulders drawn up around his ears. He stumbled on the edge of the rug, caught himself. A wedge of log fell loose, thumped to the floor.

Mrs. Cozad set her book aside. "Dear."

219

Bobby pulled off the desk, bent down, and picked up the log. "Let me."

"Let the boy do it," his mother said. Ezekiel took the log, squatted by the stove, and began laying the wood in a stack. "Where were we, Bobby?"

"His mother just married Murdstone."

"Yes," she said, "and what effect would you say did that have on David?"

Murdstone? They were reading *David Copperfield*. Ezekiel's ears blazed red. He had read the book a dozen times over.

Bobby cleared his throat. Ezekiel laid the last wood on the stack. Bobby began to pace, screwing his face, concentrating. His desk was piled with books, and drawings, and tablets of writing in the boy's fancy hand. He kept his desk orderly, pencils in a row, books neat to the desk's edge. He squirmed. "It would ruin him," he said. "It would ruin them all."

"Then what about the end of the story?" Mrs. Cozad said.

"You mean about finding Agnes again?"

"Yes," she said, "Agnes. Does that not dispute your argument about David's ruin?"

Mary, herself, had read the book with intensity when she was a girl. Her brothers had read it as boys, and she had brought it with her to Nebraska. Books had brought her a world she would not have ventured into on her own. She knew how important books were to Ezekiel as well. There was a time when she had time to discuss what he read, just as Mrs. Cozad was doing with her boys. When he was barely old enough to walk, he would settle under her arm and sit as she read for hour upon hour. She knew he still hungered for those times.

"I would not think it disputes my claim," Bobby said.

"And why not?" his mother tested. "You must support that view."

The boy studied his fingers a moment. His lank and length were elegant, his black jacket tailored to the sharp bones of his shoulders, his pants draped down the length of his long legs until they just touched the tops of polished black shoes. He seemed to have everything, yet being tested now proved him uncertain. "He was taken by her beauty."

"Perhaps," she said. "And what about his meanings regarding the lives of those less fortunate?"

"They have it hard," he said.

"And for support, what does the story say about that?"

Bobby made an actor's sweep of his arm toward Ezekiel. "Ezekiel?" he said. It pleased Mary in the deepest way that he knew Ezekiel's name. "Help me out here." The boy was joking, of course, trying some gimmick to get himself off the hook with his mother.

Mrs. Cozad allowed her attention to acknowledge Ezekiel, but Mary felt her son patronized by her, though not by Bobby. "Maybe that the weak," Ezekiel said, "are easily hurt."

Mrs. Cozad nodded, rested her hands in her lap as if she did not believe this was anything but a guess on his part.

"Yes," Bobby said. "In those times, the poor were taken advantage of."

In *those* times?

"Children were not well treated," Bobby said.

"And what about David?"

"He made friends."

Ezekiel picked up the stove broom, began sweeping.

"Yes," Mrs. Cozad said, her attention again on her son.

"He hated what they made him do," Bobby said.

"Yes. And what else?" She sat quiet, waiting.

He did not answer. He toed his shoe on the carpet, stalling. He smacked his lips to launch into some point, but said, "What about you, Ezekiel?" Again, not a sincere question; Ezekiel was not expected to give an answer.

"He pur-severs," Ezekiel said.

Mrs. Cozad squinted, looked down at the floor, confused. "Pur-severs?"

"Manages to survive," Ezekiel said.

"Oh," she said, "perse*veres*."

Ezekiel's ears flared again. Mary felt his humiliation. She knew he had read the word but had never heard it properly said.

Bobby held his hands out as if to say, "There you have it." Ezekiel slumped as if he wanted to hide. Bobby leaned toward him. "You get this at the *school?*" he said. "Mr. Young teaching Dickens now?" Ezekiel clutched the broom to himself, shook his head no.

Mrs. Cozad was looking at Ezekiel straight, now, as if finally truly aware of him. "Then what is the significance of Agnes in his life?" she said. "Ezekiel?"

"She was one more person he had to take care of," he said.

"I suppose one could say that," she allowed.

"A bit too cynical, I'd say," Bobby said, though not with scorn or teasing. Mary could see it then: From the view of their coddled lives, of course they would think it cynical.

"To love," Bobby said. And he put his finger to his lip. "Yes, by golly," he said. "He found Agnes again to love."

Bobby stayed after lessons for a few minutes, drawing at something at the table. Ezekiel passed by the parlor two or three times, peeking in. Mary was becoming embarrassed and about to tell him to make himself busy when Bobby held his paper to the light. He tipped it back and forth, set it down again and made some adjustments with his pencil. Ezekiel passed by the doorway yet again. Bobby said, "Say, Ezekiel, I wonder if I could get your help."

Ezekiel stood with his hands in his pockets. For a moment, he did not say anything. "I guess."

"Wouldn't be much trouble," Bobby said, "I don't think, anyway." Ezekiel leaned forward as if wanting to ask what but was too shy. "I wonder if you might help me kick off a few turns of the press."

Mary watched her son follow Bobby, like a sheep, toward the little room in back where Traber had the printing press. When Traber or Mr. Claypool or any of them used it, it sent up a clattering that made Mary plug her ears. She saw it sometimes when she was cleaning up. It sat like an ugly metal animal, a hulk, surrounded by pots of ink and papers and trays filled with backward numbers and letters. It was smudged, ink dark, and constructed of pulleys and plates, and levers and wheels Mary could make

223

neither tails nor heads of. Someone ran the thing several times a week, the contraption sending the hotel clattering as the men put out broadsides and printed the weekly sheet of news called *The Hundredth Meridian*.

Mary had always tried to ignore it. She did not this time. She took up a broom, as if she were about to use it, and stood back Bobby laid his hand on a stack of the papers. His fingers were long, straight, and narrow. "I have to get these out quick. Pa," he said, then caught himself. "*Mr. Cozad* needs some handbills to take with him when he leaves for Ohio this evening. Can you spell?" His face shone.

"Yes," Ezekiel said. He was eager, wanting, she could see, to please.

Bobby laughed. "Backward?" He seemed giddy, his movements nervous, quick, and terribly important. With one hand, he held up a looking glass in front of Ezekiel and with his other long arm he reached back, holding a page cut from *The Meridian*.

"I never tried backwards," Ezekiel said.

"Give it a go," Bobby said. Mary felt the smack of her son's anxiety. She knew, as small as he was, as quiet and shy, he hungered to prove himself. He yet had earned anyone to call friend.

He began to read the paper Bobby held up to the mirror. "Presi . . . dent . . . ial . . . elections. Governor . . . Ruth . . . er . . . ford B." His reading was slow and labored. Mary knew it must have made him feel a dolt. She wanted to scream out, to brag that Mr. Young had made him his teaching assistant last year, giving him charge of three students. "Gove ... nor ..." Ezekiel stumbled. She wanted to run up and rescue him. He squinted at the mirror, then said, "A misspelling."

"Where?" Bobby said.

"The first *r* in governor is missing."

Bobby turned the page to himself. "Hah," he said. "It wasn't me who made the mistake."

He put down the mirror, motioned to the machine. "Read this." He pointed to a tray filled with blocks Mary knew contained raised letters, laid backwards like in the mirror.

Ezekiel took a breath, began to read. He was no longer hesitant.

EXCURSIONS!! EXCURSIONS!!
****NEBRASKA****
Tuesday 7 o'clock pm.
_____OPPORTUNITY_____
Leaving Cincinnati, Ohio for
GREAT PLATTE VALLEY
COZAD, DAWSON COUNTY

"That's my man," Bobby said. "Let's start the presses."

Chapter 53

A thunderstorm had just blown over. A breeze rippled new-hung curtains. The curtains finished with lace from Mrs. Cozad's basket. The Cozads were not in the parlor, nor had they been in it the day before. The boys had been requisitioned by their pa, scattered to the winds: Johnny in Denver with him on some sort of business, Bobby out on the Gatewood farm helping his granddad. Mary stood at the doorway. The parlor was vacant, Mrs. Cozad was spending the morning with her mother, now and then coming into the hotel to discuss some piece of furniture, the right paper color to cover a wall, or where to hang the new lamps. Were such a room Mary's, she would never leave it.

From behind her, butter hissed in a skillet, wood thumped on the fire. The kitchen would serve a good, fat roast that day, and a gravy laced with apricot preserves and roast potatoes. Last night, Mary had assigned Rose to knead dough for honey rolls. This morning she had shown Rose how to powder them with cinnamon and dot on butter. The scent of cinnamon and honey and crackling fat lay on the hotel.

As if waiting for some acknowledgement of the work she had done on the honey rolls, Rose stood in the doorway, turned toward the front door, her broad hips obstructing the other girls' movement between the kitchen and dining room. Were it anyone else, were it any other day, Mary would have tsked her back to work. "Rose," she said. Rose's shoulders lifted barely the width of a needle; *Can she hear?* Sometimes Mary wondered. "I would like you to set out the jam and butter and bread." Rose folded her arms under her breasts and gave a slow turn away from the door toward Mary. "And I would like you to supervise the table when people come, make sure everything is laid out nice." *Would she understand these two orders at once?*

"Me?" she said.

"Yes," Mary said. "It will mean you must remain out here in the dining room while the rest of us bring out the food and while the diners take their supper." Rose's eyes gave two confused shifts as if wondering why; she was normally relegated to some job that kept her from under foot during the frenzy of getting food on the table. Mary only hoped Mr. Simpson showed that day and that she was correct in her assessment that he had an eye on Rose. For, if he did not show, and if she were wrong she feared she would never be rid of Rose.

Rose stood inert as a stump near the head of the table as people began to mill in and take their places. Each time the door opened, she gave it a glance but by five minutes after eleven, the place Mr. Simpson claimed remained unoccupied.

One of the girls brought out a steaming platter with the roast, another the potatoes and peas and a plate of carrots and celery. Just as everyone was passing the food, the door opened and Mr. Simpson came in, dusting his hat on his thigh. Rose's face colored as he squeezed into his seat.

Mary brought out the honey rolls, set them in front of him. His brows rose when he saw the rolls in the same tender manner as when one sees a pup. "Rose is responsible for our particularly delicious supper today." It was not a total lie; Rose *had* contributed. Mr. Simpson's glance settled with a lustrous weight on Rose.

Three days later, Rose showed early for work. Her hands fluttered in a manner Mary had never seen before, her fingers like butterfly wings settling here and there without focus or place. Her face shined as if oiled. When the other girls were tying on their aprons, Rose squeaked at Mary, "Missus?"

"Yes?"

"Mr. Simpson has asked for my hand. This will be my last day as cook."

Chapter 54

Somewhere from the front of the hotel, a giggle trilled, young and high. It was late afternoon. Soon town would quiet, the hammering would stop, the oxen would be unyoked and the haypress would go silent.

There came the laugh, then giggles again; they came from somewhere around or behind one of the new buildings that now blocked the view down E Avenue to the river. Mary was in the front window at the house. She had draped her feet in a cool cloth and raised them in a chair. She crooked her chin for a glance at the pure joy in their noise.

Two boys, riding bareback on a black pony, came around the corner. A large, wet, rust-colored dog ran alongside. The boy at the reins was Bobby Cozad, the rider behind smaller and hidden from sight. Bobby turned his head, spoke over his shoulder. His pants were wet to the thigh and rolled up beyond his knees. "You made me."

The child behind burbled, "Did not." All Mary could see of that child were his arms wrapped around Bobby and his dangle of thin shins. Shoes and a string of crapper fish slapped from the saddle horn. Bobby reached around behind, diddled the boy's ribs. It set up a round of hilarity.

"I'll tell Ma," Bobby said. It sent up another impossible gurgle. "I'll tell her what *really* happened."

The smaller boy slipped down, then saw Mary in the window. He flapped his arms and shouted, "Ma." His face was painted bright pink. Mary had never seen him so happy.

Chapter 55

September

Oh, Prune,

There's come a boy to town earlier this summer, a beautiful boy named Bobby who has taken my Ezekiel under his wing. He is the son of the town's founder and is some older than Ezekiel by three years, but he has called him to fish and ride along hunting rabbit. He has nicknamed my serious son Easy. This boy's friendship has changed my son. He shines now and he chatters, and chortles. I can't keep him quiet. I could kiss his new friend.

We are doing well. The weather is still warm. I dread the heat, tho it is beginning to cool more in the nights. We had the bugs again this year in July, so the gardens and the fields aren't as rich and flush as we hoped, tho we replanted our garden and have some to preserve and the farmers have had something to sell. It is a sad nuisance to see the tender shoots eaten to the ground by those fiend hoppers. I hope you never have to deal with such.

Love and kisses,

Sissie

Chapter 56

"Mary," Mrs. Gatewood said, "I am overrun with a large family coming in this evening." The table had been cleared, the dishes done, pots scrubbed. There was another new girl now, Bernadette, whom Mrs. Gatewood had put on after Rose left to get married. This one's name Mary would remember; Bernadette had been the name of Mary's best girlhood friend.

The table was full all three meals now, plus Mr. Cozad was in town. All in the kitchen were tired. "I want you to bunk these people," Mrs. Gatewood said. "I have nowhere to put them. They have paid cash on two sections east of town and are talking about buying another. They need to be put up for a few weeks until they can manage to build a house before winter. Would you mind putting them up?"

The question was perfunctory, no less than a demand. In the worst way, Mary wanted to tell her no. What would she do with a large family who spoke no English? But Mrs. Gatewood's expression bore down and left her on the short end of argument.

Mrs. Gatewood raised a just-a-moment finger and then left. She came back with a family trailing: two parents and six children. She introduced them all as the Nikodemskis and said they had spent the last four days traveling on the trains. The mother was holding a baby, and the husband was standing silently aside. The mother wore a white headscarf and a brown-colored apron over a skirt that did not reach her ankles. The father was dressed in a tight black coat and wore a mustache which billowed like some creature from his lip. He wrung a hat in his hands, and his hair was packed where the hat had sat. The children, all black-haired as their parents, stood behind in a line of descending height.

As the family gathered their things, Mary dragged herself home. Ezekiel was in his room, working a pencil on papers, drawing something. She had only time to tell him the bad news when the knock came at the door. He ran down the stairs, opened the door, motioned them in. They began bringing blankets and clothing, the parents mumbling a rush of language heavy in the throat. The children were quiet, gawping at Ezekiel, then at Mary. "Hello," Ezekiel said, and they pushed back shyly against the wall, their eyes black as birds'.

With his help, they moved the table aside and began to spread out their blankets. Mary could not make out anything of what they said, though they were pleasant. That night, their sultry breaths lay like a dew in the house. They did not stir when, in the dark, she tiptoed down from her room before dawn. She stepped around the children's bodies and clicked softly out through the door to work. They were gone when she returned at the end of the day and did not return until long after dark.

For the first three or four days, the Nikodemskis were quiet, smiling, sock-footed and silent in the house. A high color of hope and excitement lay on their cheeks.

Through a dance of nodding and grunts and pointing and sweeping of arms, Ezekiel told Mary, he had learned they were from Poland and that they were the first of their relatives to come to America. They had bought a wagon and a heavy-footed horse, and Mr. Nikodemski had ordered metal struts and fan blades and a windlass from one of the new shops.

Days later, Ezekiel learned that Mr. Nikodemski had put up a windlass on their new farm and, after a deal of pantomime, that he was starting to work on a house. Now that their farm had water, Mrs. Nikodemski bought flour, salt, sugar, and meat from Mrs. Gatewood. Mrs. Nikodemski opened one of their trunks stacked along the wall and brought out bags of spices for her cooking which she would do on a fire pit. A curious and exotic scent lingered on their clothing when they returned at the end of the day.

By the end of the second week, Ezekiel learned enough Polish words to be able to greet them, "Halo," and ask what time it was, "Która godzina?" and to count to twelve. As the days wore on, the Nikodemskis' quiet bled away and the evenings grew louder. The house seemed to vibrate with their chatter, their loud, ear-splitting laughter, their faces shining with heat and something Mary had not seen since she left Totten and Prune in Philadelphia: a family fond of one other.

Chapter 57

Letters became a bane; they required answering; they required some story. The letter from Totten regarding the trunk from Macroom had sat on Mary's bedside table for months. She did not know what to do with it. She had written Prune since it came but had made no mention of it. She did not know how to. Prune would be dying to get her hands on what was in the trunk. Either Totten thought the letter lost or tact kept him from bringing it up again.

Another came from the attorney, addressed to Mr. Edmund Harrington. It was delivered by a thin young man recently hired to clerk. Mary was in the hotel kitchen, rolling out dough, when he brought it. Flour covered her hands, and her apron, even the cross-eyed tip of her nose. The letter was sealed with wax and the attorney's stamp. She slit it open with a carving knife; it felt hot.

> *Dear Mr. Harrington,*
> *It has come to my attention that the client who expressed interest in offering to purchase your farm sometime two years ago wishes to renew the offer a second time. Your response must come immediately as my client will withdraw if my office has heard nothing from you within the month.*
> *Yours,*
> *Franz E. Hoffman, Attorney at Law*

239

That night, Mary laid the letter on the bedside table on top of the unanswered letter from Totten. It and the two previous letters from the attorney spoke of what she was helpless to do anything about.

Chapter 58

Had it been a moment of quiet, likely someone would have picked up on the rumbling in the distance. But it was Sunday, just before church. Farm wagons were rattling into town, families streaming from their homes. Children were squealing, the Lutherans thudding their dull Sunday bell; the Pentecostals would be clanging theirs in seconds. The wind whipped the women's skirts and flailed the ribbons in the girls' hair. Snow would cover town by the end of the day, but it was bright and clear when the bells began to toll. Ezekiel was gone, had borrowed a rifle from Bobby to do some hunting outside town before the weather turned.

A roast lamb sizzled in the oven, three pies cooling on a counter. Bernadette was setting out platters of tomatoes and peppers and broccoli and celery. One of the other girls was setting out dishes of mint sauce for the Cozads. Theadosia was filling a pot with water for potatoes she would mash with soured cream and onion.

Though the table still overflowed on a Sunday, the numbers of people arriving to view property was dropping as the summer, and its light, bled away and the nights began to nip. Mrs. Gatewood had told Mary she would be letting Theadosia and Bernadette go soon for the winter, and, again, Mrs. Gatewood had asked Mary— her cheapest labor—to stay on. Before Mary could bring it

241

up, Mrs. Gatewood told her she would not be working alone, that Mary would have someone to help.

Mary crossed her fingers. "Who?" she said.

"Rose," Mrs. Gatewood said.

"Might I ask why not Theadosia or Bernadette?"

"Rose is a distant cousin," Mrs. Gatewood said. "Mr. Simpson wants to add to his business, Rose's job will help him do so. Besides, it is good to help family."

So, Mr. Simpson was putting his wife to work.

The tinkle of voices bled into the hotel, the rattle of wagons; there would be a few minutes' quiet before the sermons were done and things picked up. The supper was nearly ready, the lamb roasting, biscuits in the oven. Mary removed her apron, told Theadosia she would be back in half an hour.

The Pentecostals' bell was just beginning to clang as she let herself into the house. The lowering sunlight smeared through the house's window. The panes had been clean when they moved into the house. Now, everything about it looked poor, let go, untended. She dropped into a chair, took off one shoe to rub the ball of her foot.

Outside came a thundering, then a sort of hum she could feel under the soles of her feet. The Pentecostals' bell went silent. She went to the window, the shoe still in her hand. A roil of dust rose to the south. The dust shifted and as it did came the bellowing of cows, a misery of high pleads.

One shoed, Mary ran out. *Where was Ezekiel?* A boy, playing by the river, had been trampled a year ago when a herd came through. The herd was upon town by the time anyone heard the cows' cries. Mary stood helpless as the drovers herded the longhorns directly toward town. The creatures were pitiful and emaciated, captured in Texas hundreds of miles away and they had hundreds more to go before whatever of them survived to the markets.

Mary screamed, "Ezekiel!" but could see only the cattle and the drovers. The drovers flailed and whipped. The animals rippled by, their eyes white, heads bobbing, dust rising, tails thick with terror's filth.

Someone—Mr. Claypool, Mary thought—shot out of the livery on a black mare. But for him, it was as if town froze. Families stopped in front of the churches, pulled their children close. Farmers reined in their wagons. Mr. Claypool yanked his horse to a stop, shaded his eyes with his hand. Mr. Cozad came running from the hotel, yelling, "David! David! Get them the hell out of here."

Mr. Claypool kicked the mare and ran past Mary, his eyes white as the animals'. He rode off alone toward the rage of drovers.

Mr. Cozad ran into the livery, bellowing, "Simpson, get my horse, get my horse!"

Mary began to limp-run, giving no thought to the shoe in her hand, or her naked foot. She held her arm over her face against the glare. She ran east. Ezekiel had said he would be hunting, but where? Why hadn't she asked? She ran west, began screaming his name. The updraft of the herd pulled at her.

Mr. Claypool bolted toward the herd shouting, "Who is in charge? Who is in charge?" He stopped then, his mare sidling and throwing her head. The cattle surrounded him, a clattering river of horns filled the street. "Who?" he said, his voice gaining depth. "Who's the head of this mess?"

"Who wants to know?" The drover was short, wide, and muscular and carried a rifle. The brim of his hat obscured his eyes. His fingers pulled down the lever of his rifle in a threatening and practiced way.

Mr. Claypool was not a large man but he held his ground. "David Claypool."

Mr. Cozad on his stallion shot around Mr. Claypool toward the drover. He reined the horse so hard it bucked and nearly tumbled over. Mr. Atkinson showed and Traber Gatewood. They pressed in beside Mr. Cozad and David Claypool. All the men carried rifles. Behind them, in a roil of dust, came wagons, an armada of men dressed for church, hats brushed, suits pressed.

Mary shouted, "Ezekiel!" again but the sound floated away.

The head drover was muscular in the neck, abundant in the shoulders. He held his rifle across himself in threat. He and Mr. Cozad began to rage a menace of threats Mary could not hear.

Someone else, a drover as thin as the cattle, pushed through the herd, threading his way toward her. He looked neither right nor left; he closed the distance.

Her world went silent. For a moment, he was lost in dust, then reappeared. He rode easy with a grace that took her breath; one with his horse, his horse part of him. It was a vision Mary had clung to for so long, the tenderness of a past she could barely remember, a past where he whittled a stick and made a whistle for his son that tooted off tune, a past with the power of his arms lifting her, holding her, and making some joke she laughed at, dim evenings and quiet words, the two of them together.

He stopped half a foot from her. "Mary," he said. The horse champed at the bit, blew, and threw its head.

She held onto the shoe. "Edmund," she said. She had no more words. Edmund nodded; she imagined him leaning down, scooping her into the saddle. He was here. He was not conjured, not the mist of a night's sensing. He was alive.

"The runt," he said, a bit of spittle on his bottom lip. "Where's the runt?"

"Edmund," she said again, her chin quivering, and she held up her hand to hide it.

His face was not the face she had waited for, but was thin, cruel, unshaven, teeth gone brown and barbed. "It was the runt stole my horse," he said. "He found me sick and left me out there."

There had been blood in the shed the day she went to the farm. Had Ezekiel been the cause of it? "I took a fall," Edmund said, "and would that son of a bitch help out his poor pa? Hell no. He *stole my horse*. Where is that little son of a bitch?" He raised his hand as if to bring it down on her. She held the shoe over her head against a blow, but shouts and a rough rifle shot came, and he turned. The gelding bucked and Edmund gripped the horn. And, as the horse's hooves hit the ground, he spat at her feet. He spurred the horse and left her in a spray of clods and dust, still holding her shoe.

———

Ezekiel returned home later that day, after the herd was gone. When he came through the door, she grabbed his shoulders and pulled him to her and cried, "Oh, I worried." But he did not return her embrace, made only a stiff backing away.

Chapter 59

Was it only yesterday, the cattle drive? Memory had no shape; she could not see it, could not hold it, but it took every step she took, and breathed every breath. It drove away sleep and repulsed every bite of food. All day, the weather rumbled like war, lightning stabbed, thunder rolled, and heat smothered. She sent up a prayer of thanks for the miracle that Ezekiel was out hunting that day. She could not allow herself to imagine what would have happened if he had seen his father, and his father had seen him.

Chapter 60

A heavy box full of books arrived at the post office. Ezekiel carried it home in a barrow. The box had sat on the center table three days, the twines of cord still knotted the way Prune had tied it. Whatever was in it, however loving and kind, would require response, or at least acknowledgement and some sort of lie.

She let herself down into the chair, her hand gripping scissors. She opened the blades, closed them, opened them again, and watched them close down again like a mouth uttering something she could not hear. The scissors turned then. They pointed at her like an eye, snapped open as if laughing, closed down, pressed into the softest of her middle under the cave of her ribs.

A creak from the door. "Ma?"

"Yes, dear?" Her voice seemed issued from somewhere else.

He stood in the doorway, the night behind him. The wind disturbed his hair, raised it up. She stood then, over the box. She made some effort to appear interested in it, but his gray face betrayed her performance.

Prune's note in the box said:

> *Dearest Sissie,*
> *The boys are not so interested in reading these adventures*
> *any longer, instead they are making adventures of their*

own. It gladdens me but saddens me, as well. Cornelius is packing his things to spend the last week before university begins with a friend in Massachusetts. Oliver is thinking he might want to become a doctor. My boys grew up so fast, I don't think I can bear it. My dear, I sometimes think I will bury myself in a good old Irish frump.

I have clung to these books feeling they might help me keep some part of the boys forever. Now, I want Ezekiel to have them. Having my nephew reading them brings my wonderful nephew to me. Oh that I could see you all! I picture you and Edmund in your home in town, and miss you so.

On a brighter note, I give you my love and kisses.
Prune

Ezekiel lost himself in the books for a month.

Chapter 61

Comprehension came to her in tiny stitches. She began to understand where Ezekiel had gotten the thirty dollars: On a day he should have been in school, he had gone back to the farm, had found his father sodden, fallen with drink. She could see it now as if through clean glass: Ezekiel must have wanted to speak with him, must have remembered, must have held out the same hope for the kind pa he once had. Ezekiel must have come close and Edmund struck, kicked likely, in order to raise such a profound bruise. For the mess of ruin she had seen, there must have been some tussle. Afterward, Ezekiel had stolen Edmund's horse and saddle and sold them so that Mary had money for them to live.

Had Edmund ever been the loving man she believed he was? She thought so, but was beginning to understand Edmund was an actor. For a few years, he had managed to hold onto a performance of love and fatherhood. Mary's parents, and Prune and Totten had all hinted at something they could see in Edmund but Mary had denied. Yet, he tried. It must have been exhausting. She felt a small ping of love that he had tried so hard to give her and Ezekiel a life he knew was right.

How had she been so blind? Even her son, a child, had understood. Every day, in his penurious collection of pennies and nickels, the dollars from the sale of his pa's horse, Ezekiel proved he knew he would never be able to count on his pa, something she had denied.

Ezekiel had not been in town the day she saw Edmund, and for that she thanked the Virgin Mother. But since the cattle drive, Ezekiel had turned quiet again. The Cozads were planning to return to Ohio for the winter soon; she blamed Ezekiel's silence on that.

Chapter 62

She wrapped herself into her shawl, ducked into the wind, and went to the office where the attorney did business. The clerk stood. "I am Mrs. Harrington," she said. He was young, not much older than Bobby Cozad. His voice was soft and had a lilt brought from County Clare. "I'm here to see Mr. Hoffman," she said.

The attorney's office was quiet and smelled of a put-out cigar. A desk, dark and polished, weighed down the room like a throne. Mary sat, insignificant as a lump, across from him.

The attorney was not the sort one would take note of but for the rage of speckles on his forehead and for the prominence of a goiter; she clung to its ugly, veined bulge, something sound on which to focus.

He looked at her confused, seeming not to remember who she was. "Mrs. Edmund Harrington," she said.

"Oh, yes." He wheezed himself into his chair. "Your claim."

"Yes."

He scooted his chair forward. The goiter bobbled a bit on his collar. He said, "I have clients who are interested in acquiring your property." He brought forward a map, a plat of the county, from one end of his desk. He laid a pink finger on it. "The timber claim your husband took out in your name over nine years ago." He regarded her as

253

if wondering why Mr. Harrington himself were not there. "Your husband seems to have worked the property and planted according to the requirements of a claim."

"We did," she said. *I worked it.*

"You, of course, would know nothing of the business nature of things." He did not add *because you are a woman.* "I should be speaking with Mr. Harrington," he said, emphasis on *Mr.*

He had an arrogant way of tipping back his head, looking down his chest at her. "But . . ." He held up his finger to shush. She continued, "He is not here." It had been her idea to file the timber claim. Edmund had planned to pasture feed calves on both their claims. She once had inquired what would happen if something happened to his cattle and he humored her, said it would give her something to do and if she could not handle a tree claim, he would run cattle on it. The saplings had been like children to her, tiny things she sprouted from seed and set out, small as twigs, toting water in the wagon, and praying it would be enough. By the winter Edmund left, she had set nearly a thousand.

"My client," the attorney said, "will stipulate, whether it is true or not, that you have met the conditions of planting for the first years for a timber claim." She could see Mr. Hoffman acknowledging her surprise. "Of course, to prove up a tree claim, there need to be thousands more *alive* than your husband was able to plant. Time on your claim is running out. As I figure it, your husband would have a mere four years to prove it up."

"Yes."

"My clients realize the claim is nearly worthless until proved up."

Then why do they want to discuss buying it?

"It will take time to be of any value." She knew his arguments were meant to negotiate and to bolster his clients' side. His manner was condescending, as if he were talking to a child, and that, too, was meant to bring her down to favorable terms. These things Mary knew only because she had seen the way Mrs. Gatewood negotiated in her business; nothing was given for free; a good, substantial price was paid for every transaction.

He laid the map aside, shuffled some papers. "You lived in the house for . . ." he took one up, looked down his nose at it. "A little more than five years."

"Yes."

"The claim will not be entirely proved up for another four and a half years."

"You said that already," she said and wished her tone were firmer.

The attorney shot a foul glance at her; the movement shifted the goiter, sent it shivering. He picked up another document, peered down his eyeglasses. "The cattle claim," he said, "taken in your husband's name, was never proved up either." He laid the document on his desk. "That property was sold a year ago." The attorney pinched off his eyeglasses. "Your claim, Mrs. Harrington, has been spared the auction block because of technicality, because a timber claim allows more time to prove. Apparently, your husband has not worked your tree claim since vacating the house, Mrs. Harrington."

"No," she said. A horse whinnied outside; a man yelled. She yearned to be out where they were.

The attorney sat forward, the goiter draped onto his tie. A wagon went by, the *pounk-pounk* of an off-balance wheel.

"Mrs. Harrington, I understand from your neighbors that neither you nor your husband has returned to live on the farm since you vacated the parcel."

"No," she said, "we have not."

She concentrated on his throat. "My clients are willing to make a fair offer for the property, such that it is."

"Such that it is?" She took out her handkerchief, twined it in her fingers.

"Would your husband entertain an offer?" The goiter was filled with red and blue veins. "To sell a questionable property?"

"I don't know," she said.

"My clients are willing to make what I think is a generous offer, even though the claim has yet to be proved." She could will every limb of herself quiet but for her fingers, which had twisted her handkerchief into a string. "The property has little value until it is proved," he said. *Why would someone want to buy a property if it had no value? It must have value, or the attorney would have no client to want it.*

"Mrs. Harrington?" he said. The goiter was becoming damp as if it, as well as the attorney, were under some distress.

"I have to have . . ." she said.

"More?" he said. It seemed the attorney had read her silence as a resistance to sell. He steepled his hands, put them to his lips. "My client is willing to go as high as five hundred and fifty dollars." He shook his head as if this were just *more* more than he could fathom.

Five hundred and fifty dollars! It would be enough to buy the house in town; five hundred and fifty dollars would even allow her to pay for Ezekiel's education after secondary school. He would never need to grovel for his existence as she and Edmund had done. She would still have to work, but she might be able to do something besides kitchen work. They would have a home, food, wood for the fire.

"Of course," He pulled his watch from its pocket as if time were getting short, "your husband will have to agree." He did not look at the watch.

Husband. Husband. The word began to take on shape, and to consume the room. She felt her mouth gather in as if it were about to speak. The attorney settled behind the desk like a bloated red turkey. He said, "Your husband would have to agree, of course."

She drew a breath. "I have not . . ." She went quiet again, watched her fingers play with the handkerchief. "I have not seen him." It had been merely days since the cattle drive.

"Have not seen him?" the attorney said. "Your *husband?*"

"Not for some time."

"How long?"

She could not conjure an answer.

"Hours? Days?"

"Some time." She was avoiding the truth, as if saying it

257

would give life to her last awful day with him.

"Where can he be found?" The attorney replaced the watch in his pocket, leaned forward, interested now.

"I do not know."

"When do you expect him to return?"

"I do not know."

"I see," the attorney said, and he slung himself and his pink hands forward. "A married woman's husband *must* approve. A married woman has no power in such matters."

"But it is *my* claim," she said. She had abandoned her chair, was standing in front of him now. The attorney had to look up to converse with her. It evened them, somehow.

"It is only in your *name*," he said. "You have no rights over it."

"I should be able to sign," she said. And, for the first time in a long while, she felt not hopelessness but anger.

"Ah," the attorney said, "but Nebraska law—"

"I'm the one who owns it," she said, surprised at her firm tone. It was as if her voice belonged to someone else.

"Nebraska requires the husband's approval." He tapped a finger on his chin. "Unless he has abandoned you."

"I am not abandoned."

"In that case, we can plea *feme sole.*"

"I am not abandoned."

"He's passed?" the attorney said. "Or is it that you want to claim he's passed?" The room was sucked dry. He waited. She said nothing. "To claim death, Mrs. Harrington"—*did he emphasize* Missus?—"a notice must go out to find him. Without a body . . ." He cleared his throat. "Remains . . . only a judge and the Court can certify him deceased."

Chapter 63

She could hold onto naught, not even emptiness, for emptiness implied some vessel that could be filled. She had just come from the lawyer's. She sat in the house, her shawl clinging to the cold, her breath shaped by vapor. What was the shape of nothing? Could one hold onto nothing? See it? Mold it?

Another letter from Prune lay on the center table in the light of spare dusk. It sucked her breath. She sat wearing her self-pity like a garment. It weighted her shoulders, gave her excuse. Alone, she would sink into it, but what did helplessness bequeath her son? This was truth. This was not a lie. She did not think she could count on lies any longer, no matter the tentative moment of peace and power that could rest on a lie. When a lie withered and went dry, what did it leave? Nothing.

She took the letter to her room, lit the lamp, pulled the shawl around her neck. She slid her finger under the flap.

September 30, 1876
Dearest Sissie,
It has been so long since you have written. I long for a letter. I hope you and Edmund are well and that my wonderful nephew is growing fat and strong.
Totten has not heard from you, nor from Edmund,

261

regarding an inquiry about the items from Macroom. He
says he will send another in the next mail, fearing the first
has gone astray and you never received it.

Are you and Edmund settled into your new home, dearest?
Are you faring well in all your adventures in the West? I
do believe you must be, or I would have heard.

Cornelius is down with a cold and I am afraid Oliver
might be coming down with it as he was sniffling on his
way to school this morning. Corny had gone to the Harrys'
for their daughter's birthday party (she is six, too young for
the likes of his advanced age, but her brother is in Corn's
grade) and I think he picked it up there. Totten sounded a
bit thick in the throat when he left for the bank this
morning, too. Oh, dear, I do hope the plague of colds and
coughs and fevers do not make it out your way.

Write, Sissie. I am so lonely for you. It would help my
loneliness if only I could see the scribble of your pen.

Hello to Edmund. And a great, embarrassing embrace for
your darling boy.

Love,
Prune

What had Prune ever given her? Loyalty, generosity,
love, and truth. Truth. They had been raised with the
truth. Their mother could scent a lie like a hound scents a
fox. Prune had learned it earlier than Mary. For the first
time, the only time Mary would even remember, Prune's
truthfulness gave a little slip. It was a Tuesday, a school
day. It was late spring, the boys had been excused from
class to help their father with the mill. Prune wanted to be

excused as well and pouted when their mother told her no. Prune would not hold Mary's hand as they made their way. It was blustery, the wind high. Prune stamped ahead, lost to her pouts. Mary, barely five years old, scrambled behind. A gust hit her, put her off step. She twisted an ankle and tumbled down the hill. Her arm caught under her. A pop cracked from her shoulder and she screamed.

Prune ran back. Mary was lost in the pain. Prune carried her back up the hill to the house. Mrs. Sweeney took Mary to her bed, gave a great pull to her arm. The pain took over Mary's world. She remembered nothing after that, only blackness.

She woke. A wet rag, bitter cold and smelling of the creek sat on her shoulder. The hard pain was gone, a dull ache replaced it.

Her mother and Prune stood just outside the door. Prune was crying, "Och," her mother said, "She is naught but a tiny little thing, like a leaf in this wind. You must not ha' been holding her."

"But I was, I was." A lie. Prune had been five meters ahead, her chin sunk into a powerful pity.

Their mother must have sniffed the deceit. "How, then, can Mary's sister not ha' taken a tumble as well?" Prune was quiet, unable to conjure an answer. "A daughter of mine," Mrs. Sweeney said, "can make a mistake. A daughter of mine can forget her little sister. A daughter of mine c'not always be perfect. No one in this world is perfect and I know it. But I will brook no daughter of mine in a lie." Prune hucked a sob. Mrs. Sweeney said, "Come," and the back door squeaked open then shut. A whiff of wind settled on Mary's forehead. There came voices through the walls, the words indistinct and mumbled.

When the door opened again, Prune and their ma were silent but for Prune's sniffling. Prune's punishment for the lie was to make a sign that said "I am a liar" and wear it for a week, everywhere but to school and to church.

Prune never lied again. Mary had been the cause of Prune's mistake, yet Prune never held it against her, never dealt Mary anything less than care and love. And what had Mary ever given her sister in return?

Chapter 64

The Cozads left town on a white-sky day of bitter winds and threatening snow. The night before, Bobby had knocked on Mary's door. It was dark. Mary had just come from the hotel, her hands were red from work. Ezekiel was in his room.

Bobby said, "Is Ezekiel home, Mrs. Harrington?" He wore a muffler and a cap. His cheeks were covered in a sprinkling of nervous weals. She had heard him argue with his mother to stay in Cozad. He did not want to go back to Ohio, but his mother insisted the boys return to school, the Chickering Institute, where they would receive proper education and gentlemen's training.

"He's up in his room," Mary said. She wished the boy to stay here as much as he and her son wanted it. She called up the stairs.

Ezekiel's door cracked open; a light shone down from his lamp. She caught the flicker of a sheen in his face when he saw Bobby.

"Hey, Easy," Bobby said. He reached back and under his coat. "I got something."

"What is it?" Ezekiel said.

"Something to hold you over." He pulled out a book, held it up. "Hope you haven't already read it."

Ezekiel shook his head. His nose was beginning to swell.

265

"Good," Bobby said. He handed him the book. Ezekiel wiped his nose on the back of his wrist. "When I come back, I want a report."

"When you coming back?"

"You know Ma, whenever she says so." He ruffled Ezekiel's bang and Ezekiel grinned. "There's going to be a test next summer. And you better write me."

Ezekiel sniffed. "You'll write *me*?"

"Does a jackrabbit hop?" Ezekiel's lips quivered. "You won't be able to shut me up." Bobby reached out his stretch of long arm, grabbed Ezekiel up, and pulled him in. And when they parted, a slick of mucous lay on Bobby's chest.

Chapter 65

By the time of the first snows, the trains were letting off only a few stragglers. Mrs. Gatewood pared the kitchen to just Mary and Mary was relieved to be shut of Rose. The Cozads left behind furniture but their rooms went unoccupied. The upstairs rooms held just two renters, one a woman with two children who was waiting for her husband to arrive from Virginia, the other a new man to town who took off his hat when he entered and nodded when he met Mary and reached a timid hand to shake when he introduced himself, as if she were more than kitchen help. Her hands had been wet and red and she held them out as if they were not worthy to be shaken. "Anyway, hello," he said, his teeth were crowded and white, his voice mild. "I'm Sam Schooley."

He leaned forward as if the most important thing in his life were to hear her name. She could feel the warmth of a flush. "Mrs. Harrington."

———

She had taken a cough in the summer; it seemed better in the cold but had never gone entirely away. Mrs. Gatewood had cut back the kitchen's budget for food. It meant simple meals, again, stews of turnip and potato and stringy meats that required hours in the pot, biscuits and bread served with lard, sauced apples, occasional pies. Mary served Ezekiel from preserves from their summer garden and from what she brought home in a bucket from the kitchen. The house was no more permanent than a tent, Mrs. Gatewood could sell it in a minute, anything could force her to move. She still thought of the house as the Bowers'.

Ezekiel usually read while he ate. The pages of his books were often discolored where he had spilled. He had brought down no book to the table that night and had sat looking down at his biscuit as she ladled stew into his bowl. A fire crackled in the stove, its window lit orange. She had wood she could count on now, which she paid Ezekiel to bring in and stack.

Mary set his bowl before him. He picked up his spoon, held it poised as if to dip, but he simply held it there.

"Eat, Ezekiel."

He made no move. He had been sullen, his shoulders rounded and heavy, since Bobby left some weeks ago. He merely stared into his bowl, now. "We won't ever see him again," he said, his voice low, almost inaudible.

"He will come back. Mr. Cozad is moving the family here next year, hadn't you heard?"

She thought he would be lifted at this, but was not. "Not Bobby," he said.

"Then who?"

He looked aside, a non-look seeing nothing. But he did not answer.

"Who then?" she said again.

"Pa," he said.

"Why, how can you say that?"

He shrugged. "Just know." He faced her then, his face

red.

"How can you know?"

He laid down the spoon, let his hand rest on it. He started to cry. She took his head into her apron. He closed his mouth, throttled his sobs. He began to hiccup. His ribs jumped. He looked up at her. "He left us, Ma." He snuffed and wiped his nose on the back of his sleeve. "He never loved me."

"He did," she said. "He loved you, darling, he loved us both."

He shook his head under her hand. "Then why did he leave?"

"Well," she said. It was all she knew to say.

Chapter 66

Another letter from the lawyer sat on the bedside table. Like the others, it was addressed to Mr. Edmund Harrington.

> *Dear Mr. Harrington,*
> *My hope is this letter finds you and your wife and son well.*
> *Since my last meeting with Mrs. Harrington, my client has expressed the need to move forward on a decision regarding the purchase of Mrs. Harrington's claim. Either you will respond within the next week, or my client will retract the offer altogether.*
> *I hope your response comes expeditiously.*
> *Respectfully yours,*
> *Franz Hoffman*
> *Attorney at Law*

Next morning, she returned to the lawyer's office. This time, he remembered her. Her breath came in loud pants as if she had run. "Mrs. Harrington," he said. He reached out his hand to escort her into his office. "Could I get you a glass of water?"

She could not quell her breathing. "No," she said. "I will be all right."

"Mrs. Harrington, are you well?" He seemed softer, less arrogant, now that he stood a chance of getting something

271

from her.

"Yes," she said, "I will be in a moment." He held the chair for her. She took it. She laid her hand on her chest, sat straight.

He sat behind the desk, shuffled a paper from one side of the ink blot to the other. "Well, have you and Mr. Harrington made a decision on the matter we discussed?"

"Yes," she said. Her breath came easier.

"And that is?"

"I will want to sell."

"And your husband agrees with your decision?"

Her heart came to her throat. "That . . ." Out the window, a farmer, in a thick winter coat, head obscured by a woolen cap, drove a team of two horses. She took in a breath that was audible, looked at the attorney. "That," she said again, "is something I will require your help with."

"I cannot force him," he said. "A man must do what he thinks best for himself and his family."

"Finding him," she said.

"You do not know where your husband is?"

"He is gone."

"Gone?"

A cinch pulled around her until she thought she might not be able to breathe. "Yes," she said. The attorney took up a pencil, began swirling it back and forth. "How can we go about finding some answer to this?"

"To what?" the attorney said.

"To whether or not I have the right to sell my own land without my husband."

272

The attorney smiled and the tremendous bulb at his chins pulled up with it. "Without him," he said, "it cannot be sold. We have already discussed this." He flapped his pencil, irritated. He said tiredly, "When did you say you last saw him?"

"I did not say," she said. She swallowed. "Three years ago."

The attorney blinked, his pink chins shook. "And," he said, "do you know what has happened to him?" He made his voice indulgent.

Her shoulders began to cramp, her neck to spasm. "He left in a storm."

"In a storm? Why would he not wait until after the storm passed?"

"He was desperate," she said, "not himself. I believe he was to go to Omaha."

"Two hundred and fifty miles in a storm," the attorney said.

"To the stockyards, to find some way to buy more cattle. He had just lost his herd, you see."

"All?"

"All."

"And he was setting out to get more?"

"As I said, he was not himself, or else he would never have gone. We never saw him again after that day." *God help me.* "He could only have perished."

The attorney gave his head a slow, disbelieving shake. "I see. A declaration of death will require an order of the Court. I am not sure three years has been sufficiently long." He sat back, diddled his pencil. "You will need to make a sincere effort to find him, of course. It will take time."

"The claim was taken in my name," she said, "not my husband's."

"I think we discussed that some time ago," he said. "You have no standing in business without his permission."

"And if I am a widow?"

"By law you are not a widow," he said. "By law your husband is still alive."

"Will your client give us time?"

"I am not sure."

"What will we need to do?"

The attorney set down the pencil, steepled his hands, a gesture that seemed to take on some new respect. "Notification must be made in the jurisdiction in which he lived as well as in the entire region between your farm and Omaha."

"Omaha?"

"You said you believed he was going there."

"I see," she said. She sat back, defeated.

He leaned forward. "Are you sure you want to do this, Mrs. Harrington?"

"Pardon me," she said. "I did not hear you."

The attorney cleared his throat. "Are you sure you want to go through with this?"

She looked up. "Yes."

"Then you will have to elaborate as to how you believe the individual died."

"He was not," she said, "an *individual*. He was my

274

husband."

"Nonetheless," the attorney said, "there must be a preponderance of evidence that the indiv—your husband—is dead. If he is not found after your inquiries, we can petition the Court."

———

The attorney's fees would come to fourteen dollars. Putting an announcement in all the newspapers between Cozad and Omaha would cost another twelve.

She told him she did not have that much money and he countered that the newspapers had to be paid, but that he would take half of his fee, the rest coming due when things either went through or didn't. "I must have something," he said, "for my time."

She gave him nineteen dollars of Edmund's money and held onto the irony that this was Edmund's own money after Ezekiel sold his father's horse and saddle. The announcement ran in newspapers in several towns, including *The Meridian.*

Mrs.   Edmund   Harrington   Seeking Whereabouts of Husband

Mrs. Edmund Harrington of Cozad, Dawson County, Nebraska is seeking the whereabouts of her husband, last seen December 24, 1873 at his farm about ten miles north of said town. If any person has seen or known of Mr. Harrington's whereabouts since the above mentioned date, please notify Mr. Franz E. Hoffman, Attorney at Law, Cozad, Dawson County, Nebraska.

And so began the waiting. The announcement was to run in eighteen papers for a month. Even if Edmund were not found, if there were no response, when they petitioned the Court, Judge Schulz could choose not to sign a warrant of death. The attorney said her chances for the Court to agree to separation would be higher if she were claiming to be abandoned. But death was an end.

The attorney wrote letters asking for information on Edmund Harrington to the government of Nebraska, to St. Joseph's Hospital, and to Fort Omaha Hospital in Omaha. He included Edmund's entire name, Edmund James Carraig Harrington, his date of birth, and the fact he had been born in Bandon, County Cork, Ireland.

———

The river, what there was of the winter trickle, froze over. The days went white. Ice prickled the winds, blew the streets bald, then banked up waist high against buildings. People, those who went out, wore mufflers up to their noses, buried their heads in wool caps, and wrapped themselves in shapeless coats.

Mary could not speed the wait for the Court; she had no power to speed anything. She returned to the attorney's office to ask if any word had come. "Nothing," he said. "I'll tell you the minute I hear." Then he added, "Judge Schulz is known to take his time."

So far, Mr. Hoffman's buyers, whoever they were, were willing to wait. She suspected the buyers lived in Cozad or somewhere in the county. She even began to wonder if the buyer wasn't Mr. Hoffman himself. "Meanwhile," he said, "until the matter of your husband's passing is decided for good, Mr. Harrington is indeed not yet considered deceased."

Chapter 67

It was nearing Christmas. Early on, after Bobby left, Ezekiel had received two letters from him, but none had come since. Ezekiel had not shown her either one. The Family were coming in for the holiday to spend Christmas with the Gatewoods and, hearing it, Ezekiel was chattering again, rattling on about school, complaining about how Mr. Simpson's back hurt and made him ornery, gossiping about some child at school who got the switch from Mr. Young. The change in him made her dizzy. It made her happy.

Three months had inched by since Mary's first meeting with the attorney. The announcement in the various newspapers had expired and the petition had been sent to the Court two months ago. Neither Ezekiel nor Mary had spoken of Edmund again. She did not know if he was aware of the notices she had placed in the papers, but thought he must be; he read everything.

The Cozads stepped down from the midday train three days before Christmas. They ate a light supper: ham, currant jelly, and cheesed bread, before setting out for the Gatewoods' farm. Bobby had grown even taller in the three months away, but a change had come over him; he was somber, his old buoyancy gone. Something had come on him. His face was pale, his hair gone oily and depressed. He barely greeted Ezekiel, who had excused

279

himself from school and had hovered around the hotel like a mosquito. The Family were on their way out of town with nary a nod from Bobby.

———

Mary was in her robe in her kitchen, mending a dress for Mrs. Drew. Christmas was two days passed. For a long time—years now—the possibility that Edmund might return had shrouded her life and the life she offered Ezekiel. She would have thought this would have abated, but it did not. What if he returned with the newspaper in hand? What if the judge declared her a proper widow? What if he didn't? She had done what she had done and felt it had to be lived with, but were someone to ask what she truly wanted she would not have been able to articulate a word, for what she wanted, now, at the core, no one would find acceptable: She wanted her husband out of her life. She could no longer deny his actions the day of the cattle drive, his cruelty to Ezekiel proved it. She did not want to see him again.

She could barely manage sleep, and when it did come, she would wake at the crack of a sound, which she could never identify or remember. She imagined thunder and tried to summon the season of it, the place, when it might have been. She thought if she could remember something held in it, it would explain her, answer her life. But it never revealed either itself or anything else.

As the winter season slowed work in the kitchen, Mary began taking in mending and then one day, Mrs. O'Brien had asked to be measured for a dress. Mary had taken Mrs. O'Brien's measurements and cut a muslin. She would begin on the dress the next day. Mrs. O'Brien had not quibbled about paying Mary what she asked.

She had scrubbed the dining room floor and laid out the fabric for Mrs. O'Brien's dress when Ezekiel stamped in through the door. "Ma, Ma, where are you?"

Her heart jumped to her throat. "Here."

He came around the kitchen door waving a paper sheet. "Bobby's in town. I been working with him on the press. Look."

> *NEW YEAR*
> *GRAND SOIREE*
> *SATURDAY NIGHT*
> *AT THE*
> *EMIGRANT HOTEL*
> *COZAD, DAWSON COUNTY*
> *NEBRASKA*

"Soiree means people and dancing, maybe even music," he said. "We *have* to go."

To Mary, a soiree meant more work in the kitchen.

———

Two days before the grand function, as she was preparing the supper, Mrs. Gatewood made her way into town. She spent a few minutes in her store, then came to the kitchen. "Mary," she said, "I have asked Hilda to come in special Saturday to work for the party." Hilda? Hilda had not worked in the kitchen for a year. "I want you to take the day off for yourself and to attend as a guest."

"Guest?" Mary said.

Mrs. Gatewood smiled, set her hand on Mary' shoulder. "You know," she said, "someone who comes to *enjoy* herself."

"I don't—"

"Yes, you do," Mrs. Gatewood said.

Mary was going to say she had nothing to wear.

Chapter 68

Heat from four dozen bodies, breath from eight dozen lungs, steamed over the windows until someone opened the door and let in the blessing of wind. It had been a lifetime since Mary had been at a party. She sat at the long table with her hands under her. She had once loved socials, had been able to converse, to flirt, to add something to the festivities. She sat, now, nearly mute in a dress of yellow wool she had just spent all night making for herself. Yellow was a color for spring, not for the time of year when winds and sharp snow swept dust that crept through walls. Prune had sent the wool some time ago, and Mary had saved it to fashion a dress for someone who would pay for its sunshine.

Half an hour before the soiree, Ezekiel came home from work at the livery. A blast of rude wind blew in with him. "Ma!" he shouted, his voice high and excited. She had dressed, was in their kitchen at the sink. She had pressed his only shirt, which had no holes in it and had laid it upstairs on his bed. He blew on his fingers and took off his work coat. "I filled the sink," she said, "the water is warm." His hair, his coat, and his pants were crusted with dirt and a scattering of straw. "You are to bathe."

"Ma," he said, more of a surprise than a statement. "You look . . ." He stopped then as if he did not quite know what to say. "Pretty." In all his life, he had only seen

283

her in the dullest of linsey-woolsey.

She felt so odd, now, so out of place at the hotel table, not bringing out platters from the kitchen, not nursing the pain from a burn, not serving but *being* served. Hilda came out with a pan cake and put it on the long sideboard; her face shone with heat and her hair stuck to her forehead. The perfume of oranges floated sweetly by as she laid the cake on the sideboard. She returned to the kitchen, came out with an urn of steaming tea, some honey rolls brought by some of the guests, and warm apple cider with an array of biscuits and cookies. Mary did not know what had transpired between Mrs. Gatewood and Hilda, but apparently Hilda was back in good graces.

The long room filled with people and a din of clattering dishes. When the refreshments were done, the men scooted the table aside and cleared the floor. Mr. Henry drew a wheeze from a violin; Mr. Nikodemski brought out an accordion. Dr. Chase went to the kitchen to get a pot and a spoon to bang on.

Ezekiel stood along the back wall, watching, his eyes shining with what could have been tears. He had never, she knew, seen anything like this night.

Mr. Henry's violin and Mr. Nikodemski's accordion finally came together on a note. And when Dr. Chase caught a steady beat with the spoon and the pot, Sam Atkinson grabbed his wife's hand, and together they came out to the floor, then Mr. and Mrs. Drew. At one side, women clustered in bunches and leaned toward each other and gossiped. Children ran, and played, and crawled under the table. A clutch of twelve- and thirteen-year-old girls blushed and giggled.

The party lifted people, seemed even to lift the building. The old Bobby Cozad attended that night, the loose-smiling Bobby, the cocky, flip-of-his-head Bobby. He went to one of the giggling girls and held out his hand. It set her face afire. She shook her head as if to say no, but the shake had no conviction. He took her hand and led her to the floor. They stood a moment, she as if petrified, he tall, straight, pulling himself to his full height. The girl had probably never danced before. He reached around her, took her hand in his, and held it in the air. He made a swirl that brought her with him and gave her feet no choice but to follow. Mary nearly wept at his grace.

She pulled her shawl over her shoulders and watched Ezekiel standing against one corner, his hands behind himself. There once was a time, in her youth, that she would have known how to be a part of this. She did not belong, now, a woman with no husband, a woman without standing, neither widow nor wife. She gave a little nod to Ezekiel, a signal she was preparing to leave. She started toward the door. "Mrs. Harrington," someone said. She turned, Mr. Schooley approached. They had not spoken since the first day she met him when he had given her a shy, white, jammed-tooth grin and introduced himself. "May I see you home?"

Chapter 69

The evening before the Cozads were to take the train back to Ohio, a knock came at Mary's door. The night was clear, the window letting in a cold rectangle of moon. The stove fire was spent, the coals beginning to cool.

Ezekiel was upstairs in his room, reading some book from another box Prune had sent. Mary was at the treadle. She had measured Mrs. Atkinson for two dresses that needed to be done in the week.

The knock came again, a little louder. Mary set down her sewing, tidied a strand from her hair, and went to the door. Three tall young men stood there holding ice skates over their shoulders by the laces: Bobby, Johnny Cozad, and John R. Gatewood, Traber's brother.

Bobby said, "Mrs. Harrington, is Ezekiel in?"

Mary called up the stairs. "Ezekiel, Bobby's here to see you." Her son's feet thundered from his room.

"Easy," Bobby shouted up, "want to go ice skating?" She could have kissed the boy.

Ezekiel chewed his lip. "Don't have skates."

Bobby held out a pair in front of himself. "Take these," he said. "I brought them for you. My old ones. Too small for my appendages anymore."

Ezekiel ran down half the stairs, then caught himself. It was late, after eight, a school night. "Go ahead," she said, "but not too late."

287

Chapter 70

Had she a century to imagine her reaction to the summons from the attorney's office, she would never have conjured it. It was February. She had finished the breakfast moments ago. The scent of breakfast ham still hung on her clothes. She sat across the desk she had sat at months earlier in the attorney's office, the attorney leaning back in his chair. Even the ugliness under his chin could not distract her now; she felt hollow, barren, hopeless.

The attorney had gained weight, his wattle having grown larger and redder like a red-veined balloon. He handed her some papers. There were two documents, one a death certificate with Edmond's name on it, and another for her to sign over the farm. She signed what he told her to sign and handed her a check for five hundred and fifty dollars. She took the check. She had no capacity at that moment to feel what it signified. She knew who the buyers were: The Anderssons, their old neighbors. She tipped her head back and said, "Ah."

———

She drifted toward the hotel, made her way through the midday meal, then through the preparation and serving of the dinner that evening.

She woke early and in a fog the next morning, heating the fire, fixing Ezekiel's lunch bucket, being carried along on habit. As in a dream, she opened the back door to the

289

hotel. She did not stop to take off her coat, did not pump water for the pot, did not take a skillet down from the rack, or tie on her apron. It was Friday; Mrs. Gatewood would be in early to prepare payroll. Mary knocked on the jamb of the office, and Mrs. Gatewood looked up.

"I am here to quit my job," Mary said.

Mrs. Gatewood took off her spectacles. "Quit?"

"Yes."

"What will you do then, Mary?"

"I don't know," Mary said.

Mrs. Gatewood's face puckered. She squinted, the sort of expression one makes when faced with a problem. "Then shouldn't you stay?" she said. "Isn't this abrupt? After all, I have depended on you." She motioned to a chair beside the desk. "Sit."

Mary sat. She had never been asked to sit before but had only ever been there to stand like a supplicant to ask some question or be given instruction.

"Have you plans?" It was apparent Mrs. Gatewood could see the truth: that Mary had no plans. "You must have plans, you know, Mary."

"Yes," Mary said. Her only plan was to quit; she had nothing beyond that but a ghost's dream of buying the house. "I suppose I can stay until you get someone." Then she realized in leaving it open, Mrs. Gatewood might not get someone for months, years. "A few days, perhaps."

Mrs. Gatewood's mouth pinched up, then let go as if in an instant she had forgotten her problem with Mary. "Hilda has been reminding me she wants work again," she said. "I'll get word to her. If you can stay through today, she should be able to come in tomorrow." Mrs. Gatewood rose and left the room. Mary heard her ask someone to go to Hilda's house and tell her to be at work tomorrow. Mary picked at hangnails on her ruined hands. *Is this it? Is this all?* She stood and went to the kitchen.

After supper, Mary handed over the job and a sheaf of her own recipes to Mrs. Gatewood and said good-bye.

She wandered past the stove one last time, past the pots drying, past the rack of knives, past all the familiars. The kitchen tipped. Everything that had been solid and predictable shifted. She stepped out through the door but could not bring herself to close it behind her. Frozen rain cut at her head, and mud sucked her shoes, weighted the hem of her skirt. Her hem caught on her toe; she did not think to hold it up. It caught again, ripped, and she fell to her knees. She laid her hand in the muck. The ground retreated and spun. She did not think to cover herself. She turned as if to go back in, as if returning to the mindless exhausting kitchen might make her whole. She managed a step toward the house, but had no one to tell her what came next.

———

She grew aware of time passing by the sounds and changing light. The dark growing light, the light losing out to dark, the house quiet but for small noises coming sometimes from Ezekiel's room, sometimes from downstairs. She did not get up but once, and then only to use the pot and fall back into her bed. She would learn that Ezekiel brought her tea. She would learn that, for

291

three days, he had brought her some of Hilda's thin soup from the hotel.

———

On the fourth day, her ears pinged and her head rang. She thrust back the covers and pulled herself up and sat dangling her legs. It was dark, a rooster crowing in the distance. The door was closed to Ezekiel's room. She dropped her face onto her hands. Her hair flopped forward, a rag of grease. She stank. She knew she had been in bed for days, remembered Ezekiel's nicks and shuffles as he came and went.

She was required to be nowhere. She had no idea how to feel. She breathed faster, as if fast breaths would bring answers. So far in her life she had failed; she had made an inept mother, had not been able to hold onto a marriage, or to bear more children as a woman should. She had shown her son little of life but clawing to survive, her insufficiency had carved him unfairly into a little man in a boy's knickers. What little boyhood he had came not from her, but from the generosity of another boy: Bobby Cozad.

Choice was laid on her now and it left her naked. So long, she had been suspended by the need to survive. She was dropped, now, into a free-fall.

She rose. She bothered with the small things, starting a fire, heating porridge, going out to the coop, shoving her cold hand under the hens, plucking out eggs. The hens complained. She spread grain, filled a bucket for the goat.

She greased a skillet. She cracked the eggs, slipped them, still warm, into a bowl. She could count her choices on two fingers: Move her and Ezekiel to Philadelphia to be with Prune and Totten, or return to her family in Ireland; either would put her comfortably into others' hands.

She heard Ezekiel dressing upstairs. The fire popped, the pot began to bubble for the porridge. She knotted her hair back and tied her apron around her nightgown and coat. She saw herself in the mirror: pale, her hair stuck to her face where she had slept on it. Rumpled, oily, dressed as she was, she could have been crazy Mrs. McPhearson, a toothless old woman who always wore the same shapeless coat, not unlike the one Mary wore now. Mary had a new understanding of Mrs. McPhearson, who often escaped the house where she lived with her daughter and trudged to the train depot to wait for the train. No one ever knew whom she waited for, but when the train came, she jumped and screamed until her daughter and son-in-law came to take her back to the house.

Mary turned when she heard Ezekiel coming down, drawn by the aroma of her cooking. He blinked when he saw her. She scrambled the eggs, put them on a plate, thumped porridge into a bowl. He sat, his eyes red from sleep. Seeing him there, small, vulnerable, shy, lonely, gifted with one sole friend, she knew her answer. "Good morning, dear," she said.

The next morning, she purchased the Bowers' house for two hundred and fifteen dollars. Mrs. Gatewood was happy to sell.

Chapter 71

Cozad February 1877

Dearest Prune,

I received your wonderful goods and your even more wonderful letter. I know I have been remiss in writing you. You see, I have been so taken with my own troubles I have forgotten you may have them as well. I do hope the boys and Totten are over their last sniffles and that you escaped the misery.

I have news, but will get to that in a moment. Before I do, tell Totten that long ago I did receive his letter with the news of Mother's trunk held in Customs. I have read it again and again and have imagined Grandmother's wonderful linens and her fine handwork. Until today, I could not make myself respond to his inquiry.

Oh, Prune, I am such a coward. My cowardice has kept me from responding. The truth now, you will have.

Dearest, I have been less than forthright in writing you the measure of our lives. I regret this with all my heart. It is time for me to "poot op," as Mother used to say and here it is, I will put up. It is time for me to tell the truth, dearest.

My news is not good. It has been a long time since we last saw Edmund. I fear for him every moment. He went out one day three years ago and never returned. It happened not long after an awful freeze that took his entire herd. Not one of his precious cows was spared. I believe he was leaving to find work, though he was so discouraged by then, I am not sure. It was not like him to leave and not return.

For three months, Ezekiel and I waited at the farm, and when we had no more food to eat or fuel to burn, I packed the two of us into the wagon with the hens and the goat and came to the nearest town, Cozad. I fear now that I made a mistake in coming here, and that it might have been best if we had landed in some other place. But for one family who seems to have unlimited resources, this town is struggling. A fire, and bugs, drought, and late freezes have riddled it all the time we have been here. Some new families seem to be moving in, but many have given up and gone back where they came from.

I know you will wonder how we are making it, but we are. Though Ezekiel has had to grow up far too fast, because of your wonderful books and letters and help from the mother-in-law of the town's founder, we have been able to hold on.

Ezekiel has begun to grow. He is still somewhat small for his age but is strong, a wide-shouldered rattle of bones and muscle. I am so proud of him. He excels in school, is growing to be a solitary and serious boy. The tiny laughs he once erupted in as a baby have been swept away.

But by heaven's graces, a new boy came into Ezekiel's life. He is the son of the town's founder. I believe I wrote of this boy some time ago. The boy has taken Ezekiel under his wing. He is a wonderful boy, three years older than Ezekiel and, though he laughs and makes light, I see a sadness in him as his father is mean-spirited and stern. The boy makes Ezekiel laugh as I had not heard him laugh for so long. It is for this friendship between the boys

296

that I have decided to stay here. I am able to manage it because I managed to sell the farm claim taken in my name and have bought a house in town. I will have a few resources to keep us until I am settled. I feel great pressure to rush to make my own way, now, as we have counted on others' generosity already too long.

Writing you gives me courage, darling. I feel you here with me as I write. Thank you again, my heart.

I am including the letter Totten sent for release of Mother's things. I have signed it as Edmund. I know it is another untruth, but as he is not here to do it, we will have to make do with my scratches, which I hope will suffice.

Please forgive me that I did not tell you of all my travails earlier. I am such a coward. Perhaps I will one day grow to be like my big sister who is courageous, unselfish, and loving.

My love to Totten and my wonderful nephews. And most of all, my love to my sister.

Sissie

Chapter 72

It was warm, the first good weather of the year. The river had risen and a week ago had taken out nearly all of the bridge the men had worked on for months. It was the second washout; Mary thought Mr. Cozad might decide to give up on it, but he had already ordered "the sons a bitches" to build again and make it right.

The weather would not last, but the flare of light and the squeals of the incoming birds were bringing people out to wander and to catch the freshening air. Mary went out too, stood on the tiny stoop that was now hers. A breeze shifted the hem of her skirt and settled on her the lemon scent of bergamot. And she could allow that, finally, if just for the moment on this promising day, someone might stroll by and recognize her as one who might one day belong.

———

Business at the stores picked up. Storekeepers washed down their windows, put in boardwalks, dusted and rearranged tired displays. She had never so much appreciated what she had learned during the time she worked for Mrs. Gatewood in the hotel. Everything Mrs. Gatewood did, every decision, every purchase was to bait customers to conduct business and bring in money. But still, how did one go about making a successful business? It was clear not one thing alone made it succeed, but a stew of many things went into it: the way a coat of whitewash set an enterprise apart, the manner in which a sign seemed to pull the eye. Everything about Mrs. Gatewood's Bee Hive beckoned: the building slathered in blinding whitewash, lamps lit in the windows, the clutter of hoes, shovels, flowers in pots, benches, even the sign saying *Shovels and Crocks Half Off*. Every decision was made in service of business, the Fourth of July celebrations, the broadsides, even the high-priced Sunday suppers.

———

She had not told Ezekiel she had quit her job, nor had she told him she had bought the house. The house was a mess. She took a dust rag to the front floor and coughed as she laid out all the goods from Prune to see what there was; she thought there was enough for ten dresses. She began to sort what she could save of their old clothes. She washed Ezekiel's work clothes, his outgrown coat, her old linsey dresses, and she tore into strips what was still good. The only bits worth keeping were the allowances for the seams and the backs of bodices. She piled the strips on the table, intending to braid them into rugs.

The house was filled with the dark signs of neglect; the floors were splintered, the corners coddled in lint, dust powdered everything, it gritted the baseboards and the picture moldings, the trim over the windows and door. Even the cobwebs were thick with it. The windows were smeared with smoke from the stove, the sills filled with the bodies of dead flies she had ceased to notice. Against dust, she tied a rag around her mouth and took to everything with broom and duster, and vinegar and soap.

She tried to imagine Ezekiel's response when she told him she had sold the farm. Would he be sad and need her consolation? Would the sale answer some questions for him? Complete something in him? When she did, in all her imaginings she had not come up with his reply. "How much?" he said. When she told him five hundred and fifty dollars, he said, "I think you did well."

———

In the evenings, after they had eaten and Ezekiel had gone up to his room, she began making lists: a pair of shoes for herself, two for Ezekiel, threads, thimbles, embroidery floss, hoops, hooks, baskets for displays. From Mr. Hamilton's carpentry shop, she ordered a dining table to be built and six chairs, and she made an appointment for him to repair the roof.

She had never realized how much work came with spending money. To spend it, things needed to be thought up, to be bought, and they needed to be unpacked and cared for and arranged when they came.

Daily, things changed; chairs moved; the table scooted to one side then another. Every day, as he let himself in through the door, Ezekiel had to step around a confusion of boxes of scraps and goods. The scent of vinegar filled every room.

She ordered wallpaper with designs of roses and ivy. She sent for a mannequin form she could configure in shapes to fit garments for any size. She drew plans for a long case of wood and glass and took the plan to Mr. Hamilton's to have the case built. In the evenings, Ezekiel sat with her as she laid out duties she needed him to do after school: cut wood into lengths for shelves and attach them to the parlor walls with iron brackets she bought at the Bee Hive. Together, they papered the walls in their ivies and roses. Ezekiel hammered up the shelves, which she began filling with new goods, and the fabrics she had accumulated for so long.

Mr. Hamilton and a helper delivered the cabinet of oak and glass; she had them set it where light hit it best. As the things she ordered came in, she arranged them: dress lengths, scissors, ribbons, pincushions, and threads. She and Ezekiel set up the treadle by the light of the back window. In the front window, she arranged baskets filled with rolls of cotton goods in blazes of blues and yellows and greens.

Finally, on a Saturday morning, she and Ezekiel sat together at the center table where she displayed her issues of *Woman's Journal* and *Godey's*. And together they hand-lettered a sign for the front window:

> *Fine Dry Goods*
> *New Shipments*
> *Silks, Cottons, Wools*
> *Expert tailoring*
> *Women's Latest Paris Fashions*
>
> *Mrs. Edmund Harrington, Proprietor*

———

A letter came from Prune:

23 March 1877 Phla

Oh Sissie, Oh Sissie. I am so sorry for the loss of your Edmund. It must have come as an awful shock and you must miss him so.

I order you to get on the next train. You are not to stay in that miserable place another minute. This is worse than either Totten or I feared. You have stayed in misery too long. I must see you immediately. No excuses.

So, you say my sweet nephew has found a friend. This is no reason to stay one day longer in that miserable place. Boys find friends everywhere in the city. Do you think Philadelphia has no boys? There are boys everywhere just waiting to make friends with Ezekiel.

Do you hear me shaking a finger? You cannot remain in that awful place one more minute, you hear!!!

Oh the joy to have you here. We will add a cottage in the backyard. We have acres. You will have your own home altogether. Oh, I ramble on so in my joy to see you again. Just knowing I will see you soon tosses my loneliness out the window. I will have another boy to spoil. I will have you to fatten just like your sister.

Oh, Sissie, write me immediately, telling me when I can expect you.

Your blissful sister,

Prune

Chapter 73

The world turned hot and clinging. Thunder pounded, rain made muck of the streets knee-high. It filled boots and weighted down women's hems. The horizon was a dull gray smear, its liquid heat took one's breath.

It looked as if the country might escape the hoppers this year, but the mosquitoes were making up for them. The garden was thriving and beginning to take over the back yard. School had been out more than a month, and Ezekiel tended the garden by himself, now, all but a tiny section of gladiolas and mums Mary saw to. He took pride in it, setting out a perfectionist's neat rows of lettuces, chards, beets, and cucumbers, a straight new fence, and taut strings for the beans.

In the house, Mary had transformed the parlor and the den into a mess of colors, draped a purple length over a chair and gathered a yellow beside it. She laid folded pieces on the tables, fitted the chairs with bright-colored cushions. Under the glass of her new counter she put small things: silver combs and hairbrushes, crystal bottles for perfume, soft kid gloves, arrangements of scissors with fancy handles, a selection of sterling baby cups, sachets, embroidered handkerchiefs of fine Irish linen, fancy writing pens, painted tins filled with decorated stationery. Every corner of the downstairs was being turned over to industry, the center table covered with baskets of yarns and threads and journals.

The amount of money she was spending made her gasp. She rose each day with a sour and anxious stomach. After all this, would she be able to make a living of it?

Ezekiel's only sanctuary from the fuss was his room, a place filled floor to chair rail with pyramids of books, his desk arranged with papers, squared to the edge, a trough for his pencils and pens, and an inkwell he kept filled. The Cozads were in town and she knew he was spending time with Bobby. It surprised her that she missed the hotel's buzz, the gossip, but she particularly missed the intimacy of Mrs. Cozad and the boys at their studies and she longed for a good, long tea with Fiona.

By evening, the last of the storms blew over. The air cleared, and the house felt dry. She and Ezekiel had eaten their dinner standing at the counter, as the table was full of baskets and goods. They had had a salad from the garden, milk from the goat, eggs she had boiled that morning, and corncakes left from the night before. When they were done with the meal, Ezekiel pumped water into buckets, poured some to wash up the dishes, and took some upstairs for the washbowls and commodes in their rooms.

He was a wonderful boy, but he had grown so independent, so used to going his own way; at times, he disappeared without saying a word. Sometimes, she knew he was gone only by the whap of the screen door. He continued to bring home his pay from the livery, and now from odd jobs he found hauling. At the end of the day, when she asked where he had been, he would say,

"Around." She asked what he did with all his time and he said, "This and that." How had she produced a boy so secretive, driven, hard-headed, and able?

An afternoon breeze rippled the curtain in. She sat at the writing desk in her room. There came a knock at the door. *A knock?* Wouldn't a customer come in?

She laid down her pen, stood and went to the door. Practically before she had the door open, Fiona and her one year old, and her new baby rushed her and consumed her in an embrace.

The pot whistled. The baby cried until Fiona suckled. The child, bless her heart, lay on the floor among the fabrics and slept. Mary poured tea and they talked. It was bliss.

————

It had been over a month since Prune's last letter. She broke open a tin of stationery for herself from those she had ordered to put out for sale.

> *Cozad, July*
> *Dearest Prune,*
> *Your last letter is lying beside me on my desk. I feel the wonder of your love and your care rising up from it. I have waited to answer because I had to put my mind to all that is in it, and the temptation to come to your warm arms. The comfort of knowing Ezekiel and I have someone wanting us so lifts me.*
> *My dear, you would be proud. Since your letter, your little sister has set herself up to be a businesswoman. I am putting the treadle sewing machine you gave me to good use*

to open a dressmaking business. You cannot imagine how hopeful and thrilling this is.

I have hesitated to answer your lovely letter, waiting for guidance, divine or otherwise, to shout to me what I must do. Ezekiel's love for his friend and the boy's love for Ezekiel have convinced me I cannot uproot him. The boy makes him laugh as I, or anyone else, has never been able to. Ezekiel deserves this happiness and, at least for the moment, I have the resources to allow him to have it. I cannot remove him from the one friend he has in the world.

So, my dearest, I sit among my shelves of calicoes and hope and I command you to send me your best thoughts and wishes that my endeavor will pay, and that one day I don't have to show up at your doorstep, hat in hand.

I love you so,

Sissie

Chapter 74

The night turned fresh, the remaining trace of daylight a ripple of orange and purple. The moon was almost full; by this time tomorrow night, it would be. Mary looked up from her sewing and squinted at the window. Families had escaped the heat of their houses, the women out fanning themselves, the children running circles, men smoking pipes. A dog yipped. The houses would cool but not for some time.

Her store had been open for business two weeks. She had installed a bell over the front door that had yet to ring. All the fuss, all the stuff—the bell, the sign, the pincushions, pins, the case of ribbons and threads, the baskets of dry goods—and all the effort and expense came down on her now. No one but Ezekiel and she had passed through the door since Mr. Hamilton and his carpenter's helper had brought in the cabinet and counter. She had never been one to trust her own ability and, so far, opening the store was proving her right. How presumptuous she had been to think anyone would come to buy and do business with her. What folly to think she could work anything out.

She was piecing scraps for a rug to put in the sitting room. It was make-do work, an illusion of some worthwhile activity. Ezekiel came down the stairs, passed by her on the way to the door. "Are you going out *now*?"

she said. She put her hand against a soreness on the small of her back. "It's almost dark."

"Just down to the river," he said.

————

She spent the early morning weeding the front walk and watering the nasturtiums and geraniums. Ezekiel was out working. He still had the job with Mr. Simpson but had given up the irregular jobs with Mrs. Gatewood to take up hauling, where he thought he could make more money. He borrowed a wagon from Mr. Simpson, who reduced his pay.

He had scratched "Ma" on the old stationery tin, and each day put the coins and IOUs he brought home in it. He was not quite eleven years old, yet he seemed more certain, more able and hardworking than most men. *Will his future have nothing more than this drudge and labor in it? What will become of him?* She had to see he had more than this.

A bare breeze stirred the curtains. She was wearing the only dress she had that was decent for guests, the yellow. She had fussed with the things in the parlor, arranging the baskets again as if she had not arranged them nearly every day, and was rifling the pages of a *Godey's*. The magazine's fancy designs always took her somewhere else.

The front bell dinged. The surprise made her jump. She rose, patted her skirt, and went out to the parlor. Mrs. O'Roark was standing in the doorway, squinting from the bright afternoon. "Mrs. O'Roark," Mary said, "come in."

"I heard you have set up to dressmaking," Mrs. O'Roark said.

"I have."

The woman's eyes flew around the room. Mary turned and saw things through her eyes: everything in its place, dustless, scrubbed, giving off the sense that Mary was trying too hard. Her heart cramped. The house did not welcome, did not beckon one to come in. "May I help you?"

Mrs. O'Roark took a deep breath. "I don't know." She was a straight woman, broad across the shoulders and strong. She wore a clean plain dress that had a tiny lace along the bodice. The delicacy of the lace seemed intended to give her manly build a feminine aspect, but it only emphasized a solidity that was not feminine at all. Mrs. O'Roark went to the magazines arranged on the table.

Mary said. "Were you wanting anything in particular?"

"Wanting and needing are two different things." And she laughed. "Aren't they?"

Mary felt something lift. She chuckled. "I suppose," she said. "Yes."

Mrs. O'Roark leaned over the display case, her eye on a tin of pins. The tin was small, with painted birds in blues and greens, and it was lovely. "Would you like me to take something out of the case?" Mary said.

"I'm just here to see what you have," Mrs. O'Roark said.

"I was just having tea," Mary said. "Would you join me?"

Mrs. O'Roark's hand lingered on the glass. "Why, yes," she said. "That sounds wonderful."

Mary retrieved her best cup from the cupboard, one

with a saucer that matched, and a small plate. She set three biscuits she had made that morning on the plate. She put jam in a cup and set a knife beside it. She placed them on the small, round table, which held a recent issue of the *Godey's*. The tea steamed in the light and made a lazy sort of ballet.

They sat together sipping and nibbling the biscuits and talking about things in town. Mrs. O'Roark's shoulders softened as she buttered another of the biscuits. It was as if Mary were back in a time in her youth when her mother's friends came to the house in the quiet while their husbands were at work, and their older children were cooped safely out of trouble in a classroom. The women sipped tea just like this and they gossiped and laughed and tossed off their struggles for a moment.

By the time Mrs. O'Roark left that day, Mary had measured her for a dress of blue-flowered calico and Mrs. O'Roark had asked Mary to set aside the tin with the pins until she returned for her fitting.

Mrs. O'Roark returned three days later for the fitting. She brought Mrs. Atkinson and Mrs. Spencer with her. After a tour of the cases and some small talk over the goods on Mary's shelves, Mary served tea and the two women sat sipping, nibbling biscuits, and thumbing through the *Harper's* and *Godey's* while Mrs. O'Roark stepped behind the sitting room wall to put on the dress.

Mary had narrowed the cut of the shoulders just a bit and had pleated the bodice in a way that gave the dress a softness that tiny ruffles could not. She had not discussed these amendments with Mrs. O'Roark but would change and remove them if she objected.

Mrs. Spencer and Mrs. Atkinson quietly fingered through the magazines and Mary stood by, listening to the rustle of fabric, wringing her hands as Mrs. O'Roark put on the dress. When Mrs. O'Roark came out, Mrs. Atkinson blew a little breath. "Why, look at *you*," she said. Mrs. O'Roark held up the skirt, went to the mirror. She turned side to side and her face pinkened.

Mary smoothed the shoulder, patted the pleating. "I can remove the pleats if you want."

"Oh, not on your life," Mrs. O'Roark said.

Mrs. Atkinson said, "I don't think I ever saw a calico look so elegant."

By the time the women left, Mrs. Atkinson had made an appointment to be measured for a muslin pattern and had ordered two dresses for herself.

Chapter 75

Mary drew columns in a book after the manner she had seen Mrs. Gatewood do. She had been dressmaking eight months now and was aware of the essentials of business: that one must enter more in the columns denoting income than those marked expenses. At first, the expenses won out heavily. But she knew to be enticed, a customer required choice, and choice meant cost, which was not satisfied until the choice was sold. Mary had packed the parlor with dress lengths and dry goods until there was space for no more. What money she had left from the farm sale was shrinking, not by pennies but by tens of dollars a month.

As customers came in, they brought the news. Town was continuing to build. Though the relentless work slowed in the worst of the cold, it began again as soon as the weather broke and Cozad was once again slammed with activity. People were finally pouring into the area faster than they moved out. That same spring, just five years after Cozad had mortered the first brick and pounded the first nail, it had a depot, a new post office, a new livery, a dental office, two doctors, a mill, a haypress, granary, mercantile, shoe shop, saddlery, a new hardware store, a farm implement business, and more than a half dozen streets with names and houses on them. The one enterprise Cozad did not have, and never would, was a saloon. Mr. Cozad forbade drinking.

After last spring's washout, the third in three years, men had made it through rebuilding about a quarter of a new bridge. Mr. Cozad had made another design with broader footings and an upstream edge to be built of brick. Behind his back, men said it would wash out just like the others, but they did not refuse to work on it for pay. Nearly half the men in Cozad continued to be on Mr. Cozad's payroll. When money ran short, he continued to leave town and come back with more.

Kilns sent up smoke all day and all night. Some evenings, when businesses all closed for the day, Mary wandered the town as she had so long ago searching for Edmund. She no longer searched, but carried the concern he might show again; she did not know what she would do if he did.

Town changed almost every day: new houses, a business closed, another taking its place. Bricks sat everywhere there was a business to be built. Unfired greens were stacked in the brickyard in blocks the size of rooms, waiting to be fired. A dirt track, smooth and dusty, carried from the yard to Meridian Street, where men were laying in four new buildings. There would be an opera. There would be a bank, maybe two. And, as if the community finally were solid enough for the family, the Cozads were moving their lives to town for good.

Chapter 76

By late fall, the waves of cranes, and geese, and ducks had abandoned the river and had taken their noise and fracas with them. But for the claps of the thunder and the rips of lightning, it was the beginning of the river's quiet season, left to the company of a few coots and teal. In the clear nights, the moon shimmered and often the winds died and left the river clean and flat as a platter. All that was left of the bridge was a fragment of the shadows of three footings that had survived the last washout.

In the two years since Mary had opened her business, she had learned two solid things: a woman, no matter how practical, fancied something fancy; and a woman would come to a place where she could shrug off the tedium of her day, even for a quarter hour, and, in such a setting, was apt to part with a dime or two.

Most afternoons, women came in in twos and threes, each carrying a basket with embroidery, or pieces of goods intended to be sewn together for quilts. Some of the scraps and clippings were from dresses and shirts Mary had made for them. The bell would ring and if Mary were working in the back room, someone would yoohoo and say it's just Abigail and Bernice, or Mrs. Schultz, and they would take themselves and their baskets to the dining table and pour themselves tea from the pot. And Mary would pull up a chair for herself and sit working on a hem, or finishing a seam. Sometimes Fiona came with the baby and gave Mary a hug and sat nursing her third baby until it fussed and Mary would close her eyes and know this, a roomful of laughs and gossip and naughtiness, was the color she had always wanted for her life. She only wished Prune were here.

Last year, Mary had added a room to the back of the house and moved all her mess—the treadle, the cutting table, the measuring tapes, scissors, spools of thread and scraps—into the new room and out of customers' sight. The front windows and every corner of the parlor were crammed with bolts of goods. When things were slow, she hung three sample dresses she sewed from designs she found in *Godey's*, each with gloves to match and bags she beaded at night. She sewed each with ample seams she could alter, if needed. The samples sold nearly as fast as she made them. Her customers always surveyed the shelves before going to the sitting room for tea and sweets.

She had painted the sitting room the soft color of the blush on a peach. She would have liked silk for the curtains but did not want to spend for it, so made them of printed cotton. The room sported a new display case, with an assortment of bonnets and hats and ribbons, and a long mirror for the women to model themselves in. She bought a small, round table with four chairs, and kept her fashion magazines spread on it with baskets of ribbons, dainties and a porcelain tea service with bone china cups. She took out her own subscriptions to *Godey's*, *The Ladies' Companion and Literary Expositor*, *Peterson's Magazine*, and

Harper's. She baked sweets and confections every day and kept them in the cupboard ready whenever the bell began to ding. She sometimes envied the women who could afford the dresses she fashioned and wished she herself could come into such a shop to laugh and be served tea and biscuits and fitted so intimately.

At night, before bed, she did her books. At the end of each month, now, her profits grew and she began sending half her earnings to Totten for him to manage. Even with things moving along as they were, she could never muster much of a yen for food; her nights often went sleepless, and every morning she filled her handkerchiefs with her cough. And each time, when the last dress had been sewn and an order for another had not yet come in, she feared she would never have another.

Months ago, Ezekiel turned twelve years old. He had grown and changed so much she was not sure his father would recognize him. She still searched for Edmund, but without the sense of a reason she might have been able to define. A lean rider showed one day. He sat easy as a dancer in the saddle. She watched as he rode by and her eyes followed him until he turned out of sight. What would she do if she ever saw Edmund again? She did not know.

One day, Ezekiel would be old enough for college. She would send him away for a proper education and away from the chance he might ever encounter his father again. Already, he was arguing against leaving and had begun to badger to stay in Cozad the rest of his life. She told him he could live wherever he wanted, *after* he was finished

319

with his education, that she would see to it he would be an educated man like her nephews in Philadelphia. This idea carried her and gave her strength.

They no longer spoke of Edmund, though time had not driven away the sense of his hovering over their lives.

Chapter 77

Bills, correspondence, invoices for completed dresses littered her desk. The door opened. The bell rang, and there came a footfall, the rustle of skirts, someone saying, "Mary?" The voice was rich and lilting. The bell dinged again as the door closed.

She shut the ledger and laid down her pen. Though the fall nights were cool, the day had been gentle and warm. She had cracked open the workroom windows, which overlooked the garden, and the view of it and the air seemed to quell her coughs a bit and make breathing come easier. But for squashes, the garden had been plucked clean. The squashes' leaves had gone gray as the plants threw themselves into producing fruit. Chrysanthemums were the only brightness in the patch, now, and she was grateful for them.

She rose and shook out her skirt. It had been a good year; Dawson County had been spared the bugs again, and, after months of humid thunder and rain, farmers finally were bringing in abundant crops. Silos were full, bins of beets and stacks of hay stood in the fields, and more hay to be shipped lay along the railroad siding. Mary's garden had yielded so much she had sold some to serve in the hotel kitchen. Some days, when she was cooped in the house bent over needlework and the treadle, she longed to go out and work the garden and to come back into the house with a satisfaction of blisters.

"Mary?" the voice called again.

She shrugged the tension from her shoulders. The room seemed to gain some sort of strength with Mrs. Gatewood in it. It was the first time the old woman had come to her store. Until that moment, Mary did not realize how much she had wanted this. Mrs. Gatewood did not gawp, as most women did, but simply took herself to the chair in the corner and sat. She seemed much older, her face more sagged, her breath coming in wheezes. She appeared tired. "So this is my competition," she said. And she laughed, not in sarcasm but in fun. "Ah, Mary, I find myself needing something to wear."

Mary wrung her hands, feared she would become tongue-tied, but managed, "Well, you came to the right place."

Mrs. Gatewood chuckled. She said she wanted something elegant and it had to be done quickly. She and Mr. Gatewood and the Cozads had received invitations only that day for a meeting with some foreign dignitary in Virginia. The event required gowns for the ladies and tailcoats for the men.

"I don't do tailcoats," Mary said.

"It's a gown I came for."

A length of dark green silk had sat on Mary's shelf for nearly a year. It was beautiful. Often women would ask for her to bring it out and would gently run their hands over its sheen, but seeing the price, none had asked for anything made of it. Mary pulled it down, showed it. Mrs. Gatewood said she wanted it and did not ask the cost.

And as they talked—almost as equals—Mary measured her for the dress. Mrs. Gatewood did not quibble at Mary's price.

———

The days were shortening, the air growing crisp, women putting up preserves at home, farmers carting the last of their grains to the trains and hauling in near-grown calves and pigs they had fed through the spring and summer to the stockyard. The animals, not cruelly herded as were the longhorns, would be shipped to markets in Omaha and Denver.

Mary had cooked a roast and potatoes. They would have beets and yams and some late tomatoes. She shouted up the stairs, calling Ezekiel to supper. A good part of the afternoon, he had been up there in his room.

He dragged himself down the stairs now, sat at his place at the table, and did not say a word. Silence had once been typical of him, but over the last couple of years, he had shed it for quick talk and chatter about what Bobby was up to. She knew in great detail about the printing of posters for Mr. Cozad, and even more intimately how Bobby was drawing cartoons for a humorous sheet he was calling *The Runty Papers.* Ezekiel would yammer on about stories they published in *The Meridian,* about the work on the bridge, the population of Dawson County, which would soon be two thousand, how Mr. Cozad was planning for a real schoolhouse, that some Ute Indians killed an agent named Nathaniel Meeker and had captured his wife and daughter, about a fire in Deadwood, South Dakota, that had left two thousand people homeless,

Union Pacific railroad was bribing congressmen and falling into such deep financial trouble it was selling some of its assets in order to stay in business. He seemed to know everything, yet why had he grown so quiet again?

She sat with him. "Tell me what you did today," she said. It had been so long since she had had to draw him out, it felt awkward now.

He shrugged, lifted a spoon of potato.

"Anything new to tell?"

He spooned the lump into his mouth, gave it a spiritless chew.

"Did something happen?"

He shook his head.

"How was school today?"

He looked at her then. He squeezed his eyes narrow. "Ma," he said, "they're coming our way."

"Who is coming our way?"

"Drovers."

"How do you know that?"

"It came over the telegraph." His voice was high and frightened. "Traber got it. They think it's Print Olive's men."

"Well," she said, "you stay out of harm's way."

He set his spoon beside his bowl. It was a quiet gesture, soundless, as if he wanted no one to hear. "Ma." His voice was low, nearly a whisper. "I know he's not dead."

"Who?"

"Him." He would not look at her. "I saw him when the cows came through that day."

"You were not in town that day," she said. "You were

out hunting."

He kept his eyes on his spoon. "The drovers brought the cows out by where I was. He knew it was me." His nose started to run. "He came up and he stopped his horse right in front of me and he spit on the ground and then he left." He began sobbing. "What happens," he hiccoughed, "if . . ." He broke down and could not continue.

She put a finger under his chin to lift it. He resisted. She laid her hand on his arm. "Ezekiel, he is no longer with us. He is no longer ours. Whoever we saw that day was not your pa. That pa died a long time ago."

"You saw him, too?"

"I saw someone who looked like your pa."

"Why does he hate me?"

Mary took his head against her. She was crying, too. She could only manage to get out, "Psssss, psssss."

When the new *Meridian* came out, it ran the story of how the men of town diverted the cattle drive with rifles and guns, forcing the animals to hold to the south side of the river.

Chapter 78

For two years, the hotel had lorded over Meridian Street. It was a rich thing, impressive and solid, with pitched roofs, fresh paint on its sills, and new screens in the doors. After making it their temporary quarters, The Family were moving to a large house not far from Mary's. Two weeks after they moved into the house, a fire burned it.

The community speculated who had set the fire, some maintained it was a vagrant, others swore it was the same Plum Creek criminals who burned town before. But, just as with the fire three years earlier, no one really knew. Three years ago, Mr. Cozad had raged it was "damned crooks" from Plum Creek. This time he leveled his fury at Mr. Mosher, who had written a column in his *The Hundredth Meridian* accusing Mr. Cozad of being a crook and a thief when he drove off free-roaming cattle from lands Cozad owned. His columns insisted that the open prairie belonged to everyone.

Mr. Cozad screamed he would have Mosher's hide and that he was going to sue one farmer, Alfred Pearson, who was particularly well-liked and who was grazing some animals on Mr. Cozad's land. A day later, Mr. Cozad moved his family to the safety of Denver.

With Mr. Cozad away, people grew louder and more outspoken in their hate for him. In her private moments, hemming, trimming, laying out a pattern, Mary was given to the thought that Mr. Cozad deserved every cruel censure. But with Bobby gone to Denver, Ezekiel grew despondent.

Then, over a few weeks, Bobby began returning to town often, staying on his grandparents' farm. Ezekiel's spirit lifted.

Every Friday evening, Mary and Ezekiel began taking supper in the hotel. It had been a hard spring. The river had flooded, had risen so high as to tip over a pile driver. It had taken out what was left of the bridge and threatened the railroad track and the haypress before the waters subsided.

When he was in town, Mr. Cozad picked fights. Sometimes the fights turned physical; all were loud and cruel. Everyone, even the men closest to him, could become his target. He was ruthless in his anger, softening only when he and Sam Schooley talked together, low and in a corner of the dining room while waiting for the meal to be served. His anger spared no one but his wife and his mother-in-law; even Sam could fall victim to it at times. This Mary mostly heard from the women coming into her shop; she was glad to be spared more than gossip.

By summer, Mrs. Gatewood had finally set her foot down and told her son-in-law she was tired and he could no longer count on her to run everything. She recruited Mr. and Mrs. Joseph Riggs to manage the hotel. Several times, in the worst heat of the evenings, Mary sat at the dining room table watching the Riggses as they rushed about.

Without her to tend and order it, the hotel changed from Mrs. Gatewood's speak-her-mind coziness to something stiffer and withheld. The air seemed thick, and the Riggses trod silently, Mrs. Riggs' nervous hands clasped and knuckles white. They seemed to be breaking down under the pressure of learning the work Mrs. Gatewood had managed so well for so long. Mr. Cozad often shouted that the food was "not fit for swine" and would sweep his plate onto the floor. Sam Schooley had been there one night to experience it. "Mr. Cozad," he said, his voice low, as if he wanted no one but Mr. Cozad to hear. Mr. Cozad screwed his hawk's face toward Sam and stared as if he were emerging from some awful dream. He threw his napkin over his plate and said, "Sam, I can't do everything." He got up, then, and left the kitchen girls cowering at the door, and rendering those at the table silent.

Within days, Mr. Cozad had thrown out the Riggses, and Mrs. Gatewood was back reluctantly managing the hotel. The Cozad family were making plans to move back to town and live in the hotel, once again, until a new house could be built, of brick this time.

Chapter 79

If one could believe in stability, it was a time to be lured into believing in it. Mary's business was earning considerably more than it cost to run it. Ezekiel was growing. He had turned thirteen seven months ago in May. Though he was strong, he was still small. If his parents' blood played any part, he would never become tall or large. The Cozad boys were near grown; Bobby had turned sixteen that summer, and Johnny eighteen. Bobby had outgrown his older brother, was over six feet tall, his voice a man's. He was growing into a placating, and charming young man who could also be thrown into dark and withdrawn moods. In her parlor, Mary heard the gossip that some in town called Bobby "moony." He seemed to seek comfort keeping the books for his father's business and was growing as pecuniary as his grandmother. He had, the last year, started to refer to himself as Bob, sometimes even Robert, and had less and less time to spend with Ezekiel.

But for a cough, and for troubling dreams, Mary's years had become somewhat certain, even as Ezekiel grew restless. The hinny had grown stiff and old last year and Mary had sold her. Ezekiel was beginning to talk about buying another mule when the weather cleared again.

"What for?" she said.

"Hauling."

"And what do you think you are going to haul that would earn enough to pay for a mule?"

"What people want hauled."

"I won't be paying for a mule with no more thought about it than that," she said.

"I got money."

Where did he get such cheek? "I *have* money," she said.

"Have."

"How much do you think a mule would cost?"

"I have nearly enough to buy one, now."

"And how much is that?"

"Twenty-two dollars."

She blinked. He had accumulated quite a sum all on his own. Did he still keep it in the tin? It had been so long since she last checked. "How much does a mule cost?"

"There's a young one I could get for thirty dollars at Mr. Simpson's. I would pay him the eight dollars when I made it." His jaw thrust out and set there; Mary felt there was more to this than the mere buying of a mule and wagon.

"How long would Mr. Simpson wait for his eight dollars?"

"I could do it, Ma." His expression hardened. "It's what I want to do, forever."

"You can do it after you have finished your schooling."

"That's *three years.*"

"Seven if I am counting right."

"I am not leaving to go to some university." They had spoken of this before, and he had never softened.

"You can wager Bobby will be sent to university. His

mother will see to it just as I will see to it you will."

"You're no Mrs. Cozad." This stung more than Mary would have thought. "He'll come back and I'll be here waiting."

"You don't know that."

His jaw set up again. "I'm going to do it."

"No," she said.

"I'm going to buy that wagon and mule."

"Ask Mr. Simpson how long you would have to pay it back, then."

The next evening, after work at the livery, Ezekiel went up the stairs without saying a word. At dinner, she got out of him that Mr. Simpson had sold the mule to someone else.

Chapter 80

The calendars would turn to 1882 in a week. Mrs.
Gatewood was giving the kitchen girls some relief until
after the holiday, having them put out bread and cheese
for the morning meal, serving a light dinner, then closing
the kitchen each evening for supper. Mary and Ezekiel
had settled into the habit of taking all their evening meals
at the hotel; it seemed she could manage more of an
appetite if someone else prepared what she ate, and she
began to find some comfort in conversation with Sam
Schooley, who also took most meals in the hotel.

A number of Danes were buying up land north of town,
not far from Mary and Edmund's old farm, and more
were beginning to come in droves, a slim people, tall and
with odd habits: the men often held the hands of their
wives in the clear view of everyone and were outspoken.
Their women were as blunt as their men and their men
did not seem to object. Mary wondered and envied.
What's more, the Danes let their children look straight
into adults' eyes and speak up as equals, the parent
allowing even an argument or two. To a person, the
Danes spared no low opinion of what they thought of Mr.
Cozad, called him uhøflige gris: a rude pig.

Allegiance to Mr. Cozad splintered town; people were
joining together in factions: those who tolerated and
worked with him and those who had had enough and

335

were threating to run him out of town for good. Traber escaped permanently to Plum Creek to set himself up as a druggist and dentist. He said it was because the town was larger and would have more business, but gossip held that he wanted away from his brother-in-law.

Mr. Ed Winchell took over the telegraph and post office and began helping Mr. Mosher publish *The Hundredth Meridian*. This might not have amounted to much, except Winchell was close to the faction raging against Mr. Cozad, who was beginning to think he might want to become a senator.

Between his ambitions and his businesses in Denver and Ohio, Mr. Cozad was often gone. During one of these times away, Winchell took down the post office sign reading *COZAD* and hung one saying *GOULD*. The minute Mr. Cozad came back to town, Winchell's sign was ripped from its frame and thrown into a fire outside the post office's front door. A new one, in shining whites and reds and gold, was hammered up: *COZAD*.

Men were beginning to play cards and gamble behind Mr. Cozad's back. Women, single and young and colorfully rouged, were getting off the train and moving into a house bought and paid for by a widow named Beulah Hunsaker.

Mary's customers came to her shop in clusters and spent hours filling her sitting room with gossip. The widow Hunsaker gave them ample to talk of and to speculate as to what kind of man would ever set foot in such a house. Mary kept silent as they sipped her tea and laughed. A part of her knew the desperation that might drive Mrs. Hunsaker to do as she did.

Mary *knew* some things, now, about some of her customers which, she knew, they had never shared. She *knew* Mrs. Schultz' husband had given her some infection and that she blamed Mrs. Hunsaker, and no longer took her husband into her bed. She *knew* that Mrs. Atkins still longed for a married fellow she had loved as a girl and sometimes secreted letters to him, though he lived hundreds of miles away in Ohio. For several weeks, the table gossip huffed and tsked over the doings at Mrs. Hunsaker's. Mary realized the delicacy of her own viewpoint, so as they talked she sat quiet and measured and sewed.

Some days she felt clear, that she spent her days as she was meant to, providing for herself and her son, making a home. Some days, fulfillment turned empty and she began hungering for another to share them. She could never hold onto the desire for long, for the truth cut in. She had lived her lie and it had served her. But the truth of her lie could not accommodate another in her life.

———

It seemed nothing in town could be counted on any longer. The stress and pull of the factions, the shouts and threats and ugly vitriol were taking their toll even on Mrs. Gatewood. Mary could see her grab tables and the backs of chairs as she walked, heard her sometimes yip and clutch at her back. She finally began to carry a cane.

Chapter 81

Winter clamped down. Chimneys smoked, lamps lit early in windows, and people sat in their houses and grew fat. Only church, or a quick bent-in-the wind trot to the post office or to the store brought anyone out. In a freeze, women did not bother to have dresses made, did not come in for pins, or to look at fashion plates, or to gossip, but stayed home with their families and their fires. Mary's bank account, which built solidly in warmer days, dwindled in the cold, and this kept her nervous long into the nights. And, without the comfort of sleep, the dark allowed in a hot longing for a soft touch, the whisper of a breath not hers. And when the lamp was out, under the covers of her barren bed, she moved against her own hand, and moaned low in the back of her throat until she finally gave in to sleep.

———

Mrs. Gatewood braved a particularly frigid morning. Mary saw her standing out front, gauging the front steps. Mary went out and gave her an elbow. When they were inside, Mrs. Gatewood dropped into the chair and sighed, "Oh, Mary, don't ever grow old."

Mrs. Gatewood wanted a dress to wear to a wedding in January for some relative in the east. She scheduled an appointment a week later for a fitting. The day of the fitting, Sam Schooley drove her. He helped her up the steps into the house. When she was comfortably flounced to the corner chair, he tipped his hat to Mary. "Haven't seen you at the table lately, Mrs. Harrington."

"I've been busy, Mr. Schooley."

"Will we see you again soon?"

"I am sure." She felt a heat rise in her.

He tipped his hat to Mary and turned to leave. "We should be no more than half an hour," she told him.

Mrs. Gatewood's dress was of blue wool. Mary had beaded a high collar and had cut the sleeves narrow at the wrists. She had hung the dress on the form to show when Mrs. Gatewood came in. It was lovely. Mary was proud of it, and all the while working on it, she bathed in the realization how much the old woman meant to her.

Mary reached for the hanger. Mrs. Gatewood gave out a sigh. "Oh, Mary, let's wait a minute." Her eyes went to the dress.

"Is there something wrong with it?" Mary said.

"No, it's lovely. It'll make me ten years younger and my middle ten inches narrower." She let out a tired blow that lifted her bang. "Just let me sit," she said. "You take care of me."

Mary felt a warmth. "I have tea."

Mrs. Gatewood drew up her hand, held it in a wait motion. "It's more than tea I really want," she said and threw back her head.

"I have biscuits." *Biscuits. Is that all I can give her? Biscuits?* This woman had once been so important it took Mary's breath. What she wanted was to be able to return what Mrs. Gatewood had given to her: survival. And all she had to offer was biscuits.

"Well, since it's tea you have and biscuits, we'll have tea and biscuits."

Chapter 82

The cough had come and gone for longer than Mary could remember. It never seemed to stay away altogether, never left her truly sick, but even in the coldest of days she often had a fever and took to her bed until her strength returned.

Her business leveled off some; another woman, Mrs. Mckinney, had recently set up dressmaking in town and gave Mary some competition. Even so, the year had been good and she had hired on a girl to pin, and cut, and do the tedious job of finishing seams and hems.

It should have been a time of peace; the county's crops were in, the prices had been good, and yields high. The grasshoppers had come again that summer, but their numbers had been small. People were beginning to think they had shrugged off the scourges forever. The sole bane keeping the community in a roil was Mr. Cozad.

The knowings pained her, unbidden. She began to *know* intimacies she wished she did not. She *knew* Mr. Cozad's meanness sprouted from a childhood at the hand of a cruel father. She *knew* these cruelties had left little John J. Cozad withered and small inside, beaten down until he had little to cling to but ambition and anger. And she *knew* it shamed him to *need* his wife and to depend on her. Mary *knew* Mrs. Cozad's endless mustering to keep her family from falling to pieces bled her. Mary also *knew* with

343

certainty that Mrs. Cozad harbored a secret, one that perhaps only a mother with a similar history might see: that Mrs. Cozad had had other children and had lost them to fire; Bobby and Johnny were not her first. This brought Mary to tears.

As the days began to stretch longer and the weather began to warm, the bridge became yet another excuse to battle. Every year, the potential to draw business from Nebraska on the other bank won over and every year Mr. Cozad insisted the bridge be rebuilt. As the men bent over shovels and hoists, the mud sucking their boots, sweat pouring from their chins, he stood in his frock coat and high hat, shouting invectives for their careless work. He fired them without cause, and those he put out of work shook their fists and made threats. Instead of blaming the river or his own design, he blamed everyone else. Mr. Mosher's *Meridian* ran slanderous columns, relating every word.

Mr. Cozad was being assailed from all sides. The more lands he sold for farming, the more tension and threats came from the cattlemen who insisted they had the rights to range their cattle on any land that had not been plowed and planted. Only a small, devoted cadre of men continued to back him, among them Mr. Schooley, Mr. Atkinson, Mr. Claypool, Mr. Owens, and Traber Gatewood, when Traber was in town.

Though plans were laid in for an elaborate brick home for the Cozads two years ago, it had yet to be built. Mrs. Cozad had lost weight, her complexion growing blotchy and pale. Her hair would soon be as white as her mother's. The Cozad boys were near grown. Johnny was nineteen and planning to enter college; Bob was lanky, thin as a tree branch, taller than his older brother.

Finally, Mrs. Cozad convinced her husband to relocate the family to Denver again, where she felt safer. On one hand, the town accused the Cozads of being gypsies but also took a collective breath of relief when they heard they would be moving.

The town's relief did not last long. Bobby returned to live with his grandparents on the Gatewood farm. Mr. Cozad gave him a job, assigned to run the business of the haypress and to tend to the payroll of the men working on the bridge, jobs Bobby seemed to have little heart for now. He grew sullen and dark and had little time for Ezekiel.

Mr. Cozad installed a larger, newer printing press in the back room of the hotel. He was planning a new paper, bigger, better, more cosmopolitan than *The Meridian*, and he told Bob he was to run it. Bob's first order was not to publish a newspaper, Mary would learn later; it was to print ballots and tickets for the election in a few weeks.

One afternoon, Bob came knocking at Mary's door. His complexion was a sickly and tired yellow. A thunderstorm had just passed through. The day smelled pleasant, the perfume of just-dampened earth. He held a cap in his hands. His nails, and the whorls of his fingerprints, were black. "Bob," she said, "won't you come in?"

He gave a tiny shake to his head. "I don't have time, Mrs. Harrington, but thank you. I was wondering if I could get Easy to help me on the printing press. I have some tickets need printing and some other work I could use his help with, if you could tell him I was asking."

"I will tell him," she said. "But he has some work at Mr. Simpson's right after school. I'll tell him, soon as he is home."

He said, "Thanks, Mrs. Harrington," his manner, so held in and defeated, made her stomach lurch. She found it difficult not to take Bob into her arms and pat his back.

He gave a sweet flicker of his old smile. "I'll still be there," he said, "probably forever."

Ezekiel barged in some time later. He left the screen to bang open. "Ma, I'm going to do some printing work with Bob after work." Apparently, the boy had caught him on the way home to change into work clothes. His voice was high and excited. He ran up the stairs. "Be home late."

She did not see him until well after dark. He came in stinking of metal and ink, and of straw and the dung of Mr. Simpson's stalls. His hands, his nose, the front of his shirt were covered with either excrement or ink.

He waved a sheet in front of her. "Ma, you got to see this right now." His words rushed out on mists of spit. The sheet was called *The Runty Papers*. It had a drawing of a comical figure that needed a shave and was dressed in a sloppy hat and wrinkled clothes. The crude man was waving voting tickets and screaming, "Hear Ye, Hear Ye, all good citizens be ready to VOTE OUT THE SCOUNDRELS." The sheet had some political satires on it as well, silly sayings on the worthlessness of Julius Sterling Morton and E. P. Ingersoll, Democrat and Greenback candidates running for governor. The sheet spared Runty's scorn of James W. Dawes; after all, Dawes was Republican.

"It's prepress," Ezekiel said.

"Prepress?"

"Yeh." He turned it toward himself. "A proof copy. You're the first to see it. Bob's a really good artist, Ma. Isn't he?"

The election edition of *The Runty Papers* would never make it to press.

Chapter 83

The day the boys printed the silly paper had been warm, but on a whim, the next day, the weather changed. Wind pelted the bits of dead weeds at the windows, grit crackled into one's eyes. Mary was pinning the hem on a dress for Mildred Ackerman when Mr. Ackerman knocked on the door to take his wife home. He said men had walked off work on the bridge and there was trouble. School had let out some time ago. Where was Ezekiel? She could not shake off the idea he would be in the middle of things, where the trouble was. It worried her. When the Ackermans left, she put on a wrap and went out.

Shouts rode on the wind, then whipped away again as it shifted. A stream of people were coming out of their homes. Mary's breath came short and made her stumble. When she got to the river, Mr. Claypool, and Mr. Atkinson, and Sam Schooley were standing beside Mr. Cozad near the bridge's pilings. Mr. Cozad was screaming "The bastards . . . lazy . . . good for nothing . . . nobody stops work on me." He turned toward the people lined up a safe distance away. The wind flailed his coattails, his arms bashed the air. It could have been simply one of Mr. Cozad's many tantrums people had grown accustomed to and largely ignored. But this time, the morning of the fourteenth, no one worked; the bridge, the hoist, the dredge all lay silent, the only sounds were Mr. Cozad's screams.

By the end of the day, stories about what had happened would fly up and whorl like bird flock. This Mary would soon learn: After the tantrum at the bridge, apparently, Mr. Cozad had stomped into the Bee Hive, his face the color of a tomato, his coattails flapping. No one would quite remember why he was there, to talk with his mother-in-law, perhaps, or maybe to gain sympathy.

For most who saw him that day, it was the diamond flickering in the sun that seemed most to set them off. It stood for what none of them had, for their powerlessness and anger. They joked, called him a clown, but their laughs were gargled from the backs of their throats and unconvincing.

Alfred Pearson had been one of the men to walk off the bridge. Like most everyone else, he had met with hard times. He came to Dawson County a few years before and had built a modest house for his family. When the house was destroyed by fire, he filed to homestead near Buffalo Creek and constructed another house, this one out of sod. He had run himself into debt, taking out notes for supplies and farm equipment. People knew he struggled and was working odd jobs, hiring himself out to bridge work and farming. He was also ranging some cattle. Mr. Cozad's men had recently chased his cattle from land Mr. Cozad owned, and Mr. Cozad was threatening to sue Mr. Pearson unless he kept his cattle off Mr. Cozad's property.

Pearson had come into the Bee Hive that morning shouting that he understood Mr. Cozad was going to sue him.

Mr. Cozad shouted back, "I will if you don't keep your stock off my land."

"You don't own everything," Mr. Pearson screamed.

"You're trespassing."

"It ain't your land."

Mr. Cozad screamed, "Liar!"

Mrs. Gatewood was in the store, sitting on her stool behind the counter. Mr. Cozad grabbed Mr. Pearson by the collar and shouted, "There's a lady in the house. Go outside with your lies."

They slammed out the door.

Outside, Mr. Pearson screamed again, "You can't sue me."

"I said I will unless you get off my land."

Some around town said Mr. Pearson pushed Mr. Cozad and knocked him into a pile of boxes outside the store. Some said it was Mr. Cozad who hit Mr. Pearson first and Mr. Pearson pushed Cozad in self-defense. Some said Mr. Pearson came at Mr. Cozad. Some said he was unarmed, some said he was armed, but no one knew the truth.

Mrs. Gatewood stayed in the store and later denied she could see much. Only Mr. Drew was there to see the whole thing, but later he said his view was not clear. What held, in every telling of the story, was that somehow Mr. Cozad got lodged in the boxes and could not get out. Some said Mr. Pearson punched and kicked even when Mr. Cozad was down. Some said Mr. Cozad was bleeding and kicked back in self-defense, shouting for help.

Mr. Cozad managed to grapple hold of his pistol. He fired. The shot hit Mr. Pearson in the head.

By the end of the day, the story was played, and repeated, and changed a thousand different ways. This time it was more than fist-shaking: men hammered up a platform, three steps, and a stanchion that they threaded with rope. Mr. Cozad would be the town's first hanging.

Sometime after midnight, Mr. Cozad let himself out of the hotel, and silently went, alone and on foot, out of town. By the time the sky lightened the next morning, when the men collected again to do battle, Mr. Cozad was gone. Men stood in the slicing wind, screaming that they would kill whoever harbored him. Mr. Schooley finally let them into the hotel to see for themselves that Mr. Cozad was not there. They found only two families—and Bobby.

Over the hemorrhage of shouts came quieter hysteria, the rushing of their hearts, the murmur of whispers. Mary felt the distress, the rush of blood through Mrs. Cozad's veins. She heard the snap of Bobby's teeth on the quicks of his nails, his tongue licking the blood. She heard the shallow gasp of her son's breathing and smelled the mania and worry on him. And Mary felt near buried in the town's anguish.

Mrs. Gatewood cleared out from the hotel. Sam Schooley drove Bobby out to the Gatewoods' farm and Mr. Owens emptied the hotel of the two families, told the kitchen girls there was no more work, pulled the shades over the hotel's windows, and locked the door. Mr. Atkinson brought in goods from the boardwalk in front of the Bee Hive and padlocked the door. And rumor began to take root that the hotel and the Bee Hive would go on the block to be sold.

Ezekiel went through his days as if bewildered, his face expressionless. One afternoon, three days after the shooting, he said, "What'll happen to them, Ma?"

"I'm sure I don't know," she said. "Bobby's out with his grandma, so he'll be all right."

Ezekiel trudged through his days, his face the color of paste, hair uncombed and split into oily hanks. Were it not for habit, the distraction of school, and work at the livery, Mary did not know what would become of him. He did not make another remark about what had happened but wandered the house at night and went through his days as if a shadow.

Two weeks later, Mrs. Cozad came into town on the train. Sam Schooley and Traber Gatewood met her. The weather was colder, the winds dry, the skies the color of tin and too bitter to snow. Mrs. Cozad was pale, her face dull as chalk. She wore a dark coat over a heavy skirt and a black bonnet that drew attention to the exhausted circles around her eyes. Traber drove her to the farm.

Mr. Pearson's associates followed. They surrounded the farmhouse for two nights. Traber came in from Plum Creek. The morning of the third day, Mrs. Cozad and Bob drove to town in a buggy driven by Traber. The parade of men followed again, some shouting curses, some screaming they would have John Cozad's neck. As they reached town, the commotion drew people. Mary heard the ruckus and came out to watch as the carriage passed by. She knew Ezekiel would be able to see it as the parade passed the school.

Mrs. Cozad sat in the buggy, straight faced, looking neither right nor left. Beside her, equally impassive, sat Bob. They remained in the buggy as Traber and Sam Schooley huddled on the bench, shivering, rifles across their laps, waiting for the train.

When the midday train pulled in, Traber opened Mrs. Cozad's door and handed her down. She was wearing the same dull coat and skirt as she had worn the day she came in. The skirt was so heavy, it made no more than a ripple in the cutting wind. He helped her board the train going east. Neither she nor her son looked back.

Chapter 84

Alfred Pearson was gravely wounded in the head, but did not die for two months. Mr. Cozad's charge of murder was immediate.

A day later, a knock came at the house. Mary was sitting by the stove, piecing a quilt for her bed from scraps. The coals in the stove flared and faded at the whim of the wind. But for an occasional request, her business had fallen to near nothing. As tensions grew after the shooting, she felt the sting of condemnation in being associated with the Cozads and Gatewoods. Though there had not yet been a trial, most of town had already found Mr. Cozad guilty and had put Mr. Pearson in a place only a bit less than that of a saint.

The piecing work settled her some, but it could not truly quell the anxiety at the turn of things. Whatever stability Cozad had ever held together, it was rent into pieces. Work on the bridge had been abandoned altogether, since the day the men walked off the job. What was left of the pilings sat like rotted teeth on which birds perched, and preened, and shat. Where the Cozads had disappeared to, no one was saying. Mr. Pearson's supporters hired a detective to try to find the Cozads. They hounded everyone for information, sparing no one, not the Gatewoods, or Sam Schooley, or the Atkinsons, or the Owenses. If anyone knew where they went, no one admitted it.

Traber Gatewood left for Plum Creek and made certain he would never again call Cozad home. Sam Schooley took over the post office business and what had been Traber's drugstore.

Mrs. Gatewood had not shown in town again except to conduct business. The hotel was sold to a man named Hendee, a wealthy grain dealer from Illinois. He hired Mr. and Mrs. A. T. Maryot to manage it and to run the general store. Mary missed Mrs. Gatewood. She missed even the sense Mr. Cozad gave town that it had a future important enough to fight for. Town seemed empty without them.

She kept the stove stoked always, even on warm days. All last summer she had worn a shawl while her customers came in fanning and puffing. She stoked the stove now, wore a coat over her warmest dress as she huddled near the heat sorting scraps. Yet, cold as she was, sweat soaked her bedding at night. Her coughs had grown so frequent she kept kerchiefs stuffed under her sleeves at both wrists. Though she washed the cloths, the dark of her spit was leaving a stain. She forced herself to eat rich foods loaded with fats and covered with gravies. The blouses she sewed for herself were fashioned with shirring and ruching to hide her thinness, but she could find nothing to obscure the bones along her temples and jaw. She thought Ezekiel was too busy to give thought to her, and for that she was eternally thankful.

She had chosen the brightest scraps to put in the quilt and was arranging the pieces in a hodgepodge. The freedom of working without a pattern brought her some calm. She heard the hiss of a paper slipped under the door. She laid down the scissors and stood. She patted her skirt, and went to the parlor. A tongue of envelop lay in the crack at the tread under the door. It was addressed to Master Ezekiel Harrington. It had no stamp. It had no return.

She opened the door as Sam Schooley was making his way down the steps. "Sam?"

He turned. "I didn't want to bother."

"Come in from the cold," she said. "I have tea on the stove."

"I left David Claypool minding the post office," he said.

"He can handle it long enough for tea."

Sam laughed a gentleman's laugh, open and sweet. She *knew* Sam at that moment and felt the heat of a blush in the knowing. It came to her now, unbidden: he was lonely. She was turning into a private busybody with these insights, prying into people, knowing truths they would not have revealed.

Were it anyone else, she would have told them to make themselves comfortable in her showpiece of a parlor. But Sam was not parlor, Sam was not sitting room. "The tea is in the kitchen," she said.

He set his hat on the table, pulled back a chair. She took a cup from the cupboard, set it on the counter. She knew the eternal conflicts with Mr. Cozad tested Sam, overriding his pacifist beliefs, compelling him to take up the rifle on behalf of his friend. Quaker, she realized. She had not seen this before. She took the pot from the stove, tipped it. He was devoted to peace. Steam rose from the spout. Loyalty to a man he loved had caused him to carry a firearm against others. The stream settled in the cup, clear and delicate, and in it she saw Mr. Cozad as Sam saw him: soft, and hurt, a child. Steam rose. Sam yearned. His hands were tender, his breath soft.

She set the pot in its place and, when she looked back, his gaze whispered his sense that he *knew* her as well. She felt her ears flare. She was not sure she could bear to be revealed so.

————

That evening, when Ezekiel came in, he took the letter Sam brought upstairs to his room. He carried it in his pocket nearly two weeks. Then, one morning, he forgot it on his bed stand. The script was generous and quick.

> *Easy My Boy,*
> *How's things back there in old Cozad town? We made it out all right. Ma is busy as ever, Pa is away much of the time. Johnny is doing all right. Me? Me, too.*
> *Say hello to some of the folks back in old Cozad. You can leave the others alone. YOU KNOW WHO I MEAN!!!!*

Bob had drawn a smiling, weasely face that looked like him. He signed the note Your friend, R. There was no return address.

Chapter 85

"I'm going to do it, Ma." At fourteen, Ezekiel's voice had grown unreliable: high and boyish one moment, crackling toward a man's the next.

"No," she said. *Does every mother dread this? Does a son's becoming a man mean loss to every mother?*

"What will you use to haul all these things you plan to haul?" she said.

"I am buying a cart from Mr. Owens," he said. "A dollar a month, half as payment, half to rent it until it's paid for. I have my own money, now." And, for that, she had no argument.

Hauling took a shape she could not have imagined. He had painted a sign on his wagon, *Harrington Drayage*, and had one day called her out to see it. It was well done, the letters neat and square. She yearned to pat his shoulder and congratulate him, but the whole thing, his business and the advertising for it, expressed something of ponderous trouble, a battle with her son she had to win.

"Perhaps you might conside . . ." she said.

He drew himself tall; he had grown enough to look down at her. This business interfered with what she wanted of his future, but it posed an even greater possible threat. "Perhaps just say *drayage*," she said.

"I already thought of that. There is no one I wouldn't want to see it, no one." His eyes narrowed as if he were setting a challenge, not to her but his pa.

Throughout the winter after the Cozads left, she had fought to keep Ezekiel in school. He was tired of it, and she could see some truth as to why; he had read every book, had finished every course, and passed every examination the teacher had to give. Ezekiel's old teacher, Mr. Young, had gone on to become superintendent of schools. The teacher's name was Miss Avery, now, and Ezekiel spoke ill of her.

Ezekiel made the rounds of all the houses in town, knocking on doors, asking if the families had anything they wanted moved, any work they wanted done. By winter, even as the ground began to freeze, some families were moving in, some leaving and hiring him and his wagon, and his drayage business began to take hold. His mood lifted; until then, only the letter from Bobby had taken him from a brown and murky despondency. He still checked the post office every day for another.

Little about Cozad had settled since the shooting. Mr. Pearson's family were still pressing charges of murder. From his new home in McCook, Traber had hired an attorney and was seeing to Mr. Cozad's defense.

When she began to understand how obdurate Ezekiel was about his future, Mary had gone back to the attorney's office. She had asked Mr. Hoffman what rights she had as a mother to bar her son from leaving school. "I have heard the State is considering compulsory requirements," he said, "but so far there have been none. Who knows how long it may take lawmakers to get around to making them. How old is he, Mrs. Harrington?"

"Fourteen," she said.

He took off his eyeglasses, rubbed his eye with the heels of his hands. His goiter had grown and the broad mass of it lifted the lobes of his ears.

He slipped the eyeglasses on again, settled them behind his ears. "You could refuse by withholding money like I have seen some do."

"He has his own resources."

"Resources?" His head turned aslant. "I did not know you were a wealthy woman."

"I am not," she said, "but he has arranged to set himself in a business."

"Earning his way already?"

"Yes."

"Could he feed himself, could he support his own place to live?"

"Yes and no."

"Some but not both, I assume."

"He does not confide in the amount he makes, but . . ."

"He lives with you. You provide him a home."

"Yes, doesn't every parent?"

"Not when it comes to an independent and intelligent child," he said. "Have you considered locking him out? See how independent he is when he must pay for a roof on his own?"

"I couldn't."

"Then until the laws change, or unless you tie him to a school desk, you have not the power to keep him in school."

She said she had something else she needed to discuss

with him. "I want you to prepare my will."

He stood, went to a file, drew out some papers, and he sat. And as she spoke, he began to write. She said she wanted Totten Hume to be named executor of whatever remained of her estate upon her death. She said that she wanted her son to complete as much of a college education as her estate could support, and the college would be of Totten Hume's choosing. If Ezekiel did not complete college, he was to receive none of her estate unless he married or had turned twenty-five. Until he was of age, he was to live with her sister and brother-in-law in Philadelphia.

A week later, when the will was prepared, she had two copies made, one for her and one to send to Philadelphia. She slipped her copy under her linens in the old trunk. She wrote a note to Totten and Prune:

> *Dear Sister and Brother,*
>
> *I know this letter and request will alarm you, so be forewarned that it should not. No matter its dire subject, all is well here with Ezekiel and me. I am just being fussy, and Prune you know how I can fuss. It's a mother's right and responsibility to flutter and flap and I am doing it.*
>
> *I have been giving some thought to the question of what is to happen to Ezekiel if something happened to me and I have had a Will drawn up. I am sure you have done the same, so pat me on the back for being a good parent, like you.*
>
> *Enclosed in the envelop is my Will. In it I am asking you to watch over him and take care of him if I should ever die*

before he grows up.

I am also making a copy of this letter for my son, in hopes that when the day comes for him to read it, it softens some of the cold aspects of what is in the Will.

Should the worst come to pass, I wish him to come live with you and your wonderful boys. He is a clever, hard-working boy, but I am afraid he believes he can already manage on his own and has grown quite stubborn about it. Totten, you will need to give him your strong hand, he will need it. Prune, from you he only needs your love and kindness in order to develop into the fine sort of young men you have made of Cornelius and Oliver, who I hope will welcome him as their friend and brother.

You can see in my Will that the main thing I want for Ezekiel is for him to have a home and someone to love him as I do, until he earns a college education. To this end, I wish all my resources to support that. I wish you to sell the house here in Cozad. It is paid for and has some value. I wish you to use the funds in my accounts, and the proceeds from the sale of the house, to afford Ezekiel the best education you can get for him. I insist neither you nor he wavers from this, no matter what he might think of it. He has already begun to argue against more schooling. He does not wish to leave Cozad. Cozad is a fine place, but has no more to educate him than secondary school. I am resolute, he will get a college education before anything else, whether I am here to see to it, or not. If he refuses, and I am not here to marshal him, see he does not get any of my estate until he marries, or turns twenty-five. My Will states this as well.

Thank you for accepting the responsibility it throws at you.
I realize its dry language leaves out much from what I want
my son to remember of me. So, if anything happens before
he is grown, I will say it now.
But most of all, my dearest family, love him, care for him
as neither his father, nor I were able to.
Your Loving Sister,
Mary

She received a letter a week later. Prune must have sent
it the moment Mary's papers arrived.

Phla
14 April, 1883
Sissie,
We rec'd your papers and I don't like one bit of them. Of
course, we would take care of your darling Ezekiel. But
your letter makes me worry something is wrong. Are you
well? Write and tell me you are. If I don't hear the minute
you get this letter, I shall be on the next train to
Nebraska.
Your worried sister,
Prune

Mary slept three hours, heated herself some strong tea
and sat down to write, hoping her tone would be light.

Dearest Worried Sister,
Your letter came today. Quit your worried head, my dear, I
am alive, my letter and Will should not alarm you. I

364

should have mentioned it, so you had warning, before I thrust the whole ugly thing on you.

I have been tending to the awful business of tidying things. My letter was simply no more than that. Worry if you want, but it is for naught.

So, enough of the dreary subject.

I have exciting news that will spare you the bother of rushing across the country to check on us. My news is that Ezekiel and I are planning to come your way within the next very few months.

We will see through the summer here for me to get through the dress-sewing season. You can see I am still alive enough to stitch ladies into a dress, or two.

I think we should likely make it sometime in August, in order for Ezekiel to return in time for the beginning of the school year here. It means you will have to make the bed in the guest room, and tell your Phoebe to prepare some of your fancy Philadelphia meals. We will be plunked in your lap soon enough.

I can hardly bear the wait. Ezekiel will be thrilled when I tell him the news.

All my love to Totten and the boys.

Lovingly,

Sissie

She had not told Ezekiel about Philadelphia; she knew he would not want to go. In the past, they had tussled when she suggested a visit to see his aunt Prune. When she told him about the trip, he said he did not want to leave his business.

"You will have to give it up before you leave for college."

"I am not going to college," he said. As inscrutable as he was, she did know that, after Bob left, he had made no more friends. She also knew that the friendship with Bobby was at the heart of his stubbornness to stay; he was waiting for him to return.

How she would manage all this she did not know. The attorney's comment to lock Ezekiel out of the house in order to force him to try making his own way was not possible. But she had no certain idea to replace what the attorney suggested. It kept her awake in the nights and stole any appetite she could muster. Even the prospect of seeing Prune could not quell the ache inside her. She could not give in until after her son was grown. He *must* have more choice in his life than his father had, and it meant he had to be educated. She would not bend.

Should she finally take up Prune's offer to move to Philadelphia where there were fine colleges? Or should she move them somewhere else? Lincoln, perhaps? Lincoln had a university, but she had heard it was struggling. Denver? Because the Cozads had lived there, she thought Ezekiel might soften to it, but she did not believe Denver had a university. The best colleges, she knew, were in the east. He could make Cozad his home *after* he saw some other part of the world. If he returned after that, it would be the choice of a mature and educated man.

"You will go to college," she said.

His head gave a tiny, resolute one-shake no.

Chapter 86

After a final temper of ice, and snow, and cutting sleet, winter blew itself out. Spring came and, with it, the birds. They lowered the skies and filled the county with their calls.

By the time the weather began to gentle in March, Ezekiel was in business for himself and apparently busy. He rarely came home smelling of the livery stalls, now, because his hauling work was keeping him too occupied. He quit school more than a month before it let out. Mary no longer badgered him about it. They had not argued about school since winter, but the dilemma of his education lurked. As stubborn as he was, she had to make herself more so.

Her energy was flagging, the coughs growing more disruptive, even now with the warmth of spring. Her business had picked up some since winter but was mostly limited to the spouses of men closest to Mr. Cozad. Few of them came in to gossip over tea any longer, as they, themselves, were the fodder for the town's tongues.

At some level, Mary was grateful she was not as busy as before. Until her energies picked up again, she did not think she could manage the old pace of things. She seldom cooked dinner, instead taking it at the hotel. Sometimes Ezekiel was there, more often not. He saw to his own meals, either at the hotel or by keeping a loaf of bread and jerky in the wagon and eating it with one hand, while driving the mule with the other. He was growing stronger, if not taller. The lifting and moving had given him bulk, his neck blended into his shoulders, and his thighs had grown thick as poles. She still sewed for him and could barely keep up with the changes.

She was seeing more of Sam at the hotel dining room. He and his widowed sister-in-law were living with the Claypools, but he brought himself to the dining room to eat two or three times a week, to "save the women at home feeding one more mouth." Mary suspected the real reason was something else she could not quite admit to herself, something she wanted as well.

The hotel food had grown simpler and cheaper with the Maryots, the stews more gristled and filled with potatoes, which were plentiful. Peace without Mr. Cozad lay over the building as it never had before. Gone was the long dining table and the opulent excelsior chairs. Mrs. Gatewood had taken them when she turned management over to the Maryots. In their place, they had put an assortment of mismatched chairs and three smaller tables.

It was early June. The day had been warm, the evening still. Sam had begun coming to the house before supper and taking Mary in arm to the hotel for supper. That evening's meal was better than usual, a chicken, roasted crisp with potatoes and fresh, green, fried tomatoes. There was even a dessert of cobbler. Someone at the table joked that maybe Mr. Cozad would show his face. A couple of men laughed; Sam did not.

After the others left, she and Sam had lingered at the

table. A warm breeze shifted the curtains. "Would you like to cool a little down by the creek?" he said. When she looked at him, uncomprehending. He said, "The river, Mary. Would you like to come sit with me down by the river?"

––––––

The evening was soft and lay on her like a touch. She felt young, again, and warm.

They walked as the sky had darkened and the horizon paled. Sam gave her his elbow and they took their time, slipping slowly along the way, their feet touching down before stepping, lest they trip in the dark. They were the only people out. Behind them, town's rattling wagons, the blowing impatient horses, the crying children had gone quiet. They did not speak. But for their steps and the hush of their clothes, they made no sound.

The lamps of town disappeared as they let themselves down the gentle riverbank. The scent of green, and mud, and wet feathers settled along the edges. There was a moon, but not much of one, merely a thumb's nail. The heavens were filled with a dizziness of stars.

Sam pulled a handkerchief from his pocket, shook the folds from it; it shone like a ghost in the dark. Mary felt weightless, boneless. He bent down, laid the handkerchief on the ground. "Here, Mary," he said, his voice near and soft; it was not a night for a loud voice.

She pulled her skirts under herself and sat down on the square. He took off his jacket, laid its intimate warmth over her shoulders. He sat. Their arms touched.

For a long while they breathed in the scents. Finally, he

took a long, expectant breath. "Mary," he said.

She felt something she had never felt before: a foreign and alive presence. Her life had always seemed a vapor, aloft, aloof. Since Sam came to it, the fog had disappeared. She did not trust what filled her now. It was uncomfortable but full.

She felt a chill, held herself against shivering lest he feel it and put an end to this shining night. A choir of frogs set forth. Frogs. Lovely frogs.

"I have something to ask," he said.

"Yes," she said, the first word she had uttered. She thought she knew what it was Sam wanted to say, had longed for it and feared it for some time.

"You are a widow, Mary." It could have been a question, but was said as a statement. She did not answer, did not allow even a breath. "Ezekiel told me of something." A coot scolded. "He said he had never told it to you."

She feared the change in his voice. "What is it?"

"He seemed lightened by the telling."

"Yes?"

"About his pa."

"Oh, Sam," she said, and felt the end of the thing she most wanted with Sam. She had hoped the intervening time since her legal assertions about Edmund could bring truth to them, but in truth she *knew* she was not, indeed, as she claimed.

He took her hand. "I know," he said, and let the frogs, and the coot, and the night tell the rest of it. "You are a widow, Mary. It is enough."

Chapter 87

The mail brought a letter from Philadelphia. It was written sloppily and undated.

Oh Sissie, Totten worries me so. He is losing weight, so am I. Mine from worry, his from no energy to eat. He is ill, but has no fever to prove it. I am sick with worry over him. He still goes to his office, but is always exhausted by the time he returns and it is not like him. His breath is labored, even with small effort. Yesterday, he forgot his jacket when he left the house to board the train for a meeting in New York. I ran after him with it in my hand. He stumbled home this morning and Phoebe and I had to take his arms to help him up the stairs.

We sent for Oliver, who came immediately from his doctor's college. By the time he came, Totten's forehead was clammy and cold. Oliver ordered his father to bed rest, or he was going to ship him off to the hospital where they would tie him down.

It is a godsend to have you to tell it to. I don't know who else would want to listen. I miss you so. It would bring me much relief if you were here right this minute.

I know Oliver will see to it his pa is well soon enough and for all of us to be healthy as hounds by the time you and Ezekiel come to see us. I can barely wait.

Enough of my troubles. That you will be here before fall

371

eases my frets.
Your Mournful Sister,
Prune

Mary's breath rattled. Her coughs brought up a repulsive slick and she took to setting her dressmaking appointments in the mornings, when she was freshest. She wrote Prune the day she received the letter about Totten. That night, the fevers came and soaked the bed, her breath drumming like boots on a floor.

All night she coughed and spat. By morning, the coughs had cleared some of the torment, but her chest felt fixed and solid, her ribs immoveable. By midmorning, she had to lay down her scissors, spit out her pins, and make her way up the stairs to bed. She had started sleeping two hours in the day, sometimes three, then would rise in order to ready for Sam's knock on the door at four fifteen. He had not alluded to her "widowhood" again. She suspected he was somehow aware her standing in regard to Edmund was unclear.

But for the cough and the flagging of her energy, this was, she knew, the life she had forever wished for, a home, time spent with a gentle man, a soft taking of arms, murmurings of the day, complaining of the weather, some incident at the drugstore, a mention of some story he and David Claypool were working on for *The Meridian* now that Mr. Mosher had left it. Sam liked publishing, but did not feel he was good at it. "It's Dave who does most of the writing," he said. "Leaves most of the inking to me. I'm a pretty fair inker."

She had taken measurements for a dress for Mrs. Atkinson, then had gone up to her room to rest. She planned to ask Sam to supper on Sunday. A cured ham was already soaking in a bucket. She had bought apples for a pie, and, in the garden, early tomatoes and lettuces were ready to pick. She would have Ezekiel bring them in before mealtime.

She woke from her nap with someone—a man—standing over her. The room was hot, the sun late-afternoon low. She tried to rise up on her elbows, but they would not lift her. She could feel heat on her face, the swelling of her lids. She took in a breath.

"Mary, it's Sam," he said. He took off his hat, held it in front of himself as if embarrassed. "No one answered the door so I came in." His forehead was wrinkled, his mouth drawn in. "Are you ill, Mary?"

Chapter 88

She did not finish Mrs. Atkinson's dress by the time she had promised, nor one promised for Rose Simpson, nor the baptism dress for Mrs. Hollingwood's grandson.

She rested, how many days? Mornings, Ezekiel steeped teas and brought her toast and eggs. He brought soups and dabbed her with cloths he wetted from water he kept by the bed. Sam came at night with a plate and sat with her and urged her to swallow tiny bites. Her arms, her legs were heavy as stones, her dreams burned, shapeless and iridescent. Her minutes awake were filled with Ezekiel and wonder at the weight of what he had always borne, something no boy should be made to lift.

Then, on a Friday, she woke, her sight unclouded, her breath clear. Two eggs and a buttered biscuit lay on a plate by the bed. A lazy thread rose from the snout of the teapot, wavered, then disappeared in the morning light. She breathed, her shoulders rose easily, her chest filled, and she sighed relief.

She was alone. She pulled up, waited to collapse, but her arms held. She lay there half lifted, half in bed, mouth open to a wonder of fresh, silent breath. Her cough was only a trifle. She had no fever. On her own, without help, she tried raising her legs. The muscles shook, but obeyed. She turned herself, eased her feet to the floor, and sat fully up, on her own. The morning was fresh, but she had no chill. She slid to the window, pulled back the blanket. The light coursed in. She bid her arms to lift the window. She leaned out, sucked in the air. It was as if she had been let out of a prison.

She took the plate, sat in the chair, and ate the biscuits and eggs fast as a starving dog. She gulped the tea.

———

She bathed a real bath, standing in the washroom naked, sloshing the sponge in water, rubbed it down her sharp ribs, along the knives of her shoulders. The smell of sickness rose from her nightgown. She set it in water to soak. She dressed, fully, with underthings, stockings, and shoes. She threaded the pearl earrings Sam had given her, through the lobes of her ears. And, when she was done, she went down to the sewing room and began to sew.

She finished both Mrs. Atkinson's and Mrs. Simpson's dresses that day. Sam came in just as she was beginning work on the baptism dress. He did not knock. He startled when he saw her full-dressed and bent over the gown. He was holding two plates covered with cloths and a bowl of vanilla ice cream. "Mary!"

She stood and he held out the plates and she took him into her arms.

Chapter 89

She believed it was over. She was still weak, her movements slow, and she needed to sit often, but she was able to mop the kitchen, sweep the rugs and floors, and to dust the displays. It had been months since she had such energy. The fabrics, the showcases, the static rolls of ribbon had taken on the gloom of disuse. Old, dried rains dulled the windows, a scrim of dust sat everywhere like a pall. She had once fluffed and draped goods daily to rich effect. Everything, now, seemed to have sunk into itself. She dusted and she washed and rearranged and, as the days went on, her face took back some color. She even made an attempt to try her hand at the garden again, but finally asked Ezekiel to do it.

Whenever he came in, he always stopped and said, "Ma," not so much in a tone of greeting as if to reassure himself she was there. Like snowmelt, he had begun to thaw, his brow and the worry lines aside his mouth to soften and he no longer held his shoulders up around his neck.

Every day after work, he went up to his room where he kept his account book lined with his expenses and payments and a column of what was owed by him and what was owed to him. He still kept his money in the old tin. When coins filled it, he exchanged them for bills at the bank. Weeks ago, while he was at work, Mary had opened the box. The sweet smells of paper bills rose up. There was fifteen dollars and thirty-two cents. Ezekiel had begun to hint that he might want to open a store of his own. When she asked what kind of store that might be, he was vague, saying only that his plans were "preliminary," but that it needed to be something to make him a lot of money.

Sam continued to bring food from the hotel and they sat and ate it at the kitchen table. Sometimes Ezekiel joined them. It had been nearly a week that she had felt herself again. Sam's manner had lifted along with Ezekiel's, his eyes no longer the color of a white rabbit's, his pallor lost its yellowed shade. He said he had something to discuss with her and his chest puffed like a sage grouse.

"What?" she said.

He patted the back of her hand. "Soon," he said, "when you are better."

"But I am."

"Then, Mary, come Sunday we will talk."

She should have known.

———

Saturday, her cough returned. She took the fever again. Ezekiel went for Dr. Chase. The doctor had been at her bedside twice already. He came again in the early afternoon and said to close the windows. He put a hand on her forehead, told Ezekiel to wet some cloths.

By Sunday morning, her breath came in puffs so shallow it seemed she could make it no further than her collarbone. She patted her chest and threw her head side to side. Ezekiel applied more wet cloths. The cloths calmed the fever some. He said, "Ma, I'm going for Dr. Chase again."

The muscles each side of her throat rose up as she gasped for a good breath. "Call Sam," she said, her voice loud, unnatural.

"You need to see the *doctor*."

"Sam," she whispered on the leavings of a breath.

He left. It was dark. She must have slept. She woke with Sam and Ezekiel standing on each side of the bed. She told Ezekiel, "Go to bed, now."

"I won't," he said.

"Yes," she said. She took a paltry breath, then another. "I have," she said, "something I need Sam to do. He will stay with me for a bit."

Her son shuffled out the door.

She told Sam to retrieve and read the Will and letter she sent to Prune and Totten. His eyes were damp when he put the papers back into the trunk. "Paper, Sam," she whispered and pointed at the tin that held her stationery.

On shaking arms, she pulled herself up. Sam put another pillow behind and gave her a tray from the parlor to put in her lap. She held the pen.

> *Dearest Ezekiel,*
> *I have asked Sam to put this in your old trunk where you will find it. The letter in it is a copy of what I have given your uncle with instructions for your future. Oh how I hope I am there to see it.*

Her pen began to drag a trail from one word to another and her writing became thin.

>*You are a good boy and you make me proud. I know you will*

The pen was impossible to hold. Sam leaned over, slipped it from her fingers. "Tell me what you want me to write, Mary."

She mouthed, "Water first," and he brought it, and, as he held his ear near, she said, "Write this."

>*I know you will do well, my dear, if you seek counsel from your uncle and love from your aunt. They are wonderful people and will see to it you grow into the fine man I have always known you would be. I wish I had*

Chapter 90

A shaft of sunlight sliced through a crack where the blanket did not cover the window. The shaft was long. Ezekiel was in the room. She had slept, and she knew Sam had stayed for some time, though she could not determine how long. He had come to her with an offering.

She had spent her life circling truth. She had never possessed honesty. She felt sister to the oxen, and their endless circling at the haypress. But when the oxen's day was done, their yokes and their burdens were lifted. No one removed Mary's yoke: untruth. No priest absolved it, no one forgave it. This was her penance. She would never have Sam, she would not see her son become a man. She lay in her bed knowing it. Her penance would be that. Her thoughts had no more shape or substance than lint. Her memory was no longer clear, but this she knew. This she would sleep with.

Her son stood by her bed, a cap held seriously in his hands. She said, "Hello, sweetheart," her voice soft but hers, nonetheless. She had never called him this before. She had lately gone to a place that allowed endearments. His face did not flare, nor did he turn away as he would have on another day. She could feel the thick swell of her cheeks, the dry crusts on her mouth.

She let herself sink into the coddle of pillows. She licked at her lips, but her tongue imparted no moisture.

She slit her eyes in order to see the outline of her son through her lashes, and when that became too much effort, she closed them altogether.

Ezekiel said, "Dr. Chase," in a tone both of anguish and of greeting. She tried to open her eyes. *The doctor is here?*

"Mary?" the doctor said. She heard his bag click open, heard the whip and slither of his stethoscope. She felt her gown pulled aside and the startle of cold on her chest. Her eyes opened, then, at the indecency of Ezekiel's seeing this.

Dr. Chase made a tick with his mouth. He took the stethoscope away, tossed it toward his bag. And he put one arm under her, raised her up, pulled her into his chest. With his free hand, he swatted her back. He kept this up for several swats and laid her down. It seemed her breath came easier. He said, "Is she taking fluids?"

"She was," Ezekiel said.

She fluttered open one eye. The doctor pulled a needle and syringe from his bag. Ezekiel said, "What are you doing?" It was alarming. She did not want Ezekiel to witness this.

"Giving her a physiologic," the doctor said. "And I am going to leave you something that should quiet her and help her to rest." Dr. Chase rubbed a wet rag on the high part of her arm. He lifted the skin between his fingers and pressed in the liquid. She barely felt the puncture.

"What is wrong with her?" Ezekiel said.

"Consumption," the doctor said.

He left instructions to give her broth, and water, and tea, if she would drink. And he said to put wet cloths on her face, and to rub her hands with it.

"Ma," Ezekiel said.

Her mouth wanted to form a word, but sound came without form. Ezekiel leaned forward. "What?"

She moved her mouth again, but could not make it come up with a sound. She closed her eyes and sucked at the air. She did this three times, then said in a whisper, "You are wonderful. I love you. Get. Sam. Go. To. Prune."

He ran out, thumped down the stairs.

Last she heard were his steps, the door slapping closed.

———

Came the rustle of clothes, the press of Sam's hand round hers. "Mary," he said, "I brought a letter from your sister." He read it, his breath hot on her cheek. It was short, a quick note that Totten was doing much better.

Mary tried to smile. Sam patted her arm. She tried to speak, then, but could not. As if to answer her question, Sam said, "Ezekiel is out for a moment, tending to something.

"I have something to say, dearest, and little time to say it. I've made no secret. I have loved you since the first evening I saw you in a yellow dress at the hotel." His hand gave a squeeze. She managed a little movement with one finger.

His clothes stirred and his voice came closer. "I would have been proud to call Ezekiel my son. He is a wonderful boy because of you. You have raised a . . . . Oh, Mary." His words came wet. "I wish we had more time of it."

His other hand pressured hers. "I will do everything

383

you ask. He will be sent to Philadelphia to live with your sister and brother-in-law. I will see to it. I will make sure your wishes for his schooling are carried out. He is certainly going to challenge some teachers." His voice lifted a bit at his joke.

"Years from now, he will show himself the fine, educated man you wish him to be.

"Mary, not many could have done what you have. You are a wonder, and a fine young man is testament to it. Ezekiel is capable because of his mother's strength. You have proved yourself. Mary, believe me."

A kiss.

"Believe me. Believe me."

And she did.

TELL THE WORLD THIS BOOK WAS
GOOD   BAD   SO-SO

384

Acknowledgements

The Incredible Truth

A novel only comes to life on the backs of many, and many generous people brought about *The Seasons of Doubt*. In my case, some who helped make the novel breathe are among us now. Some took their last breaths a century ago.

First, John Cozad birthed the story. He was a successful gambler who gambled (and won) enough to buy up 40,000 acres in Nebraska. In those acres, he planned to carve out the town of Cozad and make it his namesake legacy as the most important city in Nebraska. When he killed Alfred Pearson he had to abandon his dream, and to leave or be hanged. Though not the metropolis he envisioned, the town is still vibrant. Residents still live in houses he built and drive the streets he laid out. The hotel still stands and is now the Robert Henri Museum.

After the killing, the Cozad family disappeared. Only the Gatewoods and two or three of Mr. Cozad's closest allies knew where the family went. The secret held tight until the middle of the twentieth century, when The Smithsonian made public Robert Henri's diaries.

The Cozad family had ended up in Atlantic City, New Jersey. Each of them took new names; Mr. and Mrs. Cozad became Mr. and Mrs. Lee. Their older son, Johnny, took an unusual surname and became known as Frank

Southrn. In a twist of irony, the younger son, Bob, became the most known member of the family. He adopted the name Robert Henri, moved to Philadelphia and became one of the most influential American artists of the early twentieth century. I think it an odd irony Mr. Cozad, who craved notoriety and power so, lost it when he forfeited the name he had fought so hard to bring to power and influence.

Sam Schooley, the Gatewoods, Mr. Atkinson, Owens, Claypool and others are a part of Cozad history. Many of their progeny continue to live in that part of Nebraska. Other characters in the novel, particularly Mary and Ezekiel Harrington, and Mr. Simpson are knitted totally from my own imagination.

How did this story come about? As an appreciator of art, this story was handed to me when, one day, I stumbled on the book, *Robert Henri: His life and Art*, by Bennard B. Perlman. What a discovery! I had never heard of Robert Henri, yet he was hugely inspirational and influential for America's early-century artists, among them Hopper, Bellows, and Prendergast.

Some years ago, when I was in the research phase of this book, I traveled to Cozad to learn firsthand what I could of Henri. I fell into the generous and open arms of some wonderful people there who are devoted to keeping this history alive. Among them, Jan Patterson, who until recently, directed the Robert Henri Museum. The members of the board of directors of the Henri Museum: Marlene Geiger, Betty McKeone, Jane Kinnan, Earl Pharris, Della Hendricks, and Bonnie Young freely gave of their time to help a stranger with the crazy idea of writing a novel about the history they cared so much about. Thank you. I love you all for trusting me. I can only hope *The Seasons of Doubt* does you and your history justice.

——————

I also want to thank my writing buddies and critics for their care, talent, and many hours spent making the novel better than I could make it alone. Thank you, Rachelle Ramirez, Lisa Alber, Rae Richen, Jan Patterson, Anne Hawley, Sutton Stern, Mike Bigham, Carol Hirons, Dick Morgan, Loretta Goldberg, and my editors Chris Noel and Nevin Mays. *The Seasons of Doubt* would have been a mess without your help.

——————

And finally, most precious of all, dear readers, thank you. I sincerely hope you enjoyed *The Seasons of Doubt* and Mary's telling of her life and her times. As an independent writer, I rely on you, the reader, to spread the word. So, if you enjoyed the book, please your friends and family know. And if it isn't too much trouble, I would appreciate a brief review on Amazon.

Thank you again.

Jeannie

Book Club Topics

Overall, does *The Seasons of Doubt* focus on character or plot?

Did the book engage you right away, or did it take some time to get into?

In the first sections of the story, were you convinced of Mary's certainty her husband would return?

Were the main characters; Mary, Ezekiel, and Mrs. Gatewood's actions justified?

How did Mary's own past shape her actions and her life?

Ezekiel's friendship with Bobby Cozad played a pivotal role in Mary's decision to stay in Cozad. Was her decision convincing?

What effect did the times have on the lives and choices of the women of the story? What comparisons and similarities do you see between Mary's life and our lives today?

Did the story lead convincingly to the way the book ended? If so, how? If not, how?

Did Mary's relationship with Ezekiel play out in a believable way? Did his development ring true? How did his past play into the young man he was becoming?

Ezekiel Harrington's story continues:

The Opposite of Easy

Ezekiel Harrington knows about ambition and loneliness. Bitterness and striving are his sole companions since his mother died in their tiny Nebraska settlement town.

At fifteen years old, he is an orphan, forced to move to Philadelphia and thrown into the hands of relatives he has never met. Within hours of his arrival, he realizes his relatives have stolen his mother's small estate and sold his Nebraska home. Though he has no money, he flees and disappears into this strange world to carve out a life on his own.

The Opposite of Easy is set to be released fall 2019

JEANNIE BURT

The Seasons of Doubt is Jeannie's fourth book. After publishing two books of non-fiction, she turned to her love: writing fiction. Her first novel, *When Patty Went Away* came out to critical praise. Jeannie writes in the Pacific Northwest, where she lives with her husband.

To inquire about booking Jeannie Burt for a speaking engagement, please contact her publisher, Muskrat Press at info@muskratpress.com.

jeanniburt.com
facebook.com/jeannieburtnovels